Portraits and Ashes

JOHN PISTELLI

PORTRAITS AND ASHES

DEDICATION

To Lizzy

PORTRAITS AND ASHES

Part One
FALL, JULIA

John Pistelli

1. THE BRIDGE

In the choir loft of the deconsecrated church, the artist posed her naked body this way and that. He moved her limbs with his bare hands, crack-skinned and turps-smelling, tufted with wiry black hair. Caked beneath each fingernail, he had lines of that glossy blackish earth-brown color made when all the oil paints mix together. His touch felt so impersonal to her, like wood and moss and soil, that even when he took up her left leg to drape it over the blanket-heaped pew she sat on, the heel of one hand pressed bracingly on her inner thigh and the palm of the other cradling the sole of her foot, no question of sex or trespass arose. She was not what he wanted.

"Right foot touching the ground, left foot in the air," he said in his thickly-accented English. "It is a symbol."

She didn't ask of what: Julia didn't believe in symbols. She didn't believe in what she couldn't taste, touch, see. She'd always been that way: she'd stood aloof from her friends, for instance, during that vogue for dream-books in middle school, when all the girls sought the faces of their future husbands or intimations of their picturesque deaths each night. Belief, she thought, was expressed only in action. Those Soviet bulldozers clumsily chomping at gilded onion domes: pure sorcery. The domes, altars, and crosses were not symbols of something that, if you wrecked them, would continue to persist in heaven or the mind. They held all their reality in themselves. Get rid of His altars and you would also be rid of the reality of God.

"Don't look to me," the artist said. "Look to the distance."

She lifted her gaze out over the empty church and lowered it down the nave until it came to rest on the space where the altar had been. She stole glances at the artist occasionally, when he would forget about her and fix his eyes on the picture taking shape under his hand. His eyes were a bit too wide, too fierce, just the way an artist's should be, she thought: his flashing eyes, his floating hair. The old man's mouth, though tensed, the teeth clenched, nevertheless maintained a bare little smile, as of satisfaction. This felt wrong to her. Her own art never satisfied her; no, it was a constant frustration, the inability of the image on the paper to align with the image in her head. Who was he to feel satisfied? She felt a small desire to ruin his satisfaction somehow, to kick out her heel and send the canvas over the rail of the choir loft, to see what would happen if she destroyed something.

When she was in first grade, she slowly tore a religion textbook to shreds. In her little Catholic school, a red-brick building with massive gray crucifixes hanging in stony agony at the end of each long hallway, every student was assigned a homeroom desk in which to keep their schoolbooks during the day while they circulated among other teachers' rooms for their classes. During her math class, which she found dull because she did not understand it, she would keep herself awake by reaching inside the desk and slowly making small tears in the top textbook on her classmate's pile. She ripped it a little bit every day, careful not to make noise and attract Sister Grace's attention. By February, the book was in ribbons. Sister Grace sternly summoned her one Friday afternoon from her homeroom; she remembered looking up the hairy nostrils, at the dark-spotted face of the old nun, the jowls and forehead like dull clay extruded from the tight navy-blue habit.

"Did you tear this book, Julia?" Sister Grace asked, holding up in evidence, in her liver-spotted and meaty hand, the ragged strips that hung between the covers of the compulsory slipcase her classmate had made out of a paper grocery bag. Sister Grace pronounced her name with two syllables in a kind of slur: not *jul-ee-yah* but *jul-ya*.

All she remembered saying was no. She said it brazenly, not turning down her chin or dropping her eyes from the nun. She felt she had a fire in her mouth and beneath her cheeks.

"Six students sit in that desk during the day; I can't prove which one of you did it. I'll tell you what I told the rest of them," said Sister Grace. "There won't be a punishment. Not in this world, Julia. But remember this, little girl." She bent her hunched back slightly, a sharp scent of mothballs coming out of the pleats of her tan skirt. "Remember this: hell isn't a place you go when you die. Hell is what you do. If you destroy things, if you tell lies, you are already in hell. You are in the hell of your own making, where everything appears ugly and false, which is why you destroy and why you lie. So say what you want, little girl, but the truth is the truth. If your hands have been destructive and your tongue has been false, you are in hell, you are consumed from within, burning right before me, and it doesn't matter what you say."

The old nun never did know how to get along with children. She was retired the next year, and dead the year after that. Julia intermittently remembered her words. Now she had hardly any beliefs at all, but she was convinced that what she said did not in fact matter.

A customer in the café once hit on her by asking, while she prepared his espresso, if she believed in God. "Do I look like I believe in God?" she said over the sound of the machine. He frowned and narrowed his eyes, and then, after she handed him his drink and rang him up, he turned away and didn't speak to her again, nor did he leave a tip.

Eventually, the artist allowed her to relax. He had finished capturing her pose and now went to work on tones and textures; he still wanted to study her bare flesh but not in any particular position. It was five-thirty in the morning, but the painter paid her extra for his preference for working before dawn. She lay on her back, knees drawn up, imagining his tight little elderly smile.

"Can I ask you something that might annoy you?" she said.

The artist now smiled broadly with his old-world courtliness and said, "Yes, of course, but if you are too annoying I will not answer."

"Isn't painting finished?" she said. "Museums, galleries, and art schools are all about installations, performance, multimedia, various kinds of street art, new forms of interactive art. There have even been defenses on these grounds of *The Last Café*."

He grunted in disgust at her allusion.

"Then there's film, video, photography, the Internet. Whatever technological function the canvas served as a way of producing images has been entirely superseded. But even leaving that aside, didn't art considered in and of itself run its course? Didn't artists themselves bring it to an end with abstraction and pastiche and collage and blank canvases and soup cans and all of that? They took it to its logical conclusion. There's not another development anyone can imagine. What reason is there to go on making pictures of people and things after that?"

He nodded as she spoke, his chin bouncing off the top of every word, no doubt because he had already heard every word before, probably in more than one language. Then he painted in silence for long enough to discomfort her. The hairs of the brush scratched against the canvas like a whisper that echoed under the high ceiling of the church.

"The answer is very simple," he finally said. "I do it only so that it will not be finished. What you say seems as if it is true, but if I am doing it, how can it be finished? Logical conclusion, you say, but we do not live in logic. There is a way of being, of meeting, in this act that does not exist in these others that you mention. On this canvas comes together myself, yourself, this church. All are touching, which cannot happen in the machine, not even in photographs, where the apparatus comes between the mind and the mark and does its work by itself, no human touch. The apparatus itself is some other man's creation. My rival, so to say. But here is no rival, only my hand, my tool, my mind, your body, your mind, this room, this hour. All touching. This way of things coming together I do not want to see finished, so I do it if nobody else will."

"And if nobody sees it?"

"You see it, I see it. Are we nothing? You and I are not nothing."

He turned the easel to face her. There she was, palely luminescent in the candlelit greenish gloom, refracted through the viscous medium formed by his mind and his hand, which had rendered invisible the totenkopf tattooed on her left bicep, presumably excluded as a rival's vision. He had muted the neon-flame quality of her red-dyed hair to make it more nearly resemble a real fire, and he'd moreover harmonized her hair color with that of her nipples and her pubes, which were, in point of mere contemptible fact, brownish blonde. The portrait hinted that some kind of flame burned inside her, lit her from within, could barely be contained by her almost diaphanous skin. She didn't feel that way at almost six in the morning after a night of work at the café.

After he packed up his painting supplies and she got dressed, he paid her what he owed her. The two hundred-dollar bills he gave her were crumpled and smooth, so warm and soft he must have had them for years. They smelled of oil and turpentine and were worn almost to bare fabric: they hardly looked like money at all. She followed him down the dark spiral staircase leading from the choir loft into the narthex, his materials rattling and clattering against the narrow banisters. They shook hands before he went off through the huge doors into the waking city. She hesitated for a moment and then walked the other way, into the nave.

Bits and pieces of Catholic school drifted in the after-work early-morning fog of her head. Long liturgies she couldn't wait to end. The forced silence. The smell of wet stone and wood varnish. The booming of the organ through her chest. Her rigid posture on the kneelers and the nuns who would swat your ass if you bent at the waist while you knelt. She would have been horrified to learn that she might later feel nostalgia for such oppressions. What could a child know about nostalgia? Anything that vanished, no matter what it was, seemed precious just because it was gone. She stood at the end of a pew. How furious the nuns had been when the found the dream-books. "Pure sorcery," Sister Anne had said. Julia genuflected and knelt, not because she believed, she told herself, but only so that this way of things coming together would not be finished. Did she look like she believed?

* * *

The bridge was aged, undergoing repairs, its traffic reduced to one lane. The whole cracked structure shook under her feet as an early-morning delivery truck passed Julia on her walk into the city. The buildings glowed luminously gray with mist in the distance across the river, and fog hung amid the glass and cement. The silver cantilever of the central public library jutted out of the billows like a ship's prow. Somewhere the sun must be lifting itself in naked glory over the horizon, but it decorously veiled itself from her there and then. Small globes of brightly saturated green rose like cool planets through the mist, the vegetable powers coming back again. Unlike the God she had once been compelled to worship, who had died and had risen from the dead and would never die again, the flora knew infinite cycles of death and rebirth. The vegetation outlasted God's churches; their abandoned stone walls were stained green with moss and overspread with vines. God could never die again, could never be reborn, so he became feeble and senescent, the prey of time because he was infinite. That was what she was thinking, anyway, as she crossed the bridge on foot.

When she began modeling for him, the painter had politely proposed that, as he hailed from an earlier time and an older place, he should not have to listen to beeps and whirrs and buzzings and bing-bongs while he worked. She was gratified for the three hours a week of enforced silence, even if she filled it with words of her own, but she always turned on her phone as soon as she left the church. Within five minutes, she received a text from Sergey, requesting that she work tonight's shift for Caroline, who claimed to be sick.

Julia knew Caroline was not sick, except in the head. They were roommates as well as co-workers, and Caroline had felt fine the night before, well enough for a screaming fight all through the apartment with her sometime boyfriend, Charles, a fight that vibrated through the walls and kept Julia up until it was time for her to keep her appointment with the painter.

Caroline came from privilege. Her father produced human-interest stories for the local public radio station while her mother held a variety of public-service jobs in the city government. They didn't lack money, but they weren't among the truly rich. This meant, in their view, that they had to be neither selfish nor rigid. They were philanthropists, patrons of the arts, and supporters of the most humane and virtuous public figures at the local, state, and national levels. They sent their beloved only daughter to St. Sebastian's Preparatory High School and had seen to it even before high school that she was fluent in French and proficient on the violin. They were the kind of parents who encouraged their daughter to refer to them by their first names, who promised her when she was six that they would love her if

7

she said she was a lesbian. Every Thanksgiving during her childhood and adolescence they brought her to a soup kitchen and wore humbly tight little smiles of pride and beneficence as she ladled oily gravy with darlingly inexpert hands into the plastic plates and onto the ragged sleeves of the destitute. They also let her define her own self and her own interests; even when she was a toddler, they allowed her to wear what she wanted in public and treasured as precious evidence of nascent creativity the photographs of Caroline in her fairy wings at the neighborhood food co-op and then again at her grandmother's funeral. Their need to pay more attention to their only son, born when Caroline was eight and evidently troubled without being correspondingly ingenious, also allowed Caroline greater freedom. In high school she was seduced by her biology teacher and drove her sixteenth-birthday present wildly into the brick wall of the school building after splitting a lunchtime bottle of wine with him in the parking lot as he tried to break up with her. She made frightening but not very serious attempts to cut her wrists and take too many pills after transferring to public school, even though her parents' lawyer had been able to get her sentenced to community service and psychiatric evaluation rather than to a stint in juvenile detention for underage drinking and reckless driving. One night when she was eighteen, she set fire to her violin in the middle of her bed. This was the worst thing she had done, or so her father cried out when it happened, in front of the firemen, amid the burnt-hair and scalded-sugar stench of blackened varnish, a statement Caroline would never forget and often repeated. She did not attend the small liberal arts college deep in the woods they had envisioned for her. Now she was twenty-seven, working in a café alongside Julia, as big a failure as Julia was, Julia sometimes thought, though she had begun with so many more advantages. Julia's mother had had money, but had not allowed Julia to call her by her first name and did not believe that children had selves to define.

Caroline's parents had retained their soup-kitchen social conscience even as their daughter threatened to join the destitute: they paid Caroline's rent, apparently in the hopes that she would, if spared from abject need, eventually come to herself and act in the role they'd prepared for her. They also had another motivation now that Caroline's brother, Daniel, had moved in with the two women. He had just gotten out of prison for assaulting the manager of a grocery store where he'd been stocking shelves for six months after high school. The store manager, a lanky business major at the local community college, had berated Daniel for refusing, without offering any plausible reason, to take on more hours after another employee had suddenly quit; the manager spoke with a friendly smile to Daniel about the importance of seizing opportunities or, if he were mysteriously not motivated by self-interest, at least of showing a willingness to be there for the family made up by the store's employees. To the court, Daniel said only, before pleading guilty, that the manager was trying to steal his time away. He said to Caroline that the manager's neck was so thin, it looked as if his head could just be knocked off his body, like a hat swept off a rack; so he decided to try it. Caroline, who always claimed that Daniel was "mentally slow," laughed helplessly when telling this story to Julia. Daniel was nineteen, jobless, and sparsely educated. Before he went to prison, he would spend all day when he wasn't at work playing video games, his pudgy face impassive behind the flap of brown hair that mostly covered his eyes. Now he played video games most of the day in a spare room in Caroline's apartment, a room intended for an office; but he shaved his massive head and he did one hundred pushups a day and one hundred sit-ups at night and in the morning, so that the spare room smelled like a gym locker. At night he went out to drink. Julia had followed him once: she saw that he drank alone, but he was too big for anyone to bother.

When Julia reached the end of the bridge, her phone sounded and displayed her mother's name and number; she had already called twice the day before. Julia declined the call. She knew that pride prevented her mother from leaving a message, so she was determined to force her to do so by refusing to answer. Then she texted Caroline three times but received no reply.

Daniel also texted her to ask where Caroline was. This probably meant that he had spent the entire night away, probably wandering from bar to bar, and now found himself locked out. He didn't ask Julia where she was or how she was doing, even though she had been sleeping with him regularly for the last three months. She did not respond to his text.

Her mother called again. Again she refused the call.

While she had her phone out, she checked her email. She had one message in her inbox: a curt, polite rejection from an advertising agency where she had applied for a job. She'd forgotten she had even put in the application; the rejection reminded her of her desire for the job only to thwart that desire, which made it hurt worse. She knew she had attended a third-rate college and had for no discernable reason dropped out of a fully-funded MFA program, and that her subsequent employment history had large gaps of joblessness. She thought that her portfolio was good enough for a relatively inexperienced and ill-educated artist. Even now, she designed promotions and merchandise for the animal shelter she volunteered for. She had imagined that the agency might appreciate raw energy more than polished ability or the right connections. They did not, just as her mother had warned.

Her mother's warnings had been the main topic of their last conversation, and the reason Julia had no desire to start a new one. "Are you going to work in a café all your life?" she'd asked Julia as they sat over tea in Mrs. Bonham's almost flawless suburban kitchen. "Are you going to live with that flighty loser, that unbearably stupid girl who threw away even more opportunities than you did, if that's even possible? You think I'll judge you less harshly if you stand next to her? Forget it. I cannot stand weak women, Jules. I did not raise you this way. I did not invest many thousands of dollars in your education, from your excellent parochial schooling to your debt-free graduation from college, just to watch you waste your existence on laziness and drift. My God, I helped you with your first year of art school, a decision I did not understand at all, only for you to leave for no reason, for some stupid boy, not that you've ever told me the truth about that. If you want to go back to school, if you want to take some time to find a better job, I will help you. Move out of that apartment with that idiot girl and her retarded criminal brother. I will pay rent for a few months in a better place, if it's money you need..."

"I don't need money, mother. I can pay my own way."

"Julia," she said, pronouncing it *jul-ee-yah* very distinctly as she did when she was serious, "I am too old and tired to watch you turn out like your deadbeat father."

"Deadbeat?" Julia asked. "As if you gave him a chance to raise me."

"He squandered his chance. He squandered all his chances, just like you're doing. I couldn't let you stay in that house of filth, not even on weekends..."

"At least I could breathe there. I could learn things there, read books, go outside, think what I wanted to think..."

"Oh Christ, you and your freedom. You think if you do what you want, when you want, you will be free. But no, Jules: you will just be poor, and poverty is slavery. You don't know that, because I've never let you find out. I hope I live long enough to see you come to your senses, you spoiled, ungrateful child."

"I don't care whether you do or not."

Mrs. Bonham only laughed dryly, though the rims of her eyes grew red. "Bite your tongue. My God, what a thing to say to your mother. Aren't you ashamed of yourself?"

That was a month ago to the day, a gray and snowy Sunday afternoon in March, without a trace of green in the landscape.

Sergey texted again.

It was seven in the morning now, and the sun had burned the mist off the city. Everything became starkly itself for another day, the colors bright rather than hazy, the planes of the buildings incised on the blue air. By now she had walked though and past the bright façade that looked out on the bridge; she was beyond the banking and commerce of downtown and deep in the neighborhood she lived in, where filthy streets glowered in the sunshine. It was early yet. The metal gates over most store entrances were still locked. Swelling heaps of rag and blanket that proved on closer inspection to be men lay in ungated doorways. The previous night's storms had swept a Styrofoam cup, sheets of newspaper, a plastic coffee lid stained with dried milk at the lip, three desiccated pizza crusts, two burger wrappers, a plastic grocery bag, a couple of cigarette butts, a crumpled-up parti-colored ball of junk mail, a formerly pink foam toe-separator from a pedicure kit, and the jagged neck of a brown beer bottle in drifts against the curb. Many of the buildings had ornate fronts with dentil-laden cornices and Corinthian pilasters and relief panels crowded with flower and vine. This had been a prosperous neighborhood once. The ocean-green wall of the empty storefront that had once housed a seafood restaurant on the corner of her own street bore a large graffito, chalked in white: *Let Joy Be Your Spiritual Weapon.*

Sergey texted again.

She looked at her phone, but the information on the screen was obscured by the reflection of the sky overhead. It was as if she held in her palm a rectangular box, miles deep, containing clouds and empty air. She couldn't remember what she had been thinking before she received all these messages, a half hour ago when she was starting across the bridge from the old neighborhood where the church decayed, when the mist still hung over the city and the new treetops beamed faintly in the distance. Something about God and nature. She had lost it.

The phone chimed again with Sergey's last text; she had not even looked at it.

She tried calling Caroline rather than texting her, but Caroline didn't answer. Their apartment building, a hundred years old, once a palatial eight-story department store of the kind that barely existed anymore, had no bell or buzzer. According to the landlord who'd talked Caroline into renting it, this lack was made up for by the high-ceilinged interior, the exposed brick side wall, the ceramic tile of the kitchen floor, the elevated view from the bedroom windows, and the relatively low rent. "Anyway," the landlord had argued, "everybody has these phones now, so there's no need for any other means of communication, is there?"

Julia stood before the heavy red door. It was built into the brick wall between a boarded-up furniture shop, a dusty and sun-bleached couch in its crack-paned show window, and a tiny store that sold lottery tickets and cheap flip phones and cigarettes and sundry groceries and incense and religious literature.

She called Caroline one more time, but there was no answer.

She went into the tiny store, lit in degrading fluorescents but perfumed with incense, and bought a to-go cup of coffee from a gracious man who moved slowly and spoke only enough English to wish her a beautiful day, which was enough. Then she sat on the damp pavement next to the red door, her feet flat on the ground and knees tensed up to her chest so that her big black lace-up boots seemed to guard her body like columns. To pass the time, she read a stilted old public-domain translation of *On the Genealogy of Morals* from the small screen of her phone while the neighborhood began to stir around her. The coffee tasted watery, acidic, and faintly oily, but she drank it anyway.

She lifted up her head and sucked the remnants of the coffee through the plastic lid's perforation. The honey she'd squeezed into it had settled at the bottom; the excessive sweetness of the last sip needled her teeth and stung her throat. She shut her eyes against the sugary affront.

When she opened her eyes again, they were there, just across the street from her. She had never been so close to them before. There were five of them: they shuffled over the cracked sidewalk. They wore a variety of scavenged robes and coats that hung shapelessly over their bodies; the dirty hems of their long garments trailed filth. Their ash-colored bare feet whispered softly on the concrete; they scarcely lifted their legs when they walked, so their soles slid slowly over the rough sidewalk. Some trick of the street's acoustics conveyed this susurrus straight into Julia's left ear even though she sat at a distance, as if she were in a whispering gallery. Their opaque eyes appeared blind, but their pale ash-strewn faces seemed to stare ahead. Their dull gray shaven scalps did not reflect the sun even though their side of the street was suffused with morning light. They seemed not to see, but in fact they saw what Julia had missed. In the small gap between two buildings, too narrow to qualify as an alley, a clot of newsprint and trash bags concealed a man, sleeping in the small strait gap. Julia just perceived a flesh-colored square of bent elbow rising out of the trash, caught in a shaft of the sunlight.

The five surrounded him, and one bent down to rouse him by extending a thin hand from its robe and touching the exposed arm. The sleeping man flung himself upright with a guttural scream, nearly smashing his head against the bricks. When he saw them through his bleary, bloodshot eyes, he started shouting: "Get away from me! Leave me alone! Somebody call the police!" Julia knew the police wouldn't come. They committed no crimes, except for the occasional act of public indecency; some of their actions might qualify as harassment, but the news said that almost no one they touched refused to go with them. More importantly, from the authorities' point of view, they drained the city's surplus population. If there were fewer and fewer jobs, fewer and fewer places to go, then why not allow people to go underground and do whatever it was they did there if they wanted to? The ash-decorated so-called It people never coerced anyone to go with them. The police could no more stop them than they could stop priests from delivering sermons intended to convert unbelievers. There were fewer and fewer priests too. These people, or former people, the ones who seemed to merit only being referred to individually as "it" and so were called Its, therefore solved several social problems at once. There were too many of them now to call them a cult anyway.

All five now lowered themselves around the sitting man. The one who had touched his arm kept hold of it, kneading and massaging the stringy stark-veined forearm with gray fingers, pressing ash in smudges on the skin. The man kicked his legs out, but he could back no further into the narrow gap between buildings. Another of them took one of his legs and slowly rolled up the cuff to bare his yellowish and emaciated shin; it looked like an old bone feathered with dirty hairs. The It behind the It who had taken the leg undid the difficult thief-deterring knot of the man's boot; then It pulled the boot off and peeled away in strips the papery sock. This one went to work pressing its fingers into the horny, ragged-nailed, cadaverous foot. The way they touched the man's body reminded Julia of the way the painter touched her own. The man's eyes widened with panic, as if he saw his arm and leg being fed into the maw of a shark. They said nothing to him, for they kept silent at all times; the ones who were not touching him remained on their knees in a posture of worship with their eyes locked on his face. Julia's phone screen had gone dark because she had not touched it. She was transfixed by their bent gray backs, their ash-crusted robes. They paid the panicking man a kind of pure attention. His shouts and curses did not put them off, still less his filthy wasted flesh and fouled clothes.

Occasionally a pedestrian or car would go by, but not many; it was Sunday morning. An old woman who wore dark glasses and carried an umbrella shook it at them as she passed on halt legs. She told them to go back into the hole they'd crawled out of, but they didn't let her distract them. They focused on the man in front of them. The shock of their stare and of their fearless touch must have begun to fascinate him, because he stopped kicking his legs and trying to back up. His face was still rigid with fear, but now his wide eyes seemed to see not the threat he had thought them to represent, but finally to see them, without preconception. His free hand scrabbled in the rubbish around him and pulled out a flask, which he uncapped. He took a long drink, his hand trembling, one yellowish red-rimmed dry eyeball lowered on them even as he tipped up his head. One of the two who weren't touching him, with an automatic gesture, bunched its robe up around its waist and released a dark coil of shit onto the sidewalk from its uncovered asshole. The complete neutrality with which it shat, compared to the intensity with which it affixed its gaze to the man in the narrow gap, removed shitting from a context in which Julia could judge it. It was like seeing a bird shit in flight. Only the man before them mattered.

Gradually, his panicked eyes narrowed and his mouth fell out of its fearful rictus; all his features seemed to melt into the tears streaming down his dirty cheeks. He finally lowered his head, staring at the empty flask in his hand. He looked from the flask to the five gray faces and back again.

The one nearest the man extended both gray hands, palms upturned. The man set the flask gently on the sidewalk and extended his free arm. The two holding his leg slowly released it while the one who held both of his hands moved to stand. All six of them rose as one. They made a star-shaped formation, the man in the middle, and they walked in the same direction the original five had been going. The man's single boot heel scraped the pavement as the eleven bare feet whispered, all of this booming and echoing in the caffeine-enflamed caverns of Julia's head. The noise only died down when they moved to the next block.

She felt she had been watching this event for hours, though not three minutes could have passed. She shook her throbbing head and looked away from where the conversion had taken place. A spasm of nausea wrenched her stomach, soaked in the acid of the bitter coffee. She looked up and saw that the man who'd sold her the coffee had come out to watch as well; he stood in his doorway, still looking at the gap in the distance where the sleeping man had been awoken. He whispered, "Allahu akbar." Everything fell silent again.

Then her phone chimed: Sergey texted again. She still hadn't answered him about filling in for Caroline.

Across the street, a tall college-aged girl with earbuds in her ears jogged in morning buoyancy, bobbing her head to the beat she alone heard, her pink spandex tights gleaming, her lean-muscled stomach bare and tensely vibrating. She probably regarded her youthful time in this neighborhood as an important transition experience, a titillatingly grim moral education necessary to prepare her for the time she would eventually spend in some position of responsibility in the world. She planted her bright pink running shoe directly into the mound of shit the It had left, smudging it blackly over the sidewalk as she ran on.

Julia's mother called again.

She texted Sergey back to say she'd be there.

* * *

"What are you doing on the floor?" Julia said.

Caroline said, "How did you get in?"

"I asked first."

Julia shut the door behind her and leaned back on it, letting her upset stomach settle itself after her jog up the stairs to the apartment. Caroline turned her face away and said nothing. She lay Vitruvean-style on the cold ceramic tiles of the kitchen floor, her thin black dress, the only thing she wore, hung funereally from the sharp starved crags of her shoulders and hipbones. In one of her outstretched hands she held her phone, her chipped cherry-red nails tapping its smudged surface.

14

"The guy from down the hall, the one with the goatee and the snake tattoo on his neck, let me in when he came out for a smoke."

"Well, Christ, that makes me feel unsafe, Jules. He doesn't know if you're a killer or what. Just because he wants to jump your bones."

"He recognized me."

"But he's never even talked to you. You could have been somebody who only looked like you. You could have been anybody. This isn't such a safe neighborhood that he can just let strangers into the building. There's a reason people have locks on their doors. So don't hump him, anyway, Jules. Don't reward bad behavior, for Christ's sake. I know you want to. That's the thing about you: you're a sensation-seeker, a nihilist. You seem so demure, so obscure, but all you want is intensity."

Julia sat down beside Caroline and, though the nausea induced by changing positions forced her to clamp her jaws tightly shut. She gestured to the phone in Caroline's hand. "What the hell?" she said when the spasm passed.

Caroline turned to Julia and gave her customary frail little smile, a cartoonish lip-squiggle that transformed her cynical expression into a look of babyish frustration.

"I was doing a mental exercise. I resolved to hold the phone all morning, the ringer turned all the way up, but not to look at it no matter what. Not even if Charles called. I think Daniel probably called, but I don't care about that. A little time out of doors will sober up his useless ass anyway. I am sorry I missed your messages, Jules. But nobody should have to see me this way, not even you."

Julia threw her arms forward in exasperation. "So you made me sit on the sidewalk? Do you know what I saw out there?"

Caroline turned away again as if struck by Julia's anger. Then Julia told her what she had seen on the sidewalk. Caroline sat up in alarm, her legs splayed out and her dress hiked up, with a child's innocence of dignity or decorum.

"Oh my God. I thought they were, like, an urban legend, like alligators in the sewer. Something the news made up to scare people into putting up more gates. Jules, we need to get a gun or something. What if those creeps had taken you and not the homeless guy? You could be getting molested under a storm drain right now. Oh my God, what if the guy from down the hall with the snake on his neck lets them in?"

Caroline always grew more and more childishly witty the deeper she sunk into histrionic despair: the childishness made you want to protect her, while the wit gave you something worth protecting. Julia laughed involuntarily, but Caroline flung herself down on her side and started to sob, her stark-boned shoulder blades clenching and unclenching at Julia like slow jaws, their pale skin stuck with cereal crumbs, carrot peels, and a strand of fakely flaming red hair from the unswept floor. The sight of this made Julia nearly wretch, her stomach pulsing and shooting with honeyed acid. The criss-crossing lines of recessed grout between the tiles had formed an inflamed Petrine Cross in the flesh of Caroline's back, just above the low hemline of her dress.

"What did Charles say to you when he left?" Julia said.

"When I told him I slept with Bryce last week, he said that I need to learn how to be by myself. That everybody always gave me what I wanted so I never learned how to take 'no' for an answer. He said I needed someone to say 'no' to me, so he was doing me a favor by walking out."

Julia placed her hand on Caroline's arm.

"Oh stop. You think it's all true, you bitch. I don't think it's truer of me than of anyone else our age, Jules. You live the same life I do. Who says 'no' to you? I didn't say 'no' when you asked to live here. You don't say 'no' when Gerald and Donna pay the rent every month. You think it's your due for being nice to me. And all I ask from you is to be nice to me and Daniel. That's us, Jules, we're the same, you're no better than me, despite what you think. We do what we want and let someone else foot the bill."

Julia, frustrated by the renewed storm of tears and the accusations of hypocrisy and ingratitude made against her, said nothing but only moved her hand up and down Caroline's arm to massage the unused muscle, to calm the strained body. She pushed the black dress's flared sleeve aside, and she saw a fresh red wet gash in Caroline's upper arm. Julia put two fingertips in the sticky wound, an automatic gesture of curiosity and revulsed attraction. Her mouth filled with nauseous saliva.

"Don't say anything, I know what you're going to say," Caroline went on. "You're going to ask why I need you to work for me tonight. I knew you would hold that against me. And you're right to do it, but look at me. Can I go in like this?"

"No, it's fine," Julia said. "Sometimes I feel like I can't do this job at all any more. Being a waitress in my early 20s was cute. Now it's just pathetic. But that's not your fault. So what's another night?"

Julia pulled the sleeve back across the gash and renewed her massage after wiping her blood-sticky fingertips on her jeans.

"The worst part is you won't ever tell me you're holding it against me. You never say anything bad to me, Jules, that's what I can't stand about you. You talk and talk and talk, but I think it's all lies, because it's never anything bad. Do you think anything bad? Do you ever do anything bad? Tell me the truth."

Julia kept quiet.

"Well," Caroline said. "Then you must be a good person." She laughed: "You know, lying is just as bad as saying evil shit. Even if you lie by silence. They get you coming and they get you going; if you're bad, you're bad."

Caroline pulled her arm away from Julia and, with her other hand, tore her sleeve from her shoulder with such force that the black fabric ripped open to reveal the wound. The sound of tearing cleaved the air under the high ceiling and resonated for a few moments before the silence grew back around it.

"Maybe I'll just aim for my throat next time," she finally said.

Julia jumped to her feet and managed to say, "If you were truly a bad person, you'd try to cut somebody else," before the nausea overwhelmed her.

Just beneath the thudding of her boots on the ceramic tiles as she ran to the bathroom to vomit, she heard Caroline's words: "Maybe I will."

* * *

She slept uneasily for the rest of the morning. Her stomach had settled, but she felt dried-out and dizzy. She didn't want to go to the kitchen to get a cold drink of water and have to explain herself to Caroline, so she slept, her eyeballs hot and tense, her mouth full of what felt like damp sand. She thought she heard Charles's voice coming faintly from the other room. Had he returned to Caroline? She had pulled down the blinds against the bright morning, and blurry yellow light diffused itself into her small bedroom through the dust motes.

She thought she heard Daniel come in and shut the door softly behind him. It couldn't be him, not only because Caroline was here and he would not want her to know what he and Julia were doing, but because he had never entered her room before. She always went into his, as she did last night while Caroline cried and screamed at Charles, her outbursts punctuated by Charles's calm and inaudible words; he was trying to be "reasonable," or so he said, which only stoked up Caroline's fury. Julia had lain awake for a while, and then she tiptoed to the bathroom, and then, under the noise of the toilet running, she opened Daniel's door and slipped inside. He didn't say anything but only widened his eyes at her; he hardly ever said anything, so no one knew what he wanted or how intelligent he was. Julia rarely spoke to him on these occasions. She had gestured to him to put the video game controller aside. He finished the level he was on first, while she lightly brushed her fingertips down inside the hole in the front of his boxers until his penis stood up. She'd brought a condom with her, concealed in the elastic waist of her panties, as she always did, with the exception of their first time, when her avidity and his willingness had taken them both by surprise. She rolled it down on him. Then she tipped his bulk back onto his air mattress; his body displaced currents of air that stank of decayed, stagnant masculinity. Somehow his stench, his filth, his grotesque disorderliness drew her to him even more than it repulsed her, or because it

17

repulsed her. In that rancid air she took her pleasure, the way she had done about once a week for the last three months. Julia's fevered breath ran under Caroline's shouts and imprecations and the shattering of the water glasses and dinner plates she hurled at Charles.

Julia knew Daniel would never come to her, so she didn't open her eyes. She felt hands, rough and warm, traverse her body, take her by the hips. She hated that his raspy drawled compliments would make her surrender if only he would utter them, that he could flip her onto her back on the mattress if he were capable of doing so. She wanted to feel the control that comes not only from action but from refusal, as she once had, when she left school to be with her second lover, Cal, the one between Mark Weis and Daniel; she had only had three lovers in her entire life, which she could never tell the worldly Caroline, who believed her to be much more experienced. Something had slackened, some tension had gone out of her life since the time when she chose to run away with the second man, to leave graduate school and have nothing. Now she went from day to day without a mission. Her mother had been right: she'd never known poverty. She was a blindfolded woman blithely walking the rim of an abyss. Julia, I can't help myself around you, said Daniel. Caroline was now watching them in the doorway, her head shaved, her body draped in a gray robe, but Julia didn't care. In fact, she laughed. She raised her knees and girded herself for a jet of pleasure. When it didn't come, she awoke completely to the empty room. She saw her body in the mirror above her dresser, her knees raised up and splayed out, her ankles crossed, as if her legs encircled something, as if she were a saint or a demoniac, rapt by the invisible.

*　*　*

To leave the apartment, she couldn't avoid passing Caroline, who sat at the kitchen table painting her toenails black. Her feet were propped up on the empty kitchen chair, one pink foam toe-separator affixed to the right foot, the corresponding one for the left foot absent. She caught Julia staring and said, "What? I can't find the other one." Julia was actually looking at the gash-scars above Caroline's ankles. On the table, her open laptop tinnily blared out a classical music Internet station: a soprano wailed in escalating octaves over a keening cello.

There was a dent in the wall behind Caroline, toothed, as if bitten: the scalloped edge of a thrown plate had left it. There was a bite like that in the kitchen wall of the house where Julia had grown up, from a dish flung by Julia's mother at her father during their divorce twenty years before. Her mother never repaired this indentation in the wall. Julia asked her why she didn't much later, and her mother had said, "You have to wear your scars with pride."

Julia had her hand on the doorknob when Caroline said, as if to no one in particular, "It's supposed to storm again tonight." Julia turned back to fetch her umbrella from the closet. "Oh, I forgot to tell you earlier," Caroline added, still not looking up to address her, "and this is strange, because I don't even know how she got my number, but your mother called me. She asked if you were all right. I told her you were, more or less. She wouldn't say what she wanted, but she sounded upset. Like she was sick or something. She's not sick, is she?"

"Only in the head," Julia said.

2. THE WOUNDED SURGEON

When she was seven, Julia murdered a kitten. The kitten was called Mephistopheles; it belonged to her stepmother, the librarian.

To get to her stepmother's house, which was also her father's house, you had to drive away from Julia's house and into the city, where the buildings went up past the car window, unless she stretched out the seatbelt to turn her head upside down and put it against the glass and look straight up, and where people always seemed mad and in a hurry. Then you had to go out of the city again, past buildings with smoky walls and black empty windows and cars with grass growing straight into them and flowers knotted around the wheels, and then through neighborhoods with big houses and wide lawns, until you got to a little street. This street curved up around a group a trees until it came out in front of a brick house the color of the crayon called *goldenrod*. The house was half-hidden behind a huge tree, its soft branches hanging all the way down along the ground, and a garden full of spiky plants Julia had never seen before. The house faced the opposite direction from the main road, which was on the other side of the small dark forest behind the back yard. In front of this reversed house, across the little street you had to drive on to get to it, was the side of a hill, all tangled up with leaves and vines.

"Look," Julia's father said to her from the driver's seat. "It's like a forest in the middle of the city. You can play Little Red Riding Hood."

The librarian twisted her small body around in the passenger's seat and peered at Julia through her big square glasses. Her stepmother looked at her differently from the way her mother looked at her: it reminded her of going to the doctor's.

"Don't tell her that," the librarian said to Julia's father. "She'll think I have wolves. She looks scared as it is. Is she always this quiet?"

"Never. But she's just used to the suburbs, where there's nothing to see. The change will be good for her. Maybe she'll even learn something." Then he turned to Julia and said, "You can *be* the wolf."

The librarian laughed dryly at that.

This was the first time Julia ever heard her house spoken of as anything other than her house, as something strange or even bad. How could her house be bad?

There was a bird bath in the librarian's small back yard. Its bottom basin held a big pool of water; there was a smaller basin above that. The water flowed down from the smaller basin into the larger, plashing softly. On top of the bird bath was a stone angel with hair curling over its forehead and wings that were round on top and pointed at the bottom. The angel held out its hands and turned its head down to one side: the face looked kind, shy, and sad. It wore a robe that hung from one shoulder all the way down past where its feet would have been until the robe became the bottom of the small basin. Julia couldn't tell if it was a boy or a girl angel; its stone was gray with pits and patches of black. The first time she ever went to the librarian's, she stared up at it until her father asked her to come in and look around her new house.

The house seemed like it should have been smaller on the inside than it really was. The kitchen had stone walls; the metal oven seemed to be built into a cave. In the living room the bookshelves went up so high, right to the ceiling, that it made Julia feel faint to stand under them; the librarian kept a folding stepladder in the corner of the room in case she needed to get a book from the top shelves. Plants grew everywhere, out of pots along all the walls: any time you turned around, a flower or a vine would brush against your arm or your cheek, like soft boneless fingers reaching for you. Long halls with dark wooden floors ran along the upstairs; the floorboards were different shades of brown, some almost yellow, some burnt-looking and black. The walls of the bathroom were opaquely green like the ocean, and the bathtub had four big claws that dug into the floor. She told her father she was afraid to take a bath inside a monster.

"Don't be silly," he said to that. He never liked it when she chattered away with an idea he believed was impossible. He didn't think it was cute, a sign of lively imagination, the way her mother did. He worked with tools all day and cared only about what was real.

The tiny kitten was gray with black spots, a little like the angel on the bird bath. He rubbed his face against Julia's leg almost as soon as he saw her, before she'd even worked up the courage to pet him. Julia had trouble saying his name; she asked why he was called that and what it meant.

"It means the devil," her father said, sounding impatient with the very idea of the devil.

Julia looked to the librarian, who agreed that Mephistopheles was one of the names of the devil. She told Julia that this was only a little joke and that the cat would be very nice. Julia was not convinced, since the librarian rarely joked, or not in a funny way, not in a way that Julia could understand. The librarian, who smelled a bit like black pepper, crouched down and ran her thumb along the fur between the kitten's eyes: "Do you see how it looks like he has a big M on his forehead? All tabby cats have that M shape, so I always give them names that start with M. Before Mephistopheles, I had Mendel, Miller, Melville, Madrigal, Marlowe, and Mandrake." Julia laughed at this list of funny names; she often asked the librarian to repeat it.

When Julia came back to her own home after a weekend at her stepmother's house, which was now her father's house, she tried not to tell her mother that going there sometimes made her afraid. She always felt very relieved to return to the wide street where kids rode up and down on their bikes, some with training wheels and some without, the girls with pink tassels flying from their handlebars, and to the pink flowers in front of the house and the pink carpets in her bedroom and the white bathroom with its square white tub without claws, to the living room with the big-screen TV and no books, to the bright white walls that caught all the sunshine. There was nothing scary in her mother's house, and Julia slept easily within it. She didn't tell her mother she couldn't sleep in the librarian's house, because even though the house scared her, she couldn't stop thinking about all the frightening things in it and how much she wanted to look at them, even though sometimes she went right up to them and then turned around and ran away. Julia also knew from school and church that the devil was very bad, and she heard her mother complain to her grandmother about how her father and the librarian didn't go to church on Sunday, so she didn't tell her mother about the cat with the devil's name. Her mother, who didn't allow animals in her house, found the cat hairs all over Julia's clothes. She always brushed them off so hard that it hurt, as if her mother were hitting her through her clothes. Julia said the cat's name was Gray.

Julia's mother talked for the first time about not letting her go to the librarian's house anymore when Julia accidentally mentioned the books. Her stepmother had the biggest books Julia had ever seen; they didn't just have a lot of pages in them, though they did, but they were also tall and wide and heavy. Julia had to slide them off the bookshelves and then lay them down and slide them across the floor. They smelled like old wood, vanilla, or pennies. She had to crouch down to read them when they were spread open on the floor so she could move herself around the huge pages on her hands and knees. She mostly didn't read them, though, since she didn't understand many of the words; in some, she didn't understand any of the words, because those ones weren't in English, the librarian told her. It was the pictures she wanted to look at. She was getting too old for books with pictures, but these books didn't have pictures of smiling bears in overalls or pink movie princesses in them.

They had different kinds of pictures, some drawings, some photos. One drawing showed a man with a big thick moustache from the side. Above his ear, a piece of his head had been opened out like a door with hair. You could see on the side of this door stripes of bone and skin, and through the opening you could see the man's brain, folded and refolded in on itself like a dirty gray blanket. Another drawing in heavy black lines was of a skull, with all its different bones labeled; Julia tried her best to repeat the list of labels like a song or a poem. She would look at the picture and trace the lines on the page with one finger, while she pressed the fingertips of her other hand into the flesh of her face so she could feel where the temporal process sloped down to the nasal bone, which spread in turn from its ridged peak into the lachrymal bone, whose smooth expanse ran into the rigid knob of the zygomatic bone. It felt like she had mountains and valleys in her face. Then she saw the drawing of the doe, resting with her front legs folded under her and her back legs crossed behind her like a person's while she took a rest; the drawing showed the inside of her swollen stomach, where a miniature deer, red and smooth, its black eyes bulging, floated in almost the exact same position as its mother's. She saw penises, too, but they were no surprise, because she had heard about them on TV and at school.

No, the worst pictures were the photos of things that had gone wrong. A baby with one wide eye in the middle of its forehead. A child whose mouth just kept going up to the tip of the nose, a black hole in the face with two crooked teeth dangling down. A horse with a kind of huge gray veiny mushroom hanging off the side of its long snout. A silver catfish with surprised black eyes whose lips were red and meaty and split open by white bulbs, dripping a milky juice.

"Why are its lips like that?" Julia asked.

"It swam in a lake near a factory, and it contracted cancer from the poison the factory dumped into the water," said the librarian.

Julia's lips tingled and burned.

Julia only mentioned the pictures in the books to her mother once, when they were in the car and saw a deer on the shoulder of the highway, its belly ripped open, its intestines strung out pink and dull behind it. Her mother reached over and put her hands over Julia's eyes, but Julia wriggled free and said, "I can look, I saw stuff like that before," and when her mother asked her where, she had to tell her about the librarian's books. Julia's mother told her not to look at those books anymore and then didn't say anything about it again.

When Julia's father came to get her for the weekend, Julia's mother made her go upstairs so she could talk to him, and Julia heard what she said, her voice hollow and angry: "She wakes up screaming. She goes to sleep with the pillow over her face because she says if she doesn't then someone will open her head to look at her brain in the middle of the night. She won't drink tap water, she won't go swimming. What are you two teaching her? What are you letting her read? I know the librarian doesn't have children, but I can't let her take it out on my daughter. Honestly, I don't even know if I should let her go over there any more if this is how it's going to be, Frank. You know I could call the lawyer. Don't look at me like that, like you're going to laugh. I thought you'd be more responsible, though I suppose I should have known better."

Her father said, "I'll talk to her."

"I don't want her looking at those books."

"They're science books, for Christ's sake. Everything in them is true. What are you, the Holy Inquisition?"

"She's not mature enough for them yet. They are inappropriate reading material for a child."

"Don't talk to me like that, like some psychologist you heard on a talk show."

"When are you going to grow up?"

"Yeah, because your need to control everything in sight is a real sign of maturity. Jesus, remember when I married you? When you were an actual human being?"

"If you bring her back here with more nightmares, I will call the lawyer. Now get out of my house if you're going to wear those filthy boots. Have fun with your real human being. I hope her humanity makes up for her flat chest."

"I can't get over your maturity. Love the new carpet, by the way. Who could have nightmares in here? In all this pink?"

The second time her mother threatened to keep Julia from going to the librarian's house had to do with the rat fetus from the cabinet. The house had an attic. Unlike the other attics Julia knew about, it was not even difficult to get to. It didn't have a hatch and a folding ladder that you had to pull out of the ceiling or a tiny crawlspace in a bedroom closet that you had to climb up on your knees, both things Julia had seen in other houses, houses in "the suburbs," as she now thought of her weekday world. You could get to this attic by just one more turn of the house's main staircase, a turn that wound straight up to a door. Julia's father told her that she couldn't go to the attic because the librarian kept things she needed for her work there. She couldn't go inside even if she wanted to, because the door was locked. Did she want to? She felt about the attic the way she felt about the whole house: it scared her, and she wanted to see all of it.

24

One Saturday in the winter, when it got dark at five in the afternoon, Julia stayed in the house by herself. The librarian had to go to a dinner for rich people who gave money to the library, her father explained; as for him, he spent the evening in the garage, lying on a wooden board with wheels on it that let him slide under the librarian's car, which he was fixing. He put on a movie for her and told her to come get him in the garage if she needed anything. All she could see in the dark windows of the house was a reflection of herself and the couch and the lamp and the bookshelves and the television; when shiny snowflakes like glass dust flew against the window, it looked to her as if they were swirling around inside the room itself. Julia went to the kitchen to get herself some cereal. She poured the milk without spilling. Still learning her way around the librarian's kitchen, she opened the wrong drawer when she wanted a spoon. The drawer she opened had pencils and paperclips and screwdrivers in it, so Julia was about to close it when she saw an old black key, the kind she'd only seen before in books or movies about castles. The key had a circle at the end to hold onto and a long rod that ended in three small teeth, two pointed down and one pointed up. The knowledge that this key opened the attic door came instantly to Julia. One second she didn't know, and the next second she did. She also knew what she would do, as sure as if it were a memory of something she'd already done.

First, she tiptoed down the stairs to the basement, where a door led to the garage. This door already stood open an inch, so she only had to push it out another inch to make sure that her father was still working on the car. All she could see were his legs, his pants stained dark with oil. The dull gray jack that held the back of the car over his head seemed impossible to her. She wondered how a thin column of metal could lift up the whole car. An image flashed in her mind: some fingers, she didn't know whose, flicked lightly at the handle of the jack until it let go and the whole thing crashed down; then her father's legs shot up in the air, and his blood and brains burst out from under the car, splattering onto the wall. She said to herself, I didn't think that, and giggled into her hand.

She went back up the stairs, creeping in her socks, until she didn't have to creep anymore because she knew no one was there to hear her. She ran up the last two turns of the staircase, the key leaving a red picture of itself in her clutching and sweaty hand. The key squealed inside the lock as she twisted it around this way and that; finally, the teeth bit into some metal parts inside the door that clicked and rang. Then the door fell open the way it would have done if a person on the other side had pulled on it. Julia had decided when she heard the lock click that she felt too scared to look at what was in the attic tonight, but the door made a different decision: once it jumped open a little, it started to slowly swing all the way back. Even in the faint moonlight the attic's round window let in, light like a white cloud of dust, Julia could see that the room was small and mostly empty. The severely sloping roof left just enough space for some boxes along the walls. In the middle of the attic, where the peak of the ceiling rose as high as an adult, stood a tall, narrow cabinet. Julia felt along the wall inside the door until she found a light switch: a bare bulb hanging directly over the cabinet lit up. Julia's heart pounded inside her head so hard she thought it would knock her over, but she went over to the cabinet anyway.

The cabinet was old and dusty; it had feet that reminded Julia of the bathtub's, but these were more like the legs of a faun, brown and gracefully curved, hooved rather than clawed. The doors of the cabinet were made of glass so you could look inside and see what sat on the shelves. She saw jars, and inside the jars were pictures from the librarian's books come to life. None of the animals in the jars were alive. Even so, they weren't pictures: you could hold them in your hand if you put your hand inside the jars. A white worm that reminded her of a plastic tube, coiled ten or twenty times around the glass in pinkish water, like a practical-joke spring that would burst out if you took the lid off, its tiny tapered little head pointed up at the rim, drowned in the act of searching for an escape. A black rat, suspended in brown, its tail exactly like the worm, as if the worm would, when it grew up, have the whole rat for its head, the rat's arms held up and bent under, begging, its long mouth hardened in a grave frown. A frog, white-bellied and sprawled out in cloudy yellow, its neck branching into two heads, one with a mouth and eyes, the other just a lumped sphere, like a little purse full of coins. An eyeball, from what animal she didn't know, with black clouds leaking out of either side of the iris into the white. Finally, the tiny baby hairless white rat floating in a gray syrup. It was barely a rat. A tail just started under its body and a longer tail grew out of the middle of its stomach. Its arms and legs were blunt little nubs without claws, and it had two slitted mounds where its eyes should be. They reminded Julia of the time they made those shapes out of wet clay in her art class that the teacher later cooked; before Julia finished making the person-shape she noticed that you could tell it eventually *would* be a person, because it was an oval with five smaller ovals coming off it, but it wasn't a person yet, not until those ovals got fingers and toes and eyes. The rat had no eyes yet, but it also appeared to have shut its eyes out of fear. The baby rat's expression made her feel like she was falling. The jar wasn't a large one. She pulled the cabinet open, and its door creaked so loudly that all the jarred animals seemed to be screaming. The creaking scream echoed in her ears while she silently, breathlessly held herself still in case anyone had heard. There was only the snow tapping against the window and the faint noise of the TV two floors below drifting lazily up between the spirals of the staircase. With both hands she lifted the small light jar out of its clean circle in the deep dust of the shelf. Then she closed the cabinet door, shut the attic light, pulled the attic door closed, turned the key until the metal clicked, walked down to her bedroom, kissed the spot on the jar in front of the baby rat's formless and aghast head, placed the jar in an inner pocket of her overnight bag, walked down to the kitchen, dumped her soggy cereal in the garbage, threw a paper towel over it so no one would notice, replaced the key in the drawer, and went back to the television. It was an hour before she saw the adults again.

She was so relieved when no one found out that she had taken the jar from the cabinet, packed it in her bag, and brought it to her house, that she went to sleep Sunday night and then forgot about it in the rush to get to school Monday morning. Her mother found it when she emptied the overnight bag for the laundry on Monday afternoon. This time, she didn't speak to Julia's father about it at all, but she did tell Julia that if she brought anything like that home again, she would never be allowed to go to her father's again. Julia asked where the jar was. "I threw the filthy thing away," her mother said.

Her careful study of the librarian's books and her discovery of the cabinet must have led Julia to murder Mephistopheles.

One long summer Sunday about six months after the night she took the rat, Julia's father was in the back yard with some of the men who worked for him regularly. They all had chainsaws and goggles, because they were cutting down a thick-trunked oak tree whose branches hung over the lawn and scattered acorns everywhere, which made it hard to walk on and dangerous to mow. The librarian sat on the back porch and watched them over her glasses, a book on her lap and a glass of water with a lemon slice and no ice cubes on the table beside her; she never drank anything else. All the windows in the house were open, because the librarian didn't believe in air conditioning. The chain saws whined on and on, crying like a fly in Julia's ear, and the whole house filled up with the sweet, burnt smell of fresh wood scorched by the heat of the blade; both the sound and the smell seemed trapped in the sticky air. The tree wouldn't fall. The men, shirtless and slick with sweat, whooped and laughed as they backed a truck across the lawn and up to the tree. They wrapped a heavy clanking chain around and around the trunk and hooked the other end of the chain to a notch in the truck's bed. The angel on the bird bath wobbled gently from side to side as the truck trundled behind it.

All the noise made the TV hard to hear. What the men were doing interested her, but they wouldn't let Julia come close. The librarian was not very good to talk to alone.

Julia wandered through the house, down the dark hallways that seemed like they should extend out over the lawn because they were so long. Then she made up a game. She would sit in every chair in the house; she would stay in each seat with her eyes closed and count to ten before moving on.

She started at the kitchen table, moved to the dining room and the living room, and then she went up the stairs to her bedroom. Her father and the librarian's bedroom, which she wasn't allowed to go in, would be last. She even sat for ten seconds on the toilet lid to delay her disobedience, staring nervously at the claws of the tub. She walked slowly, listening hopefully in case her father or the librarian or the raucous, dirty men would call up to her and stop her from breaking the rules. In the end, no one stopped her, and she reached the door. It wasn't locked; it fact, it stood halfway open already. They had told her not to go in: they must have thought that was as good as a lock. She twisted her torso through the narrow opening without letting herself touch the door, so that it didn't open any wider. In some way, she felt that not touching the door meant that she hadn't broken the rules after all, as if she had just innocently fallen into the room through the gap between the door and the jamb. Trying not to look at the forbidden room but only to finish her game, she leaped with a single purpose into an old black rocking chair with a gray blanket on it that sat in the corner of the room. She had counted four when the blanket writhed and squealed under her. Panic made her jump partially off the chair, but when she realized it was only Mephistopheles, who in his smallness had blended in with the gray blanket, and not something any more threatening, she decided that she could finish counting to ten. She brought her weight down again and shut her eyes; the cat seemed to growl and snarl, but he couldn't hurt her because his jaws and claws were pinned beneath her. When she reached ten, it occurred to her that if she stood up, Mephistopheles would be angry at her and might scratch her face or try to bite her. This made her too frightened to release him. Frozen by her fear, she wondered how long it would take before he would stop screaming and just let her sit on him. This would be a new game, now that she looked around the room and saw that she had sat in the only chair in it, which meant that her old game was finished. The cat's cries braided together with the high-pitched drone of the chainsaws outside. Julia didn't count at all in this new game; she just waited until she didn't hear anything any more.

When she stood up, the cat lay still, arms and legs extended. It looked just like he was sleeping, except that on the side of his face that she could see, his lip was curled up over a bare fang and his eye was wide open, the black eyeball that reminded her of a marble bulging out. She ordered him to wake up. His eye continued to stare. She poked his stomach with two fingers; it felt stiff and hard.

Still nobody came into the house; nobody called her.

She wondered what would happen if she could look inside him the way the librarian's books showed the insides of different animals and people. She thought of the man with the side of his head opened up and the doe with the baby in her belly; maybe, she thought, Mephistopheles had something in his belly. Maybe she could at least see what he ate: a little mouse, maybe.

She carried him carefully into her room. Usually, he squirmed and slipped like a tube of jelly, but now it felt like carrying a piece of furry wood with flopping arms and legs. She decided that it would be breaking too many rules to get the adult scissors from the bathroom drawer, but there were children's scissors in her room for cutting shapes out of construction paper and pictures out of magazines. They had pink plastic handles. She spread Mephistopheles out on the floorboards and pushed the blunt point of the scissors as hard as she could into his white underside. From TV, she knew they should make a red line up his body, which she should be able to pull apart to look inside, but she couldn't get the point in; it just slid along the short soft fur along his belly. Then she closed one fist around the other and the inner fist around the scissors' pink handles. She held the scissors right over the middle of the cat and then raised her coupled fists above her head. She hoped this time it would go straight through so she could see inside.

"Julia," her father said. He stood in the doorway, a clear space around his eyes, which the goggles had sealed, the rest of his face streaked black with dirt. "We've been calling you." He came closer to see what she was doing, blinking the sweat out of his eyes. When he saw that Mephistopheles was dead and that she was trying to cut him open, he slowly swung the back of his heavy hand across the side of her head and knocked her down. She whimpered at the foot of her bed while he made sure the cat was really gone; she had bitten her tongue when he hit her, and she tasted blood all through her mouth, the taste that always made her think she was nothing but metal inside, under it all. Then he gathered her in his arms; he smelled like oil and sawdust and sweat and cigars, and she pushed her face into his heavy belly. She told him what happened between long, heaving sobs that almost made her gag. She kept saying she was sorry, as if she were utterly surprised at what she had done, as if he had found her sleepwalking.

"Okay," he said. "We're not going to tell your stepmother or your mother about this. I'm going to say the cat got lost. You're not going to say anything."

"I don't want to lie," she said.

"It's better to lie sometimes than to hurt someone."

She nodded, tears dripping one after another from her face.

With his rough sawdust- and oil-tipped fingers, the ridged nails stained nicotine-yellow, he gently turned her face to his. "Why did you do it?" he said. He almost sounded afraid, and her father never sounded afraid, because he knew what was real and what wasn't.

"I wanted to see what would happen."

"Well," he said, "now you know."

29

She always remembered the expression on his face, his heavy-lidded eyes turned down at the corners and his bittersweet frown, outlined by his moustache that dropped in two thick patches on either side of his lips down to the line of his jaw. No one had ever looked at her that way before; she would later recognize it as a look that passed between adults from time to time, but rarely from adult to child, a look that extended forgiveness to its recipient on the grounds that the world as a whole was so cruel that no mere fragile creature should be held responsible for any individual cruelty she happened to commit.

Julia could barely stop crying for the remainder of that day. Tears fell silently from her eyes at dinner; they ran down to a point under her chin and dripped into her baked potato. The librarian noticed Julia's morose mood even though she herself quietly grieved for the lost cat. After she mentioned to Julia's father that the child seemed more depressed than she was at the loss of the cat, he took them both out for ice cream, his favorite way of treating them, before bringing Julia back to her mother's house.

Neither the librarian nor her mother ever found out that Julia killed the cat. She never told the story to anyone; only her father knew.

The third time Julia's mother said she wouldn't let her go the librarian's house anymore came much later, when Julia was twelve. It came about because of what the librarian's friend, the tall woman with the long dark hair who never wore shoes, had said to Julia. Julia shouldn't have asked her mother what the bad thing meant; she knew it meant something wrong, even if she didn't know what. She asked because her mother, who was sad because Julia's grandfather had died the previous week, had been yelling at her constantly about her C in pre-algebra and her dirty room and her messy clothes, and Julia just wanted her to be angry at somebody else. She didn't know the bad thing would upset her mother so much that she would finally call the lawyer.

Julia never went back to her stepmother's house again after that. She only saw her father two days a year, in restaurants or parks, and he never brought the librarian with him. Even now that she was an adult, she still only saw him around Christmas and at mid-summer, and he still never proposed that she get re-acquainted with the librarian. Sometimes they would just meet at a theater, watch a movie together, and then separate again. Looking twice a year at each other's faces was the best they could do and would have to be enough. After every time, Julia promised herself she would try harder to re-establish their relationship. Their mid-summer meeting was only two or three months away, and she thought that maybe this time she would start speaking to him about all that had happened. Maybe she would triumph over her guilt at having betrayed him to her mother, and he would forget his embarrassment over what he'd exposed her to. They would forgive each other amid tears with their arms wrapped around each other, instead of trading sad stiff smiles and a tense sideways hug. His hair and his moustache were entirely gray now, and his conversation more and more predictable and querulous. He was turning to stone, as people do. How long did she have before he would be gone from her forever? What creeping paralysis did he see when he looked at her?

She wondered if he had ever told the librarian the truth about Mephistopheles, but she was too ashamed to ask.

* * *

Julia tried very hard to banish these memories during the two hours she spent volunteering at the animal shelter before crossing the bridge again, out of the city proper, to the Asphodel Café, where she would work Caroline's shift. They came back to her anyway; every seemingly new mental pathway she started down brought her straight to them.

She bottle-fed a kitten that once was white but was now streaked yellow and brown like a smoker's fingers. Someone had evidently stabbed the kitten through the eye, because a blood-crusted crescent bisected its empty socket. It lay in her arms, docile and breathing shallowly, made gentle rather than feral by what had befallen it, marked by the infinite gentleness and patience of those who have given up.

As Julia prepared to leave, another volunteer arrived to spend time with the abandoned animals. She was a kindly young woman, round-bottomed, freckled, straw-haired, and hazel-eyed. As she leaned over the boxes where the cats slept, her pendants hung straight down and chimed dully together on their leather thong: a dream catcher, a disk of onyx, and a dancing Kali in pewter. When the volunteer saw the cat's bloody eye socket, she said, "Why is it so much worse when people hurt animals than when they hurt other people?" She lowered her voice and confided to Julia, even though they did not know each other: "Honestly, I'm more horrified that someone did this to an animal than I would be if it had been done to a child. I'll tell you, if ever found the person who did this, I would cut his throat from ear to ear."

Julia nodded and turned to go.

* * *

Though it was only four in the afternoon, the windows of the Asphodel Café went black. Julia, with two plates in either hand and one balanced on her forearm, met her haggard double in the glass. The whole cavernous interior of the café, once a dank warehouse but now illuminated warmly with orange-tinted bulbs hanging high in the rafters, deepened out into the street. The glinting contours of car hoods and raincoat-clad torsos floated spectrally through the tables and chairs; when they passed the window, it looked as if they were disappearing into the canvases that hung on the Asphodel's walls. Julia served her customers and then walked back to the window. She made a tunnel over her eyes with her hands and put her face to the glass: she saw the windy electric minutes before the storm. All the trees in the river-front park across the street swayed and tossed their heads like wailing women at an Old World funeral; the wind flung up the leaves to reveal contemptuously their silver undersides. The sky had the yellowish black color of a diseased organ. Julia stepped back in time to see her reflection vanish as lightning cracked open the clouds and lit up the café in flashbulb white. Rain spattered explosively against the window, rattling the pane, bowing it inward. Julia felt the thunder: it rippled under her feet and drummed in the pit of her stomach.

"Yuliya!" cried Sergey. "Do not just stand there please. Go out and get the sign!"

The wind almost pried the door from her fingers, and she had to put her full weight against it to shut it again. The folding chalkboard sign advertising the springtime specials in bright colors had already been thrown into the side of an aluminum garbage can and was now skittering, collapsed, in the opposite direction over the elegant cobblestone sidewalk. The rain boiled on it as if it were a hot griddle; the pink and blue chalk rilled off between the cobbles. Julia got the sign under her arm and forced the door open again as the rain needled her eyes. There was a lull in the wind, and the door was sucked shut behind her. She stopped just inside the door, breathing hard, her hair streaming, her hands and blouse stained with pastel splotches.

"Do not stand there and drip like a drowned rat please," said Sergey. "You will make a puddle, a customer will fall, I will be sued, and then I cannot pay you. Don't take food out of your own mouth! My mother used to say that."

The three customers she had just served were the only ones in the Asphodel, due both to the bad weather and to the time of day, which was too late for lunch and too early for dinner. They whispered and snickered about how Sergey was running Julia ragged. They shushed each other's giggling when they saw her squinting at them through rain-stung eyes.

Sergey came over to her and took the sign from her hands. The corners of his eyes crinkled kindly as he said, "I will mop the floor. You go to the toilet and dry yourself please." He continued to look at her face as if inviting her to tell him something, to vouchsafe a confidence. She slipped past him.

The three mockers had gone when she came out of the bathroom, but Caroline now sat in a chair by the window. The rain pattered quietly at her back. Her hair was stuck in wet black lines across her face like cracks in her visage. The sodden black dress sagged heavily from her thin frame so that the tear at the sleeve gaped open, the red wound displayed proudly, a rose pinned to her shoulder. She held her phone in one hand and with the other clutched her purse in her lap. Sergey leaned on the counter, eyeing her suspiciously. The drip of water onto the floor from her body ticked like a clock in the silence. Julia averted her eyes from both Caroline and Sergey and walked straight back into the café kitchen, where the sound system was, to put on music. The public radio station was playing some kind of free jazz Julia didn't recognize, with screaming horns and beaten drums and cymbals that seemed to shake from fear. Sergey would complain, but she left it on.

"Yuliya," Sergey said as she walked out of the kitchen, but she didn't stop. She quickened almost to a run as she approached Caroline.

Caroline stood to face Julia. Her face, barred by her hair, contorted itself between laughter and weeping.

"Come on, you bitch," she said. "Did you think I wouldn't find out? Did you think the little retard wouldn't tell me?"

They caught each other, tangled up their arms together.

"How long have you known?"

"Since last night when I heard you come. I thought I'd give you a chance to tell me this morning. You didn't take it."

Caroline's face was still wet from the rain, so Julia couldn't decide if she was laughing or crying.

"But you slept with Connor..."

"Yes, Jules, I am a sexually-active young woman, even sexually incontinent, which is what you're trying to imply. Go to hell! That's different, and you know it is. You were my friend. And Daniel is my brother, and he barely knows where he is half the time. Did you think he'd say no to you? He doesn't know what he wants. You've taken advantage of him. And of me! You're a thief. No, in fact, what you are is you are essentially a *rapist*."

Julia backed out of Caroline's grasp.

"Now you're doing what you do whenever anybody tells you you're wrong. You can't say anything, because you're so obviously wrong, so you make that face where you try to look so innocent and hurt, such a sweet little girl, but it really just makes you look mean and petulant. You think you're a superior person because you don't believe in anything. So you ruin a friendship, you exploit a vulnerable adult, just to get laid? I took you in when you had nothing! When you dropped out of your MFA program to go off with that idiot Cal who wanted you to be in his performance art videos and then left you on the west coast, alone under the palm trees, and you had to blow guys in bus stations to raise the money to get back across the country. Which you told your mother you did in the name of freedom. Remember that? Go to hell, Julia! You don't know what freedom is, you just do whatever you want and call it freedom. Even your work ethic is a lie you tell to make yourself feel superior to me, so why shouldn't I let you work my shifts? 'Oh, Caroline, that bitch is crazy, I'm so put together next to her, I deserve her goddamn money because she needs me around so she doesn't slit her stupid wrists.' That's what you say to yourself, right? I almost feel bad for you, because you do anything to make yourself feel good, and then you lie to yourself and say you did it to help somebody else. Your goodness is a lie. At least I know what I am, but you think you're a goddamn saint. You hated me this morning, but you wouldn't tell me. You think that lying makes you noble. You wanted to sleep with Daniel, so you told yourself it was to make him feel better because he has nothing in his life. What do you say to yourself? 'I'll be nice to both of them'? Go to hell, Julia, you absolutely filthy liar."

Caroline turned around and opened her purse. When she turned back, she held out a small wooden-handled steak knife with a serrated blade already edged with gore.

"You're a self-righteous self-satisfied piece of shit who plays the poor little victim when you really make all the trouble yourself. You know, your mother is actually right about you. She called me again, by the way. She still can't get in touch with you. For some reason, you won't answer your phone. She wants me to tell you that your father dropped dead."

Julia leapt on Caroline. They fell in a clatter of tables and chairs; the knife slid across the floor. The music and thunder pounded together above them, making a sound like lightning-struck trumpeters: agonized squeals burst through brass beneath a drumming sky. The world blanked out red and white in front of Julia. She gripped Caroline by the throat and tightened her hands around her neck so that her thumbs touched under the chin and her forefingers at the soft-haired nape. The tendons flexing against the webs between her thumbs and forefingers caused a memory to flash up: the time her mother first taught her to take apart a whole raw chicken. Gristly little knobs of white cord stuck out of the muscle ends when she wrenched the bones wetly from their sockets.

"Yuliya!" The sound came from far away, her name being called from across a river. Louder now: "Yuliya!" as when you hear your alarm bell as a pleasant, distant carillon, and then it sounds closer and closer until it begins to rattle the walls of your dream. "Yuliya!" roared Sergey into her face, blowing hot spittle onto her cheeks. She released her grip on Caroline's throat. The café came back into her consciousness: Caroline's popping eyes and tensely opened mouth and bleeding shoulder and the red shadows of fingers on her neck; the warm low hearth-light falling softly on the pale brick walls; the abstract paintings, their dabs of color feathered at the edges into fields of white; the slow whispery baritone of the radio announcer who followed the jazz piece; Sergey in front of her, kneeling, his face falling out of its rigid purpose, the lips stretched white across the teeth, down to loose-muscled horror, eyes wide, lips gaping, the gold caps on his back molars glittering with saliva; and the reflection of her own face in the storm-darkened, rain-studded glass, her face as twisted and grimace-frozen and joyously hateful as some ritual mask. She felt a jet of pain in her stomach all of a sudden, so she looked down. The wooden handle of the steak knife stuck out of her abdomen. It was streaked with blood the way Caroline's face had been streaked with her hair. She looked at Sergey, who re-ordered his face from helpless shock to stern good sense and said, "You were going to kill her. What choice I have? You had no control of yourself."

Julia stood dizzily; her arms hung loose in front of her, swaying. Caroline, coughing in long raspy heaves, slipped out from between Julia's legs, grabbed her purse and her phone from the floor with shaking hands, and ran limping out into the rain half-barefoot. She'd lost one shoe in the fight, but it lay upside down behind Julia; Caroline, like a child paralyzed before a yard where a Rottweiler snarled behind a fence, didn't dare try to pass her.

Julia pushed Sergey away and refused to let him call an ambulance. Pressing her wound with one hand, the blood trickling out over her fingers, she gathered her belongings with the other. She walked out into the rain, which she'd hoped to find warmed through by the spring sunshine that had preceded it. A tepid bathwater shower would make her feel buoyant and afloat. Instead, it mottled her skin with cold and pressed her clothes down on her; chilling streams ran down her ribs and between her thighs. She could not stop her jaw from chattering as she crossed over to the park, nor could she still her hands enough to open the umbrella she'd taken from her purse. A car paused to let her pass. Fixed in its headlights, she must have looked like someone haunted or possessed, her teeth snapping, her hair wild, blood pooling under her. She staggered over the green and into the trees. When she finally snapped the umbrella open, a gust tore it inside out and half-flayed its skin from its ribs; it pinwheeled down the grass. Julia collapsed, her skirt billowing up around her as if she had simply vanished into the earth.

* * *

She roused a bit when Sergey put his hands under her arms and pulled her to her feet.

"No hospitals," she said, "I don't have insurance."

"I know, Yuliya. You think I don't know things? I am the one who does not give you insurance or pay you enough to buy your own. Hospitals, they take you even without insurance, you pay bill later. This is a great country. But hospitals, they ask too many questions too. Knife wound they report to police. I can't afford that, Yuliya, so I take you somewhere else, where people go when they can't go nowhere else."

He threw one of her arms over his shoulder and fastened her to his body with one hand clamped to her waist. He drew her along, her feet half-dragging.

"Wait," she murmured faintly when she saw that he was carrying her deeper into the trees, into the forest before the river, which was itself before the city, into near darkness, the rain trickling on the leaves overhead.

"I do not give you insurance, but I know where you can go. You think I come to this country and not learn a few secrets? You don't have to know, but I do."

They passed through the trees and came out on the grassy, muddy bank of the river. Rain churned up the water; it boiled brown. They pulled their feet through the sucking mud until they were stopped by a fence with a gap cut through the bottom, the severed chain links parted widely enough for a person to crawl through. He pushed her forward on her hands and knees, ignoring her cries as her hair caught on the jagged ends of the sliced links. She fell through the mud on the other side of the fence; she buried her cheek in its cool soft darkness. She wanted to say, "I'll just stay here," but she couldn't say anything.

He hauled her up with a grunt and brought her before a large drain, a person-high concrete arch in the wall bounding the river bank. He dragged open the drain's rusty grate and helped her inside. They moved down a long, dark tunnel, massively silent after the chaos and agitations of the storm; their breathing mingled and whispered up and down the rounded walls and raced on before them. They passed a point where another tunnel branched off. Julia peered into it as they went by. Some distance away, this passage emptied into a square room where a white light glowed, surrounded by people in gray coats and robes. She thought they turned their ash-smeared bald heads toward her as she stopped to watch them. Sergey forced her on: "That's not where we're going. Don't go near them, don't even look at them."

Eventually, they came out into a clearing, a square of concrete lit in garish gray by emergency fluorescents fixed to the sides of the walls under dirty casings. Julia, blinded by the glare, put her muddy hands to her eyes and fell back against the concrete wall. The last thing she saw was Sergey striding toward a metal door set into the opposite wall and pounding his fist against it; the booms caromed off the concrete and resonated in the hollows of Julia's skull.

A sliding sound, as of a panel opening in the door: "Password!" a bass voice demanded.

Sergey said, "Caduceus."

The door creaked open and Julia, still blinded, felt two sets of hands on her. She was lifted up by her arms and legs and carried up a short ramp. Then she was set onto the slack leather bottom of an old wheelchair.

When she opened her eyes, she found herself in a huge room, some kind of old basement or abandoned swimming pool, with yellow-tiled walls and floors. There was a slab in the center of the room, a mobile light above it, and equipment to the side of it, all trailing tangled bundles of wires that were plugged into the mildewed wall. Great clouds of steam rolled over a trough; the whole room, though vast, felt warm as a bath. On one cot in a corner of the room, an emaciated man with an intravenous drip lay staring out of nearly unfleshed eye sockets into the dark; in another, a small boy slept heavily, his head wrapped in bandages that extended over one eye, a blotch of blood in its center, where the pupil would be. A matronly woman with gray hair and a white apron bustled toward Julia from the trough, her plump arms red and steaming, her fingers pruned. She looked at Julia through thick glasses with dispassionate concern. The woman's kind smile was lopsided; its left half decayed into a fleshy scar, bunched and puckered, the remains of what must once have been a fierce gash. She wiped one wet hand on her apron and then extended it to Julia.

"I'm Dr. Grace," she said.

Julia understood just before she lost consciousness that she was in an operating theater.

3. SAINT MONDAY

"Julia Bonham?" said a voice out of the dark, slurring it *jul-yah*.
Julia said, "No, that's not my name."

* * *

She dreamed of Mark Weis. It had taken her a long time to notice him, because rather than in spite of his always being there, wherever she was, in classes, at parties. He never said much and had an appearance without any irregularities, either good or bad: he kept his black hair closely cropped over his evenly-distributed features and was of average height with a build that was not muscular or fat or skinny. He maintained straight *A*s without being thought of as an especially intelligent person; he was good at everything, but great at nothing.

His only stake on fame, the source of the epithet that followed him wherever he went in the social circles of the large public high school that Julia's mother had been forced to send her to after no longer being able to afford Catholic school tuitions, was a website he and his friends had created. It "randomly generated utterances in the voices of various well-known personages in the high school from a few surreptitiously-recorded keywords representing their most characteristic lexical and syntactical idiosyncrasies," as it explained on its front page. Targeted figures included beloved teachers, whose brilliant eccentricities the boys obviously meant to parody with affection, and hated authority figures, from vice principals to cheerleaders. Because they represented concentrated variants of their usual talk, their algorithmically-produced sentences demonstrated the brutality or the absurdity that they inflicted on and through language. This was Mark

Weis's rare moment of genius: he didn't only record his targets' speech, which any aspiring voyeur could do, but he shaped it into a portrait of them by stripping away what he judged to be inessential.

"Money is what matters," spoke the voice of their civics teacher jerkily on their website, "it's just that simple. Go to college and major in something useful, not underwater basket weaving. There's no two ways about it. If you're a loser, no one will want you. Would you hire a loser to fix your toilet or program your computer? It's just that simple. If you need somebody to weave your basket underwater, go to the homeless shelter. Even your mother won't love you if you're a loser. You know what people love? Money. It's just that simple. There's no two ways about it."

Mark and his friends didn't make this website to crusade for justice, but they did follow an ethical code that forbade them from going after the truly powerless. They didn't mock the most ineffectual teachers, the ones who couldn't control their classrooms and were always consequently having pieces of chalk flung at their heads or their overhead projector screens vandalized with cocks and balls in permanent marker. Among their fellow students, they refused to parody the most unpopular people, the truly shunned and reviled, the nearly autistic or the morbidly obese. On the other hand, they did take on the bullying leaders of the subcultural cliques, those who saw themselves as morally irreproachable outsiders because they had rings in their noses or pink streaks in their hair. Most importantly, they included themselves in their criticism: each of the boys responsible for the site uploaded his own sound file, in which he too spouted repetitive inanities to reveal his essential banality or thoughtlessness. This lent the whole exercise a genial, merry tone; they were only suspended for three days. Since most of their targets, from the civics teacher to the ringleader of the goths, behaved so offensively in the first place precisely because they were narcissists, a class for which there is no such thing as bad publicity, nobody much held it against the boys. Mark Weis was nevertheless for the rest of high school known as "that Internet guy."

The Internet scandal happened in his and Julia's sophomore year, though, and Julia had little recollection of it by the fall of senior year. She knew little about Mark Weis, only that he moved in her circle and took a few classes with her. Even though she'd never really spoken to him, when she called his face to her mind, it wore a smile both kindly and fascinated, the smile of someone who could probably find out how to hurt you if he wanted to, but who would not want to. One night, for no reason she could figure, she dreamed that he came to her house and cooked her dinner.

The weekend after the night she had that dream, she again found herself out in his company. About eight or nine of them, in two cars, went to the Arcadia Mall. In a dark corner of the multi-level parking garage, they bought pot from some students at the community college who had gone to their high school; then they intended to drive to the park and smoke it. Mark Weis sat on the concrete at the entrance of the parking garage, "to keep lookout," he said, though Julia, who had resolved to pay attention to Mark since he had cooked her a dream dinner, surmised that he was prudently trying to stay away from the scene of a crime. Mark never took any drugs, though he didn't moralize about it either; she seemed to recall someone mocking him for being so straight-laced, and he had said that his parents still hadn't forgiven him for his earlier suspension, so he couldn't get in trouble again. His mixture of prudence and innocence, his ingenuous guile, appealed to her, made him attractively small in her eyes.

Later, they stopped to shoot pool in a strip mall along the highway because they didn't want to get to the park too early, when there would still be five-year-olds playing on the swing sets and seventy-year-olds walking their laps. Julia's social group and Mark's intersected at one point: a friend of hers who had been dating a friend of his for a year. This meant that the two groups weren't necessarily close, and in the pool hall, they separated and played at two tables. Julia watched him, though. When he went to the bathroom, she excused herself too. She walked into the women's room and then out again, and then pretended to stare at the fliers on the cork board on the back wall of the long, low-ceilinged, dank hall. Mark came out of the men's room, rubbing his wet hands carelessly on his pants, fully as if he didn't expect anyone to be waiting for him or looking at him.

"Hey, come here," she said, and then she winced and ground her teeth because she had said, "Hey, come here," like someone summoning a pet or a toddler.

He joined her at the cork board. She didn't explain why she'd called him over, and he didn't ask. They stood there, in difficult silence at first, and then they made fun of all the amateur advertisements for grass-cutting, leaf-blowing, babysitting, math tutoring, church socials, bake sales, army recruiting, and amateur softball leagues. Across the hall, their friends grew raucous: somebody accidentally launched a ball off the tip of the cue across several tables, which made them all laugh so hard they were falling into each other; then one of his friends took out a lighter and ignited an empty rolling paper, which shot up a gout of flame in his face that had them all squealing. The bikers who otherwise occupied the dim expanse of the hall told them to shut the hell up or get out, and the red-faced old manager heaved his bulk in their direction on thin legs and told them to leave before he called the cops. Julia and Mark watched from the back of the room, not moving. "What about Julia?" one of her friends cried as they were being forced out the door.

"I'm fine!" she called back with a bright wave of her hand.

Then he leaned toward her and kissed her cheek.

Days later, in the park, they were by themselves. He told her that he had always thought she was "pretty and interesting," but assumed that she would probably not care for him since a pretty and interesting girl could go with whoever she wanted to, and anyway, he'd always managed to have girlfriends of his own. Some of them were pretty, but none as interesting as Julia. He had no more specific word for her than "interesting," though; he wasn't the type to write love poetry or strum a guitar at a girl.

She said that even if she could go with whoever she wanted, and she assured him that she hadn't found that to be true, she also didn't see what was so interesting about herself. As for prettiness, she didn't want to fish for compliments, and she wasn't one of those girls who made her face the center of her life, in fact she had contempt for just those sorts of girls; but she thought he nevertheless had to admit that she had a somehow shapeless body deliberately hidden under correspondingly shapeless T-shirts, as well as hair of such a plainly blondish brown that it practically didn't exist and a much too long and pointed nose that existed more insistently than anything else about her.

"Yeah, I said 'pretty *and* interesting.' Try to keep up," he said and pulled her face close to him so he could kiss her nose.

"But come on, what made you interested in me?"

"Remember a couple months ago in physics when Mr. Starr went on that incredibly long tangent about what you could do with numbers, and he wrote the proof on the board demonstrating with absolute logical validity that one equaled two? And then he looked up and said, 'What's my point in telling you this?' Nobody said anything. And you raised your hand, even though you never, ever talk in that class. You just like to sit in the back and watch. Do you remember what you said?"

"I don't remember any of that."

"That's because you do too much of this," he said and knocked the blunt out of her hand and into the grass. "You said, 'The point is that we made up numbers the same way we made up words, and we can lie with either of them. But the truth is what happens, not what somebody says about it.'"

"Jesus, I said that? What did he say?"

"I don't remember, I was too busy noticing for the first time that you were hot. I think he called you a nihilist or something. Oh yeah, and an *antinomian*. I remember, I wrote it down to look up later, and then I forgot to look it up."

"You think a girl's hot because she says something smart and sort of depressing? You must be a very serious person. Don't you want to know why I noticed you?"

"No," he said. "I just want it to stay this way."

41

They were together all of senior year and the summer after before they went to separate colleges and inexorably turned from each other.

It was in the spring that they made love, in her mother's house.

His own parents dealt with him gently and rewarded him for meeting their demands, but they were also somewhat remote, an older couple who perhaps, as he was slowly coming to understand, hadn't planned on having a third child so long after they'd had his brother and sister, themselves close in age and twelve and fourteen years older than he was, respectively. His father was an insurance inspector and his mother a retired music teacher who sang in the church choir, and they took no intense interest in Mark's life unless they thought he was ruining it, as with the sophomore year suspension. They were polite to Julia and had said nothing against her to Mark, which signaled their mildly indifferent approval.

Julia's mother adored Mark, doted on him, deferred to him. She asked him to repair her computer, to look under the hood of her car, to re-ignite the pilot light in the oven. She praised his good grades, his facility with machinery of all sorts, his abstention from cigarettes and alcohol and drugs, his college plans, and his mature ability to hold a civilized conversation.

"I was worried you would find some clever and unambitious screw-up like your father," she told Julia. "Somebody who would enable your tendency to drift. You get that from his side of the family, you know, that awful dago laziness, that failure to take life seriously, to take any responsibility for things. But this boy, I can't believe him. He's no joke. I think he's really good for you, Jules. Listen: let's not tell grandma he's Lutheran."

Julia's mother, Mrs. Bonham, had a strange attitude toward the prospect of Mark's having sex with Julia. She knew enough to know it would be Julia's first time, and she knew too that an eighteen-year-old girl had to lose her virginity eventually, probably sooner rather than later, and almost certainly prior to marriage, which in any case should come only when Julia was much older, after she had finished her education and begun a profitable career. As for safety, she had no fears: Mark Weis was a responsible boy. Mrs. Bonham also kept up her religion as a social form, though nobody, least of all her daughter, knew what she really believed or how seriously to take her usual platitudes about how whatever happened was evidence of "God's plan." For these reasons, Mrs. Bonham explicitly discouraged them from making love, while, with almost theatrical verve, failing to take any steps to prevent it. She demanded that Julia keep the door of her bedroom open when Mark visited, but then she was always discovering when they were up there that she had run out of paper towels or butter and would consequently have to go to the store and leave them alone.

One time after she left on one of her shopping runs, Julia asked Mark to strip completely naked, the first time he had done so in front of her. She not only remained clothed but also tied her painting smock around her waist and retrieved an easel, canvas, and oil paints from her walk-in closet. She brought out crumpled balls of old newspaper, which she then unfolded and spread on the beige carpet before positioning the easel. "My mother would be more upset if she came home to find me painting over the bare carpet than she would to find us doing it," she explained. Mark lay on his side on her pink bedspread, chin resting on one hand, his down-turned head inviting, his slim ankles crossed like the legs of a fawn she had once seen. She painted his portrait all afternoon. Mrs. Bonham stayed out for two hours that day, but Julia and Mark never touched each other.

Mrs. Bonham was in fact at home with them when it actually happened. She was sitting on the front porch, smoking a cigarette, her pink-slippered feet propped up, because she wanted to watch the rain. Huge black clouds had banked up suddenly, even though it had been a hot, sunny Saturday afternoon in April. Mark and Julia had gone to a pre-graduation class picnic at an amusement park, but they pulled up in Mrs. Bonham's driveway in his car earlier than expected and ran to the porch, just ahead of the rain.

"We were going to leave early anyway," Julia said. "We were riding in the paddleboats and some kid accidentally dropped his giant drink off the bridge right overtop of us." She showed her mother the streak of bright red down the front of her white shirt. Then she ran upstairs to shower the sticky sugar out of her hair as the rain started thudding dully on the aluminum awning over the porch.

As he told Julia later, Mark settled down to watch the rain with Mrs. Bonham and to have a conversation with her, but she said, "Sweetie, do me a favor and go tell Jules to make sure she rubs the stain-stick on that shirt." She took a long pull on her cigarette.

"I thought you were trying to quit," he said.

"I am trying. I'm just failing."

She blew a long, widening column of smoke out over the porch until it disappeared into the slanting rain.

He went inside and up the stairs, deliberately stomping his feet to alert Julia of his approach. She was already in the shower and couldn't hear him. He opened the bathroom door and called her name, and she screeched with terror behind the white plastic curtain; then she started laughing breathlessly at her own needless fears. She pulled the curtain aside and faced him naked through the steam. "Hey, come here," she said, laughing. Before he dropped his pants, he opened his wallet to get the condom he carried. They ended up on the floor of the tub, the water gently tapping the curtain above them just as the rain tapped the small eye-level window set into the shower's wall. Bruising her elbows and knees against the warmed white ceramic, Julia felt as if she were in a wave-tossed, rain-lashed boat, battered and washed at sea. When they tried to get up, their feet kept slipping, and eventually they tore the shower curtain halfway down; the metal rings spun and chimed on the rod. They couldn't stop laughing. She aggressively dried his short hair, abrading his scalp with each pass of the rough towel. Then he hastily got back into his clothes. He kissed her cheek, told her to put some stain-stick on her shirt, and went back down the steps, taking them two at a time.

When she came down fifteen minutes later, her whole body sore and charged, the returned sun, amplified by every raindrop still affixed to the front windows, filled the house with blinding white light. Mark and Mrs. Bonham were in the kitchen now, talking and laughing: she read him ludicrous stories from the newspaper, while he stood at the counter and chopped onions, carrots, and celery in preparation for cooking dinner. His hair was still wet. "Oh, listen to this one: 'Local woman claims her dog predicts social collapse.' As if you need a dog to tell you that!" Their uproarious laughter was spiced with the scent of onion and of soaked spring leaves, bruised and bloody from the storm, drying in the sun. Julia watched through the kitchen door at a distance for a long time, not announcing her presence.

Years later, after their relationship had peaceably faded into the distance between their two colleges, she shipped the nude portrait to him.

* * *

"Well, 'Julia Bonham' is what it says here. Anyways, you look like you're doing all right. When people get here, they're usually too desperate to ask any questions, but if they make it through whatever their emergency is, they start to wonder about Dr. Grace. She's okay, though, despite what you might be thinking. Maybe people have to pay for the things they do wrong, but she has a goddamn gift, and I don't see why the rest of us should suffer for the lack of it just because she screwed up her own life. That's how she makes up for it, I guess: she stays down here in this hole and takes the folks nobody else will. It's pretty seriously illegal, of course, but there are people who say the cops know all about it and help her out here and there. You've heard the joke, right? What's the difference between a cop and criminal? A badge! Well, I wouldn't laugh either if my stomach was all sewn up. But I like to add something to that: what's the difference between a doctor and a patient? Luck! That's the long and short of it there, Ms. Bonham. So, yeah, she killed a kid, and nothing's ever going to fix that, but the way I see it, she's saved a hell of a lot of people since then. I'm happy to do some volunteering down here after she helped me out so much; she was the one who suggested it, actually. And a lot of other people besides me want to help her keep this operation going on the sly. If the cops ever bust it up, well, they can put me away. Frankly, at this point, it would be a relief."

Julia opened her eyes, still smelling onions, expecting to see old Mark Weis, whom she hadn't thought of in years, and his shy, amused smile. Instead she saw a man in his fifties or sixties with a plump body, a drawn face, sunken cheeks, and luminous blue eyes. He had a kind of randy smirk. His long head shook, describing a very small circle in the air as he spoke, jostling the scant pale hair over his forehead. Numerous questions clogged Julia's throat, and the one that finally escaped in a kind of cry wasn't really what she had wanted to ask at all: "What happened to you?"

"Honey, you wouldn't believe me if I told you." When she didn't say anything to that, he leaned toward her and said, "Okay, try this on for size: strychnine poisoning. I was in *The Last Café*."

He was right: she didn't believe him. She didn't have time to ask any questions, though, because Dr. Grace came up behind him and said, "That's enough for today, Tom. Let's let Ms. Bonham rest."

"She says that's not her name."

"No, no, it *is* my name. I'm sorry, I was confused."

"That's perfectly understandable," Dr. Grace said. She led Tom away from Julia, across the large mildewy yellow-tiled vault toward another bed, where a young man lay with staring eyes, his shoulder wrapped in bloody bandages. "Can you wash up and then change his dressing?"

Tom disrupted his involuntary tremor to nod; then he went about his work. Looking down at the blood-soaked bandages, he grumbled, "That'll teach you to play with guns, kid. We all come here to learn something, and there's your lesson."

Dr. Grace stood over Julia with her arms akimbo, her authoritative smile half-kindly, half-mangled.

"Was he really in *The Last Café*?" Julia whispered.

"I don't know for sure, but he really ingested a nearly lethal dose of strychnine." Dr. Grace pulled down the sheet and examined Julia's wound. She said as she did so, "I remember when I first heard about *The Last Café*. I thought, This is truly the end of our civilization. We've sunk to a depth of degradation that nobody could have imagined even ten years ago. People out of work, cultural fragmentation, political polarization, no one having anywhere to turn, nobody helping anybody: maybe when a society gets to that point, it inevitably falls prey to the evil nihilism of *The Last Café*, the end of any faith or kindness or decency. But that filth found defenders, people who called it art, a radical work of art. Academics mostly, so what do you expect? But still..."

Julia nodded in polite agreement.

"So what else did talkative Tom tell you?" Dr. Grace asked.

"Oh, I don't even remember."

"Thank you for saying that, Ms. Bonham. But the fact is that I was an alcoholic, and I did lose my medical license and serve a five-year prison sentence after an incident in which I operated a vehicle while intoxicated. I struck the side of another car, where a four-year-old boy named Peter Dunn rode as a passenger. He died on impact."

She reached into her the front pocket of her white coat and retrieved a laminated wallet-sized picture of a boy with a buzz cut and a gap-toothed smile; he'd been photographed against a gray backdrop crisscrossed by brightly colored lines. Dr. Grace held the photo up a long time, to make sure Julia truly saw it.

"It's moreover true that I operate this hospital illegally, though with the tacit cooperation of some local and state authorities, who appreciate its mission, which is larger in scope than that of your standard medical center. If you suffer from any malpractice caused here, I will do my best to make reparations in a way we both can agree on, but I ask you not to jeopardize this hospital, which serves so many people with nowhere else to go, and in ways well beyond the care of the body. If you attempt to involve police or attorneys, I think you'll find them unsympathetic to your cause, either at first or in time. You may also find yourself personally inconvenienced. Do you understand what you've just heard?"

Julia nodded uncertainly.

Dr. Grace's posture relaxed: "Good. Now that I've made my little speech, we can talk, girl-to-girl. You're going to be fine. It really wasn't a very deep wound, though you must have tried to pull away, because the muscle tissue was slashed horizontally. I know Sergey, very well actually, and I know he wouldn't do something like that out of malice. Not at this point in his life, anyway. You're going to be very sore for a few days, but after two to three weeks of stitches and rest, and by 'rest' I mean no stretching, no lifting, no motion above a slow walk, you should be fine. In fact I can discharge you today."

Julia nodded again and started, very gingerly, to rise from the cot she lay on. Dr. Grace placed her hands on Julia's shoulders and carefully pushed her back down.

"But there is something else you need to know. Something I'm very sorry about."

She seemed to search her patient's face, but Julia only blinked.

"You suffered a miscarriage before you even arrived here. It was over by the time I saw you. There was nothing I could do."

"A miscarriage?"

"Ms. Bonham, I run this hospital on a strict principle of 'no questions asked' until my patients are well again. Given my history, I can hardly set myself up as the judge of the mistakes that bring people here, though I do take steps, as you might find out, to discourage them from making more mistakes in the future. This is why the authorities find me valuable. Just ask Mr. Thug over there if I've said a word to him about his dangerous lifestyle yet," she told Julia with a lowered voice, nodding her head toward the wide-eyed young man with the bloody shoulder. "But my old friend Sergey told me what happened with you. I don't have any advice at all to give, and no right to give any if I had it. Everybody has their own journey to go on. All I'll tell you now is that I don't think you should look at this loss as a bad thing, considering the circumstances. And I think you might want to ask yourself very carefully from now on, 'How do I want to live my life?'"

Julia averted her eyes from Dr. Grace's serious gaze and looked out over the yellow-walled theater and up at the expanse of dank darkness above the fluorescent lights that hung overhead. An odor of mold stuck to everything. Tom was silent as he meticulously flushed Mr. Thug's bullet wound. The boy with the bandaged eye lay with one leg crossed over the opposite knee, carelessly bobbing his foot in the air, reading a comic book with a stern expression on his face. The emaciated man now sat up on his cot as another volunteer soaped his long, wasted legs; he stared down his own atrophying body with startled eyes, amazed to see his skeleton slowly rise into view through his very person.

Finally, Dr. Grace said, "You know, I just love your hair. Sometimes I wish I was twenty years younger, so I could try to pull it off. But everything goes, and you don't get it back. Anyway, what's the color called?"

"'False Alarm,'" Julia said.

Just then, a clamor echoed up the long ramp that led into the theater. A teenaged girl and boy, brother and sister from the look of them, emerged into the light, nearly crushed under the weight of an enormous black Doberman they carried in their arms, its long sleek body sagging between them.

Through gasping breaths, the girl, who was the older one, said to Dr. Grace, "We heard you're a doctor who helps people without any money. Daddy said we have no money for a vet."

She smiled patiently and said, "I'm not a veterinarian, but I'll see what I can do."

"You can help my brother too," the girl said. "Caesar bit him bad. That's why I had to hit him in the head with the bat. But we don't want him to die."

Dr. Grace, with practiced and deliberate care, lifted the unconscious dog out of the siblings' arms. Then the boy silently raised his black shirt, which masked the blood, to show her the wound in his side.

No one noticed Julia slip out of bed, into her clothes, and back up to the light.

* * *

"Hello?"

47

"Sergey, it's Julia."

"How are you? Dr. Grace take care of you?"

"Yes, very well. But listen, Sergey, I don't think I can come in today."

"Of course not. We call it 'Feast of St. Monday' in the old world, when worker doesn't come in after the weekend. After big party."

Julia laughed.

"Don't worry, I do all the work anyway. I ask Carolina not to come back too. I can do hard work, unlike you girls."

"Sergey, I don't know if I can..."

"Don't say nothing please, Yuliya. I was your age once, long time ago. You think I didn't make all my mistakes? I made all my mistakes."

"But I just called to say..."

"Don't say nothing please. Good luck to you. I am always here when you need me. And God bless you."

* * *

She was, as usual, looking over her fellow bus passengers to evaluate their sanity when it occurred to her that, because she had only been able to retrieve some of her clothes on her hasty way out of Dr. Grace's hospital, the other passengers probably thought of her as the crazy one.

A prim old man in a rumpled hound's-tooth suit sat across from her and peered at her with wide rheumy eyes through horn-rimmed spectacles. Those eyes traveled from her unlaced black boots up her pale bruised legs to her paper hospital gown with the leather jacket, its lining stiff with dried blood, draped over it. In his lap, he held a package carefully; he sat very still with his long wingtips flat on the floor, heels together. The jostling of the bus across the winter-pitted asphalt rocked his stiff body from side to side, and the mobile tessellations of the hound's-tooth sent rhythmic waves of pain between Julia's temples. As the bus shook, she superstitiously kept her hand cupped over the location of her wound like a medieval horseman, cleaved from sternum to pommel, swaying on his headlong mount, trying to hold his guts in.

Toward the rear of the bus, where the young and healthy congregated, a group of men loudly discussed, with interspersed bursts of laughter, ways to evade the family courts' pursuit of back child support. A lone man sitting apart from them shouted into his phone that he needed a ride to his next court date. Nearer to where Julia sat, a bearded student with eighteen-gauge talons through both ears slouched across two seats reading a book of radical political theory with some kind of Constructivist painting reproduced on the cover, red triangles at war with white circles, the kind of book that she would have tried without much success or interest to read in her art theory classes in graduate school. Every so often he would lift his eyes, under angrily bunched brows, from the page to her face, as if testing the book's propositions against her reality and finding a recalcitrant misalignment. A woman younger than Julia texted furiously while the two children in her care played some kind of game where they ran from empty seat to empty seat in the front of the bus. The children's shrieks shot from the wound in Julia's abdomen up to her back bottom teeth. The texting woman smelled of vanilla, and Julia allowed herself to drift amid her sugary atmosphere during the brief moments when the pain released her. She felt relief that no one had tried to call or text her since she had emerged from the underground hospital.

Her head kept growing heavy and falling forward; she imagined that the front of her face was full of stones. The clattering bus, its windows rattling in their frames as potholes snapped at the wheels, faded gradually in and out of her consciousness, like an emergency light with a slow cardiac blink. She knew where she would get off the bus, but she didn't want to let herself know. She wished someone would come along and collect her, gather her up in a pair or a quartet of arms, and take her to some asylum or lazar-house where she could stare at the wall and allow a sister of mercy to sponge her burning forehead until she finally died in peace.

"Are you okay?" one of the children asked her.

She jerked her head up; the little girl wore a glitter-decorated kitten T-shirt, and she stared at Julia solicitously, if also with an air of judgment.

"I think she's drunk!" cried the other girl, perhaps the less sensitive of the pair.

Julia turned away from this high-pitched accusation as if she'd been struck. This movement twisted her torso along the torn flesh and muscle of her stomach. A burst of pain like an orange flare flashed across her eyes.

The girls' guardian was still texting, her head stubbornly bowed. Julia wanted her to reprimand these children before they turned the whole bus against her. The old man now carefully studied her again; she thought she saw him clutch his package more tightly.

"Who's drunk?" said the bus driver.

Julia opened her mouth, but nothing came out. Her dry and constricted throat made a kind of clicking sound.

"Are you gonna throw up, lady?" said the girl with the kitten shirt; its glitter hurt Julia's eyes.

"Who's going to throw up?" demanded the bus driver. "If you're drunk and going to throw up, then get the hell off my bus," he said to no one in particular, articulating a general principle.

Both girls now stood in front of Julia, trying to think of what to say next.

Then one of the men in the back of the bus shouted, "Look! It's the It people!"

The bus was stopped at a red light, so everyone had time to look. The little girls both ran to kneel on the seat opposite Julia and press their noses against the dirty glass. Everyone, even the texting woman and the fastidious old man, turned to look out the window. Julia took the opportunity to tilt her head back and close her eyes. She didn't need to see the It people, because she had seen them already, just yesterday, though it felt like years ago. Voices came and went at her out of the dark.

"What are they doing to her?"

"They're like giving her a massage. That's how they get you to go with them."

"Wish they would come give me a massage. I'd go with them too."

"I'll give you a massage, baby. I mean, these kids aren't yours, are they?"

"Some dirty creep touches me, he, she, or it is getting popped in the face. I hear they live in the sewers."

"Can't tell if it's a male or a female. They don't want you to know."

"I hear they piss and shit right where they stand."

"Language, dude. We got minors here."

"They're like this movie I saw once where there were a lot of fish in the ocean, and the fish all moved together, that's called a school, and no fish ever went by itself because they all went everywhere together, and when one was sick they would all swim around it and carry it..."

"Yeah, yeah, yeah, I saw that movie too!"

"Shut up, dummy! No you didn't!"

"They're the revolutionary multitude, all of the excluded, man as species, affect generalized, the persistence of life apart from consciousness, the sublime purity of the conatus against all territorializations. Immanent being without intent or control. They aren't subjects. They're post-humanity. What comes after the subject. The reign of love."

Julia opened her feverish eyes in time to see that the old man had turned from the window and faced her again. He said, very quietly, through thin white lips, his eyes wide and wet, as if addressing only her, "Essenes. Desert Fathers. Bogomils. Albigenses. Fifth Monarchy Men. The rejection of *this* world."

* * *

"I will of course want to paint you again. But so soon?"

"This will be the last time. I'm going somewhere. I'm going on a trip. I don't know if I'll be back."

The artist hesitated on the other end of the line; then he said, "Tomorrow in church, yes?"

"Yes. I would really like that. I would really, really like that."

"My dear, are you sick?"

* * *

The man with the goatee and the green snake wrapped around his neck leaned against the big metal door to the apartment building. He smoked a hand-rolled cigarette and stared into the distance. She had to stand in front of him for a while before his abstracted vision gathered her into focus. Then he stared at her, his eyes darting from the hospital gown to the dried blood on the lining of her coat to whatever slack or twisted expression her face wore; she couldn't tell anymore, because she no longer had any inner vision of her face.

"Whoa," he said. "You all right?"

She asked him if she could smoke some of his cigarette. She had given up the habit years ago, but she felt she needed a strong sensation to wake her from this feverish confusion. He handed it over and said, "Keep it," probably worried that whatever she had wrong with her was contagious.

She concentrated very hard on sucking the ashy smoke into the back of her throat. It felt like a metal rake dragged over gravel. When she contracted her muscles to pull the smoke through the paper-wrapped cylinder of tobacco, a spike of pain went from her stomach wound straight through her body and exploded out her back. She heard a sound, a long creaking hissing groan, which insisted in her ear like a fly. She realized it had come out of her own mouth.

The snake man raised his eyebrows and put the key in the lock. He held the door open for her. "You should go upstairs," he said. "Your other two roommates aren't there. They left this morning and didn't come back. But I let in this other lady about an hour ago. I bet she'll take care of you. She said she was your mom."

When she passed under his long branching arm as it held the door open, she saw that the snake coiled around the muscle, and its tail rested on the elbow, dangling down with the bunched skin that hung from the extended joint.

"Why a snake?" she said through her parched throat.

He turned the left side of his face toward her, where the snake's mouth opened wide just below his ear.

"The snake stands for knowledge. I want him to whisper what he knows to me."

"He hasn't?"

"Not yet." The snake man smiled. "But I have faith."

* * *

Mrs. Bonham looked awful. Her eyeliner was off-center, which made her seem to have two sets of subtly mismatched eyes superimposed on each other. Long cracks in her face, sedimented with dusty foundation, surrounded her mouth. Her pink-tinted lips had set into a permanent just-parted, half-pursed expression, a startled beak, as if she were always suddenly being told news that alarmed and disgusted her. She was too skinny, lost in her purple sweater with its fashionable scarf-like collar, out of which her neck emerged, strung with tense veins and tendons under scaly, exsanguinated skin. Julia was sure she would lose consciousness after climbing the stairs, and she felt her senses failing one by one, but she nevertheless noticed every defect in her mother's face. They came to her through a tunnel of clear perception that ran through the darkness that encroached on her vision. Death had been visiting her mother in the night, leaving scratches and bruises all over her, in impatient anticipation of the day when he would finally carry her off for their consummation. What did Mrs. Bonham see when she looked at Julia?

"First of all, little girl," Mrs. Bonham said from her seat at the kitchen table, "don't you ever go for this long without answering your phone when I call you. Do you have any idea what you put me through? You are selfish. Selfish! You are twenty-eight years old. You are too old to be acting this way, Julia."

Julia crossed the kitchen carefully and sat down opposite Mrs. Bonham at the table. "Second of all?" she said hoarsely.

"I don't care how old you are, I'll smack your smart mouth, you little brat."

Julia laid her head between her arms.

"Look at me," Mrs. Bonham said, but Julia kept her head down. Her mother put both hands on Julia's arm and said, "Sweetie, your father is dead."

Julia said into the table, so that it echoed, "I know."

"Don't you want to know how it happened?"

"What difference does it make?"

Mrs. Bonham let Julia's arm go and leaned back, seeming to think about the question. She folded her arms across her chest and started talking.

"Well, Jules, let me tell you what difference it makes. Let me tell you this story, and you pay attention, and then you can tell me if it gives you a clue about where your own life is headed. It seems that your father and the librarian were up to their old tricks again. The same tricks that led to my request for sole custody when they were shacking up with that obscene piece of bohemian trash, you remember her, back when I realized they had no business raising my daughter, not even on the weekends, not even on the part-time basis that I think should disqualify a man from the title of 'father.' Well, this time they were careless. Even more careless than usual, if you can imagine that, and they are very careless, very irresponsible people. They invited another girl in, the way they invited in that Alice woman fifteen years ago, the one who ought to be in jail for the part she played in *The Last Café*. This girl, and she is a girl, not much older than you, was apparently living in one of your father's buildings, and, whenever he went over to fix the oven or unplug the drain, he must have noticed, with a little help from her simperings and insinuations, I have to imagine, that she was poor and unemployed, that she couldn't take care of herself, because he started giving her money. You know your father, even his goodness is bad, naïve and arrogant, because I guess he, who walked out on his own wife and daughter, thought he could save this stranger. So he brought her home like an animal to the librarian's house. Anyway, this girl had a boyfriend or ex-boyfriend she was keeping secret from the two of them. This boyfriend got wind of the fact that she was spending her time in a nice house in a nice neighborhood, and then he got a bright idea, probably the only bright idea he ever had in his stupid life, that she should let him in so he could take whatever he wanted. See, he didn't work, he probably couldn't get hired even if he wanted to because he was some kind of felon, and he relied on the girl to support him, for which I say a big thank-you to the feminist movement, by the way, and he came up with the plan that she should support him by helping him commit robbery. A whole crew of lazy, selfish, naïve, irresponsible people is involved here, Jules, so pay attention, try to keep it straight. Anyway, this stupid little girl lets her boyfriend in, and your stupid father wakes up and finally tries to take some genuine family responsibility for once in his life by defending his wife's house. But it's too late for family responsibility now. He should have started twenty years ago if he didn't want to find a thief in the night. Your father doesn't know he's a fat old man now, so he tries to go one on one with this boy, who's probably been in prison for all we know and was probably strung out on some kind of dope too, and your father drops to the floor and dies with a heart attack while his loving wife, the librarian, apparently left him there gasping for breath, because she was trying to get out of the bedroom to prevent the thieves from taking any of her beloved books and carcasses. How such a smart woman ever got to be so stupid, I'll never know. Then the boy and the girl took what they wanted and tried to burn the house to the ground on top of that, but the librarian got out in time. This happened last week. The police caught the stupid girl trying to use the librarian's credit cards, and the weak stupid girl spilled the whole story. The boyfriend is on the lam somewhere. And do you know how I found out about this? I saw it on the news. That's the father of my only child, and I saw it on the news. Nobody cared to tell me. Nobody cared. Then I tried to call you, and apparently you didn't care either. And on the one hand, you know, I say that's what your father gets. I told him twenty years ago, 'This is all going to bite you on the ass someday, Frank, don't think God's going to let you get away with this,' and he got that look on his face, you get it yourself, Jules, like he just wants to laugh at you because he's so smart and superior and you're so stupid and simple for believing in things like responsibility and decency and God. And here we are, Jules. That's what he gets, and I honestly don't give a damn, myself. But the way you're acting isn't right. You ought to care. That was your father, you only get one. You should care. Don't you care about anything?"

Julia raised her dry eyes to her mother, whose eyeliner was running blackly down her face, into the lines around her mouth.

* * *

"Yeah?"

"It's Julia."

"Yeah?"

"Where are you?"

"We went back to our parents' for a while. It was Caroline's idea."

"Listen, I'm out of the apartment for good. You can both go back. You don't have to worry about me."

"Yeah?"

"But I need to say something to you."

"Yeah?"

"I enjoyed spending time with you."

"Yeah."

"But if it was wrong, I'm sorry. Was it wrong?"

"I don't know. Maybe. I mean. I don't know. My sister's pissed, so."

"I know."

"Yeah."

"I probably won't ever see you again."

"Yeah?"

"Yeah. So if there's anything you want to say to me..."

"I don't know. I mean."

"Forget it. Listen, stay out of trouble, okay? And take care of your sister. Tell her..."

"Yeah?"

"No, don't tell her anything, forget it. Just please take care of yourself."

For some reason, neither of them hung up for a while.

"Are you, are you crying?"

"No."

* * *

They were shooting a pornographic film on the altar. Not the real altar, of course, as the church officials had taken that when they gave over the building. The filmmakers had brought an altar of their own, plastic, light enough for one man to carry, its face gilt and baroque with sunbursts and scrollwork and cherubs. Silver candle holders, elaborate if also tarnished, stood at all four corners of the altar, and tall red candles flamed into the gloom, their sides running with melted wax. Between the candles a woman writhed as she pleasured herself, her cascade of red curls hanging over the altar's side. When the director said, "Cut," she sat up, put her glasses on, and smoked a cigarette, sitting on the altar's edge, swinging her legs in the air, scarlet toenails flashing in the gloom. Her green eyes glimmered in the low light as she traded sexual taunts and insults with the camera crew. The director said ran a meaty hand through the sweat on the fat-rolled back of his bald head. Their raspy laughter rose and dissipated like smoke before it reached the vaulted ceiling.

The artist looked down on the scene from the choir loft with a bemused, tolerant, seen-it-all smile. "Everyone worships in his own way now," he said. He turned to face Julia, who had undressed while his back was turned, just as he always insisted that she do in his courtly way. His smile dropped off as he gasped at the sight of her stitched-up stomach, the flesh swollen and purple against the tensed black threads.

She waved her hand through the air before he could speak. "I want you to paint me now," she said. "Everything will be all right, I promise. But I want you to paint me now."

Instead of sitting on the blanket-heaped pew or allowing him to pose her, she simply stood, her back straight, her chin up, her arms at her sides and slightly extended. His eyes resigned and serious, the artist took his place behind the easel, rested his palette on his right arm, and went at the canvas with his left.

Filming had resumed at the altar; the woman's cries echoed up to the choir loft. Small, vulnerable breaths followed each deep moan.

At first, the painter made slow, delicate strokes at the edges of the canvas without even looking at Julia, but then his hand began to go faster and faster. By the end, he violently slashed at the canvas in huge vertical strokes. He usually took two or three hours to paint her, but this time he finished in twenty minutes. Neither of them spoke. He turned the portrait toward her: she was just a haphazard set of pale cuts in a greenish gray gloom, topped with a red blotch and sliced through the middle with a dark red gash that went past her body and out into the darkness, crossed with faint black lines.

"I go quick, you see, because I think you need to leave here, to rest, maybe in a hospital. But don't be sorry, you do me a favor. It makes me go straight to the heart of things, not waste my time with details."

He dug in his pocket for his wallet; she saw that his hands were shaking.

"I don't need money," she said.

"But I want you to take it, go to a hospital. I pay if you can't afford."

"No," she said. "I don't need anything now." Without getting dressed, she began to walk toward the stairway behind him. His face reprised its ancient smile. He had forgotten himself by getting so excited by her plight; he had forgotten how old he was, how much he had seen. Whatever she was doing, he had encountered it before. Whatever she was becoming, he recognized it. As she passed him, he touched the paintbrush to the palette on his arm and then to her bare shoulder. It left a red mark. The wet paint sent a convulsing chill through her, even though it felt as warm as if it had been secreted by a live body.

* * *

A crowd gathered around the naked young woman who stood on the concrete steps of the deconsecrated church. Two children couldn't stop giggling as they pointed at her. A man in a baseball cap pretended to use his phone to call the police or an ambulance, but he was in fact surreptitiously recording her bare breasts. He tried to crop the picture to keep the infected-looking wound on her stomach out of it. A middle-aged woman said she worked as a nurse, and she climbed the steps on her creaking arthritic knees to take the strange girl's pulse and check her pupils. The girl didn't resist, nor did she answer when the woman asked her if she had taken any drugs or if she was experiencing various symptoms, such as facial numbness or difficulty speaking. The nurse ordered the laughing children to stand in front of the naked woman, facing forward, to shield her from the eyes of passers-by.

The children scattered in all directions when they saw the group of bald people in ash-covered coats and robes slowly climbing the steps toward them on bare feet that were, like their faces, roughly the color of the concrete. The man in the baseball cap turned his phone to record this sighting of the so-called Its or It People or It Brigade or whatever the media was calling them. Such sightings were becoming more and more common, but he still thought he could get a viral video out of it. The nurse cried to the Its to get away, to leave this sick girl alone, but they surrounded her body anyway.

Julia lifted her arms to them and let them palpate her hands with their gray fingers. They smeared her palms with ashes. "Let me go with them," she murmured to the nurse. "Take me, take me, please," she said.

She threw herself down on them, no longer able to stand. They lifted her on their shoulders and carried her body like a bier down the steps of the church.

Part Two
SUMMER, MARK

John Pistelli

4. THE GOOD BURGHER

It was perfectly reasonable. Mark Weis needed money, and she was offering. In return, he only had to do all those things she couldn't ask her husband to do.

He found the ad on the Internet one July afternoon in the central public library, where he spent his days now that he'd been laid off from the architecture firm he'd worked for since earning his master's degree two years earlier.

Because his wife, Melissa, had informed him that she was pregnant five months before he lost his job, he decided not to worry her needlessly or compromise his child's gestation by inducing maternal stress. He did not tell her he was out of work, because he feared it would disturb her image of him, sometimes expressed to her friends when she thought he wasn't listening, that he was a rare find, a man both strong and gentle, dependable but playful, one she could rely on but who would never seek to dominate her. While he believed she would prefer him to become weak rather than brutal if he had to decline one way or the other, he didn't want to be weak in her eyes. He intended to find another job before their child, little Lila or Henry, was born; five months, he was convinced, would be enough time.

He went to the library during the hours of his former workday and used the slow, dirty, old computers there to tweak his résumé or to prepare cover letters in answer to job postings he'd seen on his phone, which he checked so compulsively at home, sometimes even in the middle of the night, that Melissa accused him jokingly of having an affair, though she knew he would never do such a thing to her. There was no way he could justify taking his and Melissa's communal laptop during the day, since she used it as the main computer for her online business. *All Tomorrow's Patés: Gourmet with Attitude* was a subscription Internet cooking show, complete with twice-weekly videos, slideshows, paid advertisements from local and national businesses, and promotional tie-ins to vintage fashion sellers, whose wares Melissa "rocked," as she said at the end of every episode when giving the sellers' web addresses for those who wanted to rock their clothes too. Melissa "directed her culinary activities to an audience of young women committed to bringing a slangy casualness and a curatorial but fashion-forward eye to domesticity's formerly stodgy and politically regressive trappings," as she'd written on the grant applications that she asked Mark to proof-read for her.

Despite his relatively good income in the middle five figures and her impressive revenue stream from the website, Melissa and Mark were trying to moderate their expenses since they had just moved from the suburban house they'd been renting to a loft in the city, nearer to Mark's office. Melissa wanted to give Lila or Henry the cultivation that came only from a childhood spent in urban parks and museums, amid people who spoke all the languages and worshipped all the gods and ate all the foods of the world, and Mark agreed with her that this was the ideal way to rear a child. Lila or Henry certainly deserved to live in one of the safest neighborhoods, but rents in the safest neighborhoods were costly. Melissa and Mark would probably also have to enroll their child in a private school of some sort, since the city schools even in the safer neighborhoods had, as Melissa said sadly to her friends, "a lot of disciplinary problems that no child should be exposed to." Maybe one of those classical schools that taught Latin to kindergarteners, they mused, though Melissa always added with a nervous laugh, "Definitely not a religious school, we hope." These projected outlays would be added to the college loans both Mark and Melissa were paying back, not to mention the incidental expenses of car payments, reasonably healthy food, and soon enough, all that went into the care of a child. Mark was lucky enough to get his health insurance extended through the end of his former company's fiscal year, which would carry them through Melissa's due date. By then, he hoped, he would have a new job with new insurance and maybe even better pay, the high five figures, say.

Melissa was due in August, and soon the end of June arrived. Mark had had a few interviews, but his industry, like so many, was highly competitive, full of bright, poised young people who'd earned bachelor's and master's degrees from more prestigious universities than Mark had matriculated in, had studied in European capitals, or had won international prizes in fields like sustainable development before the age of twenty-four. At the beginning of his joblessness back in late April, Mark decided he would take the opportunity offered by his enforced time in the library to master the more theoretical side of his chosen profession, to revisit some big ideas he hadn't encountered since his undergraduate days. He started with Plato's *Republic*, to learn how the disposition of the people in the city replicated the internal order of the soul, and then he moved on to Vitruvius's understanding of the human body as the natural original of the ideal architecture's proportions. He intended, with excitement, to go on to Alberti, to Ruskin, all the way to Loos and Le Corbusier and Mies van de Rohe, and on through them to the present, but the time escaped him somehow.

Mark sometimes just sat in the library with a book in his lap. All around him, the other patrons seemed to be suffering from some collective respiratory disorder: they hacked and wheezed, their lungs phlegm-rattled. He tried to imagine being somewhere else. Failing to find interest in architecture theory, he tried to read novels about slavery and the Holocaust to persuade himself that other people had been in far worse troubles than his own. He had more success with romance novels, which he concealed within the library's giant folio reference volume of *The Stones of Venice*. The romance novels allowed him to persuade himself that Melissa would forgive him when she inevitably found out the truth, because theirs was true love, destined love, the type of love that always overcame mere contingencies, customarily in airports.

Eventually, he took up works of pessimistic philosophy. They argued that human life was inherently miserable and brief, only the latter fact making the former bearable; that no argument could justify the pain even the luckiest sentient beings would inevitably endure; and that no action he, Mark, could take would ever alter this fact, not any more than a mayfly could choose to live longer than one day. *Man is born unto trouble, as the sparks fly upwards*, and soon enough he would be flying upward, his glow dimming slowly; he would contract to a pinpoint of light and then fade into the dark of the sky.

Mark's unemployment coincided with the time when the library had its suicide problem; three people since the beginning of the year had leapt from the fourth floor gallery down onto the marble tiles of the atrium.

Sometimes, Mark fell asleep in the library. The security guard would have to come by and shake his shoulder and say, "Sir! Sleeping is not permitted! Did you hear me? You can't sleep here, man."

* * *

One day, toward the end of the seventh month of Melissa's pregnancy, Mark, browsing a social network at the library computer to kill time before another job interview, learned that his most serious girlfriend from high school, Julia Bonham, had gone missing. He hadn't spoken to her since the summer before they each went to different colleges, when they were both eighteen years old, and the last time he had heard from her was when she'd sent him a nude portrait she had painted of him while they were dating.

He'd thought little of the portrait, because while she was painting it all he could think about was whether Julia would take her own clothes off and get into bed with him when she finished. She didn't though, and they didn't have sex until months later, seemingly encouraged by Julia's crazy but alluring mother, who one day sent him up to the bathroom to tell Julia something or other while she was showering. The mother sat right downstairs, on the front porch, while Mark went into the shower with Julia and fumbled in the steam with her until they blundered into a somewhat effective rhythm, Mark nervously goading himself all the while with the fantasy that a naked Mrs. Bonham might pull back the curtain and join them.

He'd opened the large painting, which he'd had to haul in its slippery wrapping paper all the way from the campus post office, in his dorm room. When he saw it, he thanked God that his roommate was gone for the weekend. Julia had made no real attempt at a likeness; his face was a blur of flesh-colored paint against the white wall of her bedroom. She had in a few deft strokes, with little detail, captured his pose remarkably, even embarrassingly, as he lay on her bed with his face propped up on one hand and his legs overhanging the foot of the bed, crossed at the ankle. She made him look somehow eager to please from the neck up, his head thrust awkwardly too far forward. The painting gave the impression that she had caught his body unawares: his torso was twisted so that his hip rose with an exaggerated curve, while his penis nestled snugly between his thighs, and his long legs were primly and demurely entwined. He looked like a zoo animal in her picture, all teeth and muscle going to waste, domesticated, made cute and caressable. She had somehow violated him by painting this picture, he felt, fully as much as if she'd hidden a camera in his bedroom or bathroom. This painting reminded him of a photograph not because it faithfully replicated physical reality, but because it recorded a truth about him that he couldn't have seen for himself through his own eyes; it revealed the weakness and vulnerability in a position he had deliberately assumed to communicate sensitivity and relaxed strength. He thought his way of behaving toward her, toward women in general, signaled that he *could* hurt them, but that he never, ever would. Her painting, by contrast, declared that he'd never hurt her because in fact he couldn't: he was powerless. He interpreted Julia's sending him the portrait as an act of malice, even though they'd parted amicably when they separated for college. He asked himself what he had done to make her hate him enough to force him to look in the mirror of her awful picture.

There were no knives in his dorm room, but he found a fork and used it to tear a hole where his body had been in the painting. He carried the mutilated canvas down to the dumpster behind the dorm and shoved it violently in among the cereal boxes and liquor bottles and stained underwear.

He hadn't thought of Julia Bonham much since then, not until he noticed that a distant high school acquaintance, now a busybody housewife who had insisted on friending him on a social network he'd joined only to make business contacts, linked a news item about Julia's disappearance. She had tragically gone missing soon after the death of her estranged father during a bungled robbery. Despite its luridness, which he could not quite associate with Julia's calm intelligence, Mark read the article with desultory interest. Julia's roommate claimed she'd been acting erratically and suspected suicide; Mrs. Bonham was sure foul play must be involved, especially considering the dangerous neighborhood Julia insisted on living in and the unfortunate company she kept; her boss at a local café optimistically imagined that she'd run away to start a new life; most strangely, a local artist she'd worked with in some way swore that she ran off with the It people, that growing and little-understood cult of ash-gray wanderers who eschewed all signs of personal identity and all individual ambition for a communal life of bare subsistence in the name of nobody knew quite what.

A comment under the article, from someone called Cal, read, "Jesus, Julia. I loved that chick, but she was crazy, like cuh-razy. One time we were sitting on a leather couch in some chain café off the coastal highway, this is like three years ago. We were young and in love, you know the drill, couldn't keep our hands off each other. Practically laying there on the couch is what I'm saying, people were looking right at us, and I'm thinking, go ahead and look, jealous bitches. She was staring into my eyes in that intense way she had, like she was trying to see into my brain through my eyes. Then, before I know it, she grabs a metal candle-holder off the coffee table in front of the couch and jumps right up on the cushions and starts bashing in the head of the guy sitting at the table behind us with it. I'm like, Julia, for Christ's sake, stop! The guy's got blood running in two streams down his face like one of those statues you hear about in like Columbian churches that are always crying blood. So I pull her down and we run for the car and tear the hell out of there, right down the coast. I say what were you thinking? and she's like didn't you hear him chewing? He was eating some kind of pastry and chewing and smacking his lips, I tried to ignore it, but it was all I could hear, and I just like blanked out and then I was hitting him. And when she's saying this, I'm thinking, man, I need to get away from this chick!"

While Mark had never known Julia to be physically violent, he remembered the stare. He supposed that as she got older, she became more and more extreme in defending it. She didn't want anyone to intrude on what she saw, maybe, and it made her destructive, so she decided to turn away from the world rather than attacking it. No, he didn't know. He had never figured Julia out.

On reading the article, then, Mark mainly felt grateful that someone else was doing worse than he was. All the happy photos the social network offered of the smiling children and the exotic vacations of former classmates and colleagues had made him ashamed of his failures; having company among the lost and miserable relieved him, and having Julia for company again reminded him of better times. This made him wonder just what had become of Julia and her crazy mother to lead them to such a grotesque crisis. He tried to remember the sordid story of the girl's absent father, which neither she nor her mother had ever told him in full, but he couldn't call to mind even what parts of it he used to know. That upset him more than anything else: not only had Julia vanished, but so had his memories, his experiences. He had lost so many whole days, and carefree days at that, days when he didn't have to sit among wheezing, masturbating men and pretend that his life had not become a cage he couldn't imagine ever getting free from, days when he'd thought nothing of tearing down a shower curtain to make love to a pretty girl. He even wished he'd kept her portrait of him, if only to have tangible proof that he'd been that young and done those things. When he remembered the image of himself on the canvas, though, leaning and awkward and girlish, he was glad he had destroyed it, glad she was gone. Maybe she'd had the right idea. Maybe her life had also become a trap, so she'd run off with the It people and stopped caring about this world at all. Maybe he should do that too, cover his face in ashes and vanish to the sewers. The story now almost piqued him enough to make him want to investigate further, find an article, if there was one, about her father's death, but the sallow woman at the computer next to him, stringy silver hair hanging out of her dirty straw hat, started talking to him about Jesus. He hurried away and headed out of the library, to catch a bus to go to his interview, but when he arrived he was informed by the sorrowfully smiling secretary that the position had already been filled.

He didn't think any longer that day about Julia Bonham and her mother, but at night he dreamed of her. In his dream, he found himself in the kitchen of Julia's childhood home in the suburbs. Mrs. Bonham stood at the kitchen counter talking to a stranger while he leaned against the pink floral wallpaper and watched her. She caught his eye and gave him an ironic, provoking smile, as if he had done something very perverse.

She walked over to him and put her hand on his arm and said, "Do you really think you should be trying to pick up women at your wife's funeral?"

He said, "My what?" with a nervous laugh.

She threaded her arm through his and led him from the kitchen, through the dining room, into the living room of her house. It was full of soberly dressed people talking in low voices; they looked at him as he entered and nodded sympathetically. At the front of the room, before the picture window that would have looked out over the front lawn if it weren't permanently screened by off-white muslin curtains that diffused the light of that bright summer afternoon into a vanilla glow, lay a white coffin on a bier, its top panel open. Mrs. Bonham gestured to the body in the coffin with an I-told-you-so smirk. Melissa lay inside in a pristine smock, her hair in bright orange curls like a gentle fire on the satin pillow beneath her head. Her lips, always so mobile in life, wrinkling in on themselves to make her appear perpetually bemused or pleasantly surprised, were thin and still now, her freckles washed out on the waxy skin of her face, her pert nose tilted down rather than up, though she'd always held it up in life, not arrogantly but bumblingly, as if to hold her glasses on. She wasn't even wearing her glasses now, and she didn't need them, because her eyes were closed, the lids heavy, lacking even the twitches and flutters of sleep. Her hands rested atop one another on her flat baby-bereft stomach, arranged to make it look as if they held a spray of lilies, though the flowers in fact had been pinned to her smock; a solid shade of white, they resembled doll hands, the fingernails merely a hint of a depression in the surface to suggest verisimilitude.

"She's dead," said Mrs. Bonham, "and she lost the baby too, and I think you need time to mourn before you move on."

He walked away from the coffin, his head pounding in a blood-rush panic. The light in the room faded around him as if he were walking into a tunnel, because he had ordered his days around Melissa and organized his imagination of the future around their child; now he didn't know what he would do from minute to minute in her absence, their absence. He seemed to walk out of the tunnel, back into the creamy light of Mrs. Bonham's living room, when another thought occurred to him: he was free. He could move into a much cheaper studio apartment now, and it didn't much matter where he worked because he had only himself to support, and all the lies he'd told had become irrelevant because the person he'd told them to was gone, gone to her death thinking him innocent, thinking of him fondly. No one alive depended on him. The constant subtle sensation of uncertainty he'd felt during the last two months spent in the library, in a failed scramble to retain what he had lost for the sake of his wife and unborn child, simply stopped. It reminded him of when the almost sub-sonic buzz of some insect finally ceases, and only when the creature flies away do you realize how much louder it had been than silence, how insistently it had forced you to clench your jaw and bunch the muscles of your shoulders to repel its subtle, droning affront. It was over. He could do whatever he wanted to do now.

When he woke up suddenly in the dark, he felt tremendous relief, until the anxiety began to creep back over the borders of his awareness. He suspected that he was not free, that tomorrow would mean another weekday at the library, that he still needed to find a job, that he had simply been asleep. All his troubles ranged themselves around the bed in a ring, patiently waiting for him to return fully to consciousness. He cautiously turned to squint in the slight moonlight at the contour of Melissa's shoulder beneath the comforter; sorting the dream from reality, he had to make sure she was there. Only when he saw her did he feel relief that she was alive and not dead, and still pregnant with his child. If someone had asked him whether or not he'd give them up to escape his troubles, he knew he would declare, "No, I can't imagine life without them at all; I'd kill myself before I'd let them go."

* * *

"Are you all right? You look sick."

"I just didn't get a lot of sleep."

"Yeah," Melissa said, "I could feel you tossing and turning. Are you having trouble at work? I don't think I've heard you say anything about work lately."

"No," Mark said, "it's pretty much the same. I go in, I work on designs, Paula and Jerry tell me what's wrong with them, I fix them, I come home."

"It sounds like you need more satisfying work," Melissa said, smiling abstractedly. She stood at the kitchen table, bent tensely at the waist. Her seventh-month belly swayed heavily out of her T-shirt as she cautiously piped purple frosting into the shape of grape clusters that overhung with bacchic luxuriance the middle layer of a three-tiered cake. From the kitchen counter where he stood and ate his cereal, Mark spied her: she ran the tip of her tongue slowly back and forth along her upper lip as she worked. She always did that; it was one of the signatures that made her Melissa and not anyone else, one of the things that would be irreplaceable if she were lost. He put his bowl in the sink and then walked over to her, the heels of the dress shoes he customarily wore to work clacking on the varnished floorboards too loudly. He feared that they would call attention to his lies, warn her to listen more closely to whatever he said about his job and about how he spent his days. She didn't even turn around.

When he was sure she had finished piping the grapes, he encircled her with his arms and cupped her pregnancy-swollen breasts in the palms of his hands. He put his nose into her flame-colored curls; they tickled so much, he thought he would sneeze. Between the strawberry fragrance of her shampoo and the vanilla icing smeared on her hands and her shirt, she smelled like an ice cream shop. She laughed distractedly as his penis stiffened against her hip.

She thrust her elbow back at him and said, "Get away, I'm working! Even if I felt like it, which I don't, by the way, because you try to have a five-pound parasite pulling your spine out of whack and then tell me you'd like to do it, I still have to get the final cake done before I prep today's shoot. I don't know how many of these I can get in before I calve, so I don't have any time to waste. We need the money, Mark, in case you didn't realize. You don't know, it's easy for you, you get up and go to work every day, you have a trajectory, you signed a contract. But I'm on my own, it's catch as catch can out here. So what's happening is that I'm at work right now, earning money for our family, and you're distracting me, taking food out of our little creature's eventual mouth. Your desire to have sex right now is doubly inappropriate because it's insensitive to the physical limitations of my present state. And whatever you do, please don't make one of those vulgar jokes I used to hear shock jocks and fraternity brothers make about screwing pregnant ladies, to the effect that you're afraid you'll poke the baby in the eye, or, worse, that you want it to give you head."

Melissa always spoke in these spates of verbiage when she was nervous, her diction at once overly formal and helplessly obscene. All that involved her work made her nervous, being on camera most of all, which meant that her haplessly worldly and risqué monologues were the star of her web series, maybe more than the food. Her audience of similarly anxious young women, caught between a professionalism that couldn't satisfy them and a domesticity they weren't supposed to want, evidently saw an intensified version of themselves in her jittery, awkward, and sarcastic attainment of culinary perfection, a perfection both domestic and professional, even lucrative. Sometimes Melissa's ability to capitalize on her fears annoyed Mark, whose own fears went unexpressed, for the good reason that they rightly interested no one.

"You're not on your own, 'Liss," he said, as if the words he were responding to were the only words of hers he'd heard. "I go to work every day for us. You don't know how hard I work. Christ, I was up half the night"

His own voice sounded tinny and petulant and distant to him, coming from somewhere else, the bathetic whine of a child who hadn't yet had enough practice at disguising his wounded self-interest in a mature pose of dispassionate argument.

"Whose fault is that, honey? Because it's not mine. I appreciate what you do, but you're projecting. Don't blame me if you don't appreciate it yourself."

"Why wouldn't I appreciate it?"

"We both know it's not what you wanted. Remember last year ago when you turned that promotion down? You didn't want to get stuck in the company because you hoped in five years you'd have your own firm? And now you have four years to go, and a kid on the way."

He dropped his hands from her breasts and took a step back, his erection having long subsided.

"I knew you'd throw that in my face. I knew as soon as you told me you were pregnant that you wouldn't be able to resist bringing that up."

"What did I say? I said it was bothering you, not me. I mean, would it be nice to have the money now? It certainly would..."

"Don't do that, Melissa!" he said, his voice deepening to a shout, his use of her first name rather than some diminutive revealing that malice had entered his heart. "Don't try to criticize me and then disown it by pretending you're just speculating on what thoughts you might have if you were a more petty person. Just be as petty as you want. Forget what you used to say about working for love and being against materialism. Forget the way we used to make fun of my parents, of your sister, and their narrow-minded interest in nothing but cash. Go ahead and say it: 'Mark, you don't make enough money.'"

"Well, Mark, sweetie, look it at this way: I'm not in a position right now to think of money as a petty concern. I'm sorry I can't be the way I was when I was twenty-two and didn't actually know a shitting thing about the world. It's life and death right now. And you don't feel it in your bones like I do, because, let's face it, you don't have to, you just go to work and come home and go to sleep and dream about some better way things might someday be. Which means you're still twenty-two for all intents and purposes. This uncertain future is not growing inside your body and kicking you every so often to remind you that your life is very precarious and that there's no time for dreaming."

"Oh, that's a nice way to talk about our child."

"It's not our child till it comes out and stops leeching the nutrients out of my body. Until then it's mine, and I'll talk about it however I like. And nice doesn't pay the bills. You think if everybody is nice, everything will work out. But nothing will work out. It's people who have to work, even at things they don't want to do."

He opened his mouth to reply, the unsticking of his tongue from the roof of his mouth making a loud click that echoed in the air. He couldn't think of anything to say.

"Aren't you going to be late? Or is going to your job on time too petty for you? Why don't you just quit so you can wait for some entrepreneurial opportunity to fall into your nice little lap. Then you can have the best of both worlds, a working wife to keep and feed you while she's barefoot and pregnant in the kitchen."

"Whose projecting now, Melissa?"

"Do you have any idea how hard this is for me, Mark?"

"No, obviously I don't have a clue. I don't know anything. So there's no point in continuing this conversation, is there?"

He congratulated himself later on having slammed the apartment door with wall-shaking vigor when he walked out. When he got in the car, he noticed he had left his briefcase behind. Then he emerged from his angry conviction that he was working harder than Melissa understood, and he remembered that in fact he didn't need his briefcase at all where he was going. He drove out of the apartment's back lot, not looking at the windows of his loft as he passed them, to demonstrate to Melissa whether she could see it or not that he didn't need her or care about her. Then he headed in the direction of the library.

* * *

That day, he saw the ad. He had seen some like it before, but it had never occurred to him to study them in any detail. The baby's due date was in two months, though, and the health insurance would run out in three, and the lack of money in his checking account would, if Melissa saw his receipts, call for an explanation. The things she had said to him that morning made him want to hurt her but also prove to her his devotion, his willingness to do almost anything, no matter how unsavory, for his family. He wanted to hurt her and then have the privilege of watching her pity him, because she had forced him to do it.

The ad said, "WF, petite blonde, 28, seeks M 20-60 for BDSM and other fetish play, NSA, no questions asked, our little secret. Applicants with financial difficulties prioritized."

Mark did not frequent websites advertising or soliciting prostitution, but he understood that the last sentence of this ad implied he would be paid for his services. What the WF asked for was not exactly to his taste. In fact, Melissa sometimes had to ask him to be less cautious, more rough and quick, though whenever he obeyed he still kept asking her, "Is this okay?" and "Are you all right?" until she had to say, "Just shut up and do it!" He looked at the WF's request like an architectural commission: when the client paid the requisite fee, his or her aesthetic supervened upon your own. When you receive an honest wage, you should do an honest job. The ad was just an hour old when he saw it. He replied quickly and, before the sixty-minute allowance of library computer time had ended, he'd made an appointment with her for that afternoon at four, when the WF would be finished with work and free for light play. They were to meet at the apartment of a journalist friend of hers who was spending six weeks in China; their meeting would last one hour.

During the rapid composition of emails back and forth with the WF, he felt his cheeks enflame and his ears redden, as if everyone in the library could somehow see what he typed, even though the words they used in their emails were very chaste and business-like, the mere logistical discussion of an impending exchange. He looked from side to side with what he hoped was a casual air. The elderly woman to his right slowly clicked with a serene smile through photos of her grandchildren at play by the ocean on a social networking site, while the teenager to his left wore huge black headphones and watched a music video set in a women's prison, the inmates cage-dancing in orange bodysuits, linked at the ankles by a rusty chain.

He had a nervous six hours to pass in the library until four o'clock. The prospect of architectural employment seemed more distant than ever to him; to study that topic would consequently feel like nothing but a cruel joke. Thinking to research his new job, he wandered through the human sexuality stacks, but each book he picked up mentioned the risk of venereal disease on the one hand and the importance of love, respect, and intimacy on the other, two topics that worried him each in its own way, given the circumstances. The nature of the job being what it was, he decided he should avoid needless worry. The circumstances obviously also ruled out more of his furtive romance-novel reading, while books about people in life-threatening situations, such as those that had formerly comforted him by depicting lives more difficult than his own, would now make him wonder too darkly about the impending meeting, the vacant apartment, the friend with business in China, the sadistic woman who only wanted her desires gratified.

Self-improvement, then. When he wanted to read something serious, Mark mostly read non-fiction, books about architecture, history, science, or philosophy, books that would make him more intelligent and knowledgeable, while he only perused fiction very occasionally, without taking it at all seriously, for the sake of entertainment or consolation. He had once heard an old professor on TV holding forth to the effect that an acquaintance with the classics of literature fortified the mind and disciplined the passions by subjecting them to the scrutiny of controlled intelligence, as manifested by all the historical varieties of rhetorical eloquence mastered by the great authors. The graybeard had gone on to observe that nothing in popular culture, still less in so-called new media, could match this passion-regulating function of the best that had been thought and said. While this old man, with his wisps of white hair at the sides of his head and his wrinkled chambray shirt, which looked as if years' worth of pipe smoke must have been caught in its folds, had obviously gone on TV to promote some conservative agenda, Mark, a pragmatic liberal who thought it worse than useless, even cruelly obtuse, to scorn the needs of one's own time and to protest or try to resist historical change, and who could moreover only imagine the professor emeritus's scornful reaction to Melissa's web series with its zippy sarcasm and outbursts of profanity and proliferating pop-culture references, nevertheless saw the benefits in his present circumstance of both acquainting himself with a variety of passions and learning how they might be controlled.

He went in search of the classics. In the literature section on the third floor, he found many guides to them, some advertised for resentful truants and morons, others for solemn aspirants to high culture. He noticed that the former usually had some kind of school motif on the cover, the title made to look as if it were written in chalk, for example, while the latter tended to have reproductions of Michelangelo or Vermeer or Waterhouse on the front, some rippling-muscled Biblical hero or attractively pensive and stolid Dutch bourgeoise or perishingly sad-eyed English waif, all suggesting what literature might do for your sensibility if only you'd follow the guidance of the books' authors.

He paged through a few of these volumes looking for promising titles, ones he'd heard of, works he'd be proud someday to say he had read, and eventually he settled for *The House of the Seven Gables*. He thought its architectural motif would allow him to grasp more quickly the complexities of Hawthorne. In tenth-grade English, he'd been made to read *The Scarlet Letter* and had, like most of his classmates, found it unforgivably dull. He did recall the frustrating, tantalizing sense that if he were just a little older or just a little smarter he would be able to decode some kind of raciness and forbidden truth between or behind the novel's sentences. His teacher back then, a girl recently out of college and younger than he was now, as he realized with a start there in the library, unfortunately gave him no help. Her big idea had been to make the students decorate red letters representing their own most notable sins and then wear them for a whole schoolday, an activity designed to enrich their later class discussion about whether or not shame effectively deterred anti-social behavior. Mark had asked his casual girlfriend of the time, the easygoing basketball player he'd gone out with before more seriously dating the much odder Julia Bonham, to inform him of his besetting vice.

"Remember that Internet thing?" she'd said. "Where you and your buddies decided to judge everybody?"

Not wanting to be taken for an adulterer, he added an R to his A and drew them as one combined letter, fashioned to resemble a drafting compass. The compass's central branch formed the stem of the R and the stroke of the tilted A; the A's other stroke represented the compass's drawing branch, and the lobe and leg of the R and the crossbar of the A served as so much intricate vine-twisted ornament, as if the compass-smith had been a monomaniacal aesthete of the Baroque determined to smuggle curvature and involution into even the most utilitarian instruments. Mark himself was a reasonable man and therefore usually favored a much cleaner visual style, but this excessive mode, which he generated by combining examples from various reference books, seemed to embody the concept he pinned to his chest, as suggested by the basketball player: AR for *arrogance*.

He never did finish *The Scarlet Letter*.

* * *

The summer had been mild and white-skied so far, but had become violently hot that day. By the time he arrived at the traveling journalist's apartment, he looked rumpled and sweaty. If the woman noticed when she opened the door, she gave no sign. Because he'd forgotten his briefcase, the book stuck out of his back pocket, and she chose to focus on that. "Did you think you'd be bored?" the woman asked, pointing to it as he passed through the apartment's main door while she held it open for him. She meant to signal a hard-boiled eroticism by the question, apparently, a breathy suggestion that if he thought he'd be bored with her he had another thing coming. Her actual tone, though, was half genuinely-offended, half cutely kid-sister-playful; she didn't seem to have sexy huskiness in her repertoire. As he followed her up the steps, he observed her more closely, the WF, whose name, Katie, he'd learned from their emails. In a black pantsuit that she wore awkwardly, as if she had not yet aged into it or aged into her social role more generally, she was obviously a professional. He noticed too that she had never learned to walk in high heels. She lacked the art of throwing her shoulders back to recenter her mass around her upthrust pelvis; the deficit caused her to lurch in a forward hobble like a deer staggering on its hind legs. No doubt because he'd feared he would meet someone sinister in this strange apartment building, he found it immeasurably touching.

"What do you do?" he said as they continued to the third floor.

"I work in the non-profit sector," she said. "But let's try to keep this as anonymous as possible." She giggled after saying this, like, he thought, a girl embarrassed to exert her shy self for a command role in the school play the teacher had peremptorily recruited her into. Then she recovered herself and said, "You just do what I tell you, and I'll give you the money. Don't worry, my husband's out of town."

He agreed and resolved to force himself to endure any awkward silences from then on.

The journalist's apartment proved to be mostly bare: it held a futon, a television, and a crooked half-empty bookshelf divided evenly between foreign correspondence on the one hand and New Age self-help on the other, with a few stuffed animals in the middle. The living room's back wall was decorated with a giant poster, an ad for some NGO that showed aid workers in sunglasses and camo vests distributing bowls of rice to black girls beaming with good will and gratitude against a red desert vista. The apartment resembled a hostel more than a home.

"She travels a lot for various magazines and websites," Katie said. "If I told you her name, you might recognize it. So I won't."

He shrugged.

She said that there were water bottles in the refrigerator if he needed one, but otherwise he should be quick about following her into the bedroom.

The apartment wasn't air conditioned, despite the heat. He stood in the foreign correspondent's empty kitchen and drank down a bottleful of frigid, plastic-tasting water in one gulp. The bottle crinkled loudly in the silent apartment as he sucked out the last drops, chilled streams running down both sides of his chin and dripping onto the greasy linoleum.

When he entered the bedroom, Katie lay stiffly on the bed, fully clothed. Undressing her would be his job, he guessed. She had taken off her high heels, which rested, one upright and the other on its side, next to the doorway, and he suddenly realized that he could smell her feet in the small, airless room. This almost turned him around and sent him out, because he associated such grotesque intimacy with monogamy alone, with fidelity, marriage. He had already betrayed his wife, betrayed her absolutely, just by standing there, inhaling the particulates of this other woman's body; then he understood that he could not go back through the door even if he wished to. Katie, evidently inexperienced in intrigue, had left four crisp hundred-dollar bills on the nightstand, and he was no longer in a position to think of money as a petty concern.

Katie held up a narrow strip of diaphanous pink fabric between her small, outstretched hands, her wedding ring glimmering in the low light.

"Tie this on," she said.

* * *

He did everything she asked.

It didn't take a full hour. Within thirty minutes, she was sated, more than sated, as sick as if she'd gorged herself on birthday cake and ice cream.

She pulled the comforter up to her nose as he dressed himself. Again she saw the book, its top half bobbing out of his pants' pocket.

"Read me something," she said, her voice strained and hollow.

He couldn't refuse; he was still on the clock, after all. When someone pays you an honest wage, you have to do an honest job, he reminded himself again.

He had already read about thirty pages in the library earlier; the decade since high school had not ripened his tolerance for Hawthorne's dense style and viscous pace. He had marked an early passage in the novel with a little yellow golf pencil pilfered from a tray next to the library catalogue computers. He opened the book and read it aloud.

"'In this republican country, amid the fluctuating waves of our social life, somebody is always at the drowning-point. The tragedy is enacted with as continual a repetition as that of a popular drama on a holiday, and, nevertheless, is felt as deeply, perhaps, as when an hereditary noble sinks below his order. More deeply; since, with us, rank is the grosser substance of wealth and a splendid establishment, and has no spiritual existence after the death of these, but dies hopelessly along with them.'"

"Huh," Katie said. "Not too sexy."

* * *

After a month, a month during which he had not yet gotten a job, Katie ended the arrangement. She said it one afternoon when they had finished, when she had the blanket up around her face. She spoke with a curt voice raw from screaming. He felt an icy burn in the pit of his stomach when she told him, and sweat broke out all over his body. He objected that his wife was due to give birth in a month and that his bank account and credit would both be maxed out without the wage she paid him. She said she was sorry to hear it, which made him want to punch her right in the face. She was sorry to hear it, she went on, but she could no longer betray her husband. The satisfactions of having her fetishes catered to were merely physical, transient, whereas she recently understood, due to her husband's absence, that her connection with him was both spiritual and enduring. She could not jeopardize it. Then she began to speak of him; she had never done so before in Mark's presence. He sat dizzily at the foot of the bed and hardly heard her.

"The problem is that he's basically too pure," she said. "Too good. I just couldn't ask him to do these things with me. It would be, I don't know, inappropriate, I guess? We met in college, when we were both officers of the campus women's organization, you know? He's a filmmaker. You may know of his work, his documentaries. *Wasteland Wonderland*, about the homeless garbage artist of Queens? *Sonatina*, the one about the child-prodigy classical composer who was a refugee from Rwanda? That was on cable; it won an Emmy. Right now, he's working with migrant women, if that's the appropriate term. He's been on the Mexican border all this month. The best and most gentle man I've ever met. The *best*. I mean, if it's ever okay to rank people like that. If it is, he's the best. I'm the luckiest girl in the world. And do you know what the worst thing is? It's that if I told him what I wanted, he'd do it. He'd do it all. In a heartbeat. Just to make me happy. Ha!"

Her laugh was without mirth. When Mark didn't say anything, she went on:

"Do you know what he'd say? He'd say that just because something is a damaging social construct doesn't mean it's not real. Signifying that my desires are symptomatic effects, I guess, of social structures? But no less real, no less in need of satisfaction. So, in other words, how could he refuse? It's not that he'd refuse. If I thought there was even a chance he'd say no, I might have asked him. If I thought he'd spit in my face or say, 'Who the hell did I marry?' or call me a dirty slut. But he wouldn't say anything like that, not ever. So I couldn't ask. Even though I wanted it so badly. I can never say a bad thing around him, never lie to him, except about this. I just want to be the best possible person, you know? But I guess I can't. Is that normal? Didn't people just used to do whatever and not question everything all the time? Back when there was so much ignorance and prejudice. Does everyone question everything every minute, does everyone live that way now? I'm sorry to talk your ear off. Maybe you want to say something, but I kind of don't want you to? I don't want to know you, really. If I'd known you were, you know, smart, I guess, I don't think I could have gone through with it. I wanted someone who wouldn't even understand. Someone who barely spoke English maybe. A migrant worker!"

She emitted more mirthless laughter, and then her tone turned urgent, pleading.

"Am I bad person? It's just that I didn't know anything about you, and you aren't what I was expecting. When you ask for someone with financial difficulties, you think, you know, 'homeless,' not, like, 'reads Nathaniel Hawthorne.' I'm sorry. God, I'm such a bitch. I'm really sorry. We should really go. Please don't say a word. Thank you so much."

She touched his shoulder with her knuckle, as if they'd played a brave but losing game against an unbeatable team. He turned and took her hand and held the back of it against his burning cheek for a moment.

* * *

The loft was sweltering, humid as a jungle, when he got in. Melissa had turned the air conditioning off. She stood at the stove, a huge cauldron-like pot on the burner in front of her, almost equal to her own height. Steam roiled up from it in clouds and floated in the dense air. Her hair tied back severely, her face a bright mask of perspiration, she turned her head fiercely when he opened the door and then quickly turned back to the stove.

"Jesus Christ, it's hot," he said. "Is the air broken? With what we pay, we should be able to get the property manager here the same day in this heat."

She didn't say anything.

He walked over to the thermostat. "Did you call them about it yet?"

The tone of her voice stopped him even before he understood what she was saying.

"I turned the air conditioner off because we can't afford it. We can't afford it because you lost your job. You might have made enough money playing sex games with some rich slut to afford air conditioning, but I'm not going to let you spend that money on me. On principle, if you know what that word means, Mark. I know you're probably thinking, Well, why can't I spend it on myself, since I have to live here too? But you don't have to live here too. I'd really prefer that you didn't. In fact, I want your ass out of here tonight. I won't spend another night under the same roof with you. This is my place, and I'm not leaving, but I want you out."

"Honey," he began. Possibilities jumbled together in his mind: find out how she knew, deny everything, explain in a way that mitigated his actions, scream at her for not understanding how difficult this had been for him and how her unreasonable expectations of life made it all the worse. "Who told you?" he said in a strangled voice. She still hadn't turned around; she faced the pot of boiling potatoes, the sweat running down her face and onto the floor.

"Oh, that's a good story," she said. "Your little slut's douchebag husband came over crying. He really was crying, as in, sobbing, his whole body shaking. He said she had to tell him because of how much she respected him, but she begged him not to do anything to you. He made her turn over your email address anyway, in case you were a sexual predator, and a few quick Internet searches brought him here to tell the truth. On principle, he said. There's a lot of principle going around tonight, I guess to make up for the lack of it these last few months. He said I deserved to know. And he very charitably said he'd watch my web series, since he is, on top of everything else, a quote-unquote film director. I asked why he didn't you film his vicious skank of a wife's escapades, so he could really make some money. He didn't like that too much, so he left. Then you came in, and now you'll be leaving."

"Honey," Mark said with the force of a sudden insight, "all this stress and anger is not good for the baby."

"No, it isn't," she said. "So take it somewhere else."

"Listen, I wanted to tell you, but I didn't want to worry you. I thought I'd find another job right away, and you'd never have to spend any sleepless nights worrying about it. But I couldn't find a job, and my money was running out, so I did it."

"Instead of bagging groceries, stocking shelves, driving a bus, any number of honest occupations?"

"I have a master's degree in architecture," he said quietly.

Her contemptuous laugh trembled as it trailed off, but she kept her face averted, her body stiff.

"Get out, Mark. There's nothing more to say."

"You can't just throw me out. We're having a baby, for Christ's sake. And we went in together on the deposit for this place, it's mine too. You can't just unilaterally decide. I *love* you."

He had paused after each of these assertions, but she didn't say respond to any of them. He compulsively filled her silence with protests and justifications and reasons she should forgive him, his voice sounding progressively more like a whine, a bray, an annoying buzz in his own ear. The starchy steam made him feel faint, his whole body heavily damp on the outside, but desiccated and hollow within. He wanted to come up behind her and lean on her, but her body looked as defended and unapproachable as a fortress.

"There was no sex," he finally said. "No penetration, I mean."

She spun around and whipped a weighty ladle across the room at his head. He tripped out of its way; it punched a chunk of plaster out of the wall. Mark lost his balance and fell on his hands and knees. "Melissa," he said, but she had already turned back around. He watched her from below, her back rigid, shoulders stiff, shirt soaked through. From the back, he couldn't tell she was pregnant. He tried to stand but felt dizzy and nauseated; anyway, the air on the floor was clearer and cooler, not so fouled with steam and heat. He crawled to the bedroom to pack his bag.

5. THE DEAD MALL

Returning to your childhood bedroom as an adult prepares you for death, Mark decided after drinking half a bottle of cheap, bitter red wine pilfered from his parents' liquor cabinet. The room had once been filled by his dreams and desires, as one would be able to say of the world itself when he was gone. He lay on his old bed and stared into the now-empty corner where once had stood his miniature drafting table. On it, he would draw with T-square and drafting pencil future cities, their silver spires connected with mile-high skyways that resembled medieval bridges, ellipsoid aerocars drifting beneath their ogivals. Against the headboard he now reclined on, a girl first raised her shirt in front of him; her breasts were goose-pimpled in the open air, a few fine hairs glinting in the after-school sunshine. The room was empty of all that now, just as the world itself would eventually be empty of him. He doubted, though, that the world itself would be filled in his absence with his not-yet-retired father's desk, home computer, several metal filing cabinets, and teetering piles of paperwork the way his childhood bedroom now was.

In fact, he could have slept anywhere in the house; his parents were only three days into a two-week cruise, a summer vacation deliberately scheduled for a month in advance of their grandchild's due date at the end of August. He hadn't even bothered to call and tell them he would be moving in for a while, because he didn't want to hear their customary quiet disapproval, their calmly disappointed reception of the news that he had failed in his marriage, with a baby on the way, no less. Anyway, Melissa would forgive him, he was sure of it. She couldn't, in his view, abandon him forever with their child about to be born; if nothing else, he only had to wait for Henry or Lila to be born. Then the play of his own features in the tiny pink face

78

would recall Melissa to her love for him. In the interests of optimism, he had brought only a week's worth of clothes with him. Though his former bed had been carelessly shoved into a corner to make room for his father's office, he decided to sleep there anyway, on the theory that it would inspire him with the verve and buoyancy he'd felt as an adolescent. His father's office would give him a stable and professional base from which to renew his job search, so that when Melissa asked him to come back, he wouldn't have to return empty-handed. He knew he couldn't contact her; he needed to allow time for the red haze of her anger to dissipate so that her solid, durable affection for him could re-emerge. His head liquid and his eyes watering from the rancid wine, he collapsed into his father's computer chair on his first night without her and turned on the desktop PC. He intended to begin scanning the job listings immediately. When he opened the web browser to the search engine homepage, he typed "Julia Bonham."

* * *

She was one of those girls who always walked around with her arms folded across her chest. He thought this habit said two things: one, "Don't lay a hand on me, don't even come near, I am armed at all points," and, two, "Please come to me, hold me, I am so parched for touch that I must embrace myself." She clearly had something inside herself she didn't know how to manage; even at seventeen, he could see that. This granted her, in his eyes, a depth, an inwardness, that so many of the other girls, and boys for that matter, lacked. Their availability and generosity was false, because they obviously had no idea what they risked by opening themselves. Such lack of self-awareness also made them dangerous: if they themselves didn't know what they were capable of, how could you trust them? Julia's self-protectiveness, on the other hand, announced that she had a self to protect. He listened whenever she spoke, even though she almost never spoke to him until that night in the pool hall, with a flare going up behind them from those idiots' empty rolling papers. She kept her manner calm and quiet, as if to assert that she was both in command and committed not to making a fuss. When he brought his lips to her warm cheek, inhaling her scent of too much make-up and too-strong shampoo and, deep under them, the saltily sweet olfactory signature of her own particular skin, he did it to show her that he could take the lead if she wanted to set down the burden, and that he didn't mind at all if she made a fuss over him.

All their sexual interactions tended to begin with a light flirtation initiated by her, sans any coy game-playing chase; there was just the invitation, quiet but unmistakable. He remembered her turning her blue flicker-lit smile on him in an empty movie theater while an ice storm swept its chiming crystalline dust over the trees and streets outside. He slipped his hand inside the waistband of her skirt and fingered her while the film's heroine crept in her underwear before a tilted camera down a dark corridor toward the closed bathroom door behind which her roommate almost certainly lay in red water with a gash in her throat. His heart going so fast and high that little sparks winked in the theater-dark at the corners of his vision, he fixed his eyes to the screen. He had never been so frightened at a horror movie before.

She only ordered him around when she wanted to paint him. Later, when he grew more experienced with human psychology, including his own, he understood her problem to be her mother. Mrs. Bonham was the one who gave all overt commands and therefore forced Julia to cultivate a more sly and secretive way of making things happen. Mark preferred the mother's way, her whole pageant of emotion and desire, because with that at least you knew where you stood, even when she did something as outrageous as more or less asking him to climb the stairs of her own house and screw her only daughter in the shower. Melissa was that way too: unambiguous, frank in her needs and secure in her judgments, open-hearted enough to find an audience as far afield as France or Korea to watch her make cupcakes or mashed potatoes, because her feelings could be understood even if not all of her words could. No one would watch Julia, though, because she made no sense, not on the surface anyway. Maybe this explained her disappearance. Searching her on the Internet turned up next to nothing except for the news that she'd gone missing. Though the article about her vanishing mentioned that she was still an artist, she'd maintained no artist's website of her own, no online portfolio, no profile on a gallery's or university's web page, no blog, no social network presence. Evidently, she had disappeared before she disappeared: running off with the It people only made it official. He imagined her folding her arms around herself until she was intricated into a knot and then knotted into the air around her, evanescing into herself, never to be seen again. Because she was the most unusual girl he'd ever been with, he always wondered how different, how unbounded by conventional expectation, his life might have been if he'd ended up with her. She was an artist, apparently so pure an artist that she stopped making any pictures at all; then she went to the impossible place where the pictures come from. She wouldn't have cared if he had a job. Would she have had bis baby? Would she have cared if they starved to death?

His head faint with the sour wine, he imagined her stalking as in a horror movie down the darkened suburban street, her head shorn, her face ash-smeared, her ragged gray toenails scraping the sidewalk as she turned her steps toward his parents' house. She would come to take him with her, underground with the refusers; she would cover his face in ash. He would go with her.

He collapsed in his clothes onto his old bed and fell into a dazed and drunken sleep.

* * *

On waking, even before he brushed his teeth, though after hopefully and fruitlessly searching his phone for word from Melissa or from potential employers, Mark returned to renew his search of the job listings. When he opened the browser, though, he found himself researching the Its instead. Their emergence in the last few months had strangely coincided with his troubles, so he had paid only distant attention to it as it seemed not to affect him or to promise him any relief from unemployment and a failing marriage. He had never seen them in person.

He found in his search that the members of the It people or the It group or the It brigade or simply the Its, as the media variably referred to them, wore gray coats, robes, or gowns and never wore shoes; they shaved their heads; they covered their exposed skin in ash or dust; they eschewed names both first and last; they maintained vows of silence, poverty, and chastity; they touched each other continuously, so that any individual member at any given time was in flesh-to-flesh contact with one or more others; and they had insisted in the only written communiqué ever reliably attributed to them that if any one of them had to be referred to individually, only the pronoun *it* should be used. They did have hierarchies like any organization, no matter how they tried to avoid it. More elite members of the group went further than just ascetic behavior and dress. Advanced members, for instance, had their tongues surgically removed to prevent even the possibility of a return to the alienation of individuality, marked by the pretense that any given individual had anything to say. At the highest levels, the men had their testes and penises removed, while the women underwent radical mastectomies and hysterectomies and infibulations, supposedly performed in secret underground operating theaters by renegade doctors in sympathy with the movement. These rumored doctors, though, were not to be understood as members themselves, since members were forbidden from practicing any trade or profession and especially from taking any action that might prolong or extend life beyond the bare consumption of food and water. This latter fact should not be taken to imply that they endorsed suicide: in fact, they proscribed it, perhaps because taking an easy escape from the trials of this world was no less disgraceful than capitulating to them by leading an ordinary life. You could recognize a true adept of the Its by its starved yet swollen features, the eyes staring with impersonal fervor out of a face as gray as its body's clothing, its head coming to resemble a stone. The adepts did not desire to monopolize their status, however. They hoped instead that eventually everyone would don the gray suit, take the ash upon them, have the surgeries, and bring collective human life to its calm and quiet end: cross-legged ascetics in gray on gray hilltops, expiring one by one, leaving the deserts, oceans, and jungles to reclaim the cities until nothing would be left to testify that humanity had ever stained the silence. Were they religiously inspired, a heretical Christian sect? A Gnostic revival? An ecumenical but extreme Buddhism? Were they secular radicals, anarchists, deep ecologists, who wished to diminish humanity so that the earth could flourish? Perhaps they were really fascists, following that ideology to its logical terminus in the collective's ecstatic self-immolation. Maybe they were communists, at last willing to drop the utopian ruse and admit their true belief that the penultimate equality was abjection and the final equality death. No one knew, not even their escaped members, because they neither spoke nor wrote; they made no arguments and elaborated no philosophy. They only acted.

Almost all of this information, Mark found, along with its ambiguities and absences, came from those escaped members of the group. "Escaped" was not the right word for these renegades, though, because the Its did not prevent anyone from leaving or joining at any time. As long as one wore their costume and performed their daily activities, one was a member. The small number of people who had left had simply walked out, out of the underground tunnels and into the light.

The few escapees who were interviewed by the media tended to converge around the following theory of what motivated the Its: consciousness and individuality were a disease, a disease both causing and worsening the differences between us. Eliminate the differences of language and sex and appearance and skin color and clothing, eliminate even the vanity of existing as a body apart from other bodies, and you will have eliminated our loneliness, a condition not known to the so-called lower lifeforms, though zoologists report that some of the higher primates were already showing symptoms, adopting moldy logs as their own babies, for instance, and so might one day need to form It cults of their own.

Many didn't trust the escapees. They tended to be sons and daughters of the rich, and there was reason to believe that they had not chosen to leave, but had been carried out by private police forces retained by their well-to-do families, who could not stand the thought of their lavishly-educated children hanging around train termini and public toilets and sewer tunnels with their heads shaved and ashy, wearing greasy gray coats and palpating other vagrants, when they had instead been destined for medical school or corporate boardrooms. For certain wealthy families, to let a child go like that would be, on top of everything else, a wasted investment, as well as a failure to repay society for their own privilege by returning it in the form of their children's talents. When the wealthy youth were recovered, often sedated and on stretchers, government-trained deprogrammers worked with them to break the habits of thought encouraged by the so-called cult. Assisted by pacifying drugs that dimmed the will to resist and that perhaps also counteracted what were rumored to be experimental psychoactive compounds in the ash that the Its spread over everything, deprogrammers mainly tried to restore the escapees' individuality by surrounding them with its tokens: favorite movies, TV shows, music, items of clothing, food. Food indeed often proved to be the key. One bite of filet mignon, one taste of chokecherry ice cream, served as bait enough for the deprogrammer to reel the alienated person back into daily life as him- or herself. Television worked almost as well: an episode of a familiar TV series, especially one that had not ended before the escapee joined the Its and so promised answers to the questions of what would become of the characters and their journeys, often proved so seductive that the deprogrammer could lure the escapee out of whatever psychic cell the cult had led her into. Frequent text messages from family and friends, often paradoxically combined with those same friends' and family members' exclusion from the escapees' surroundings, also drew the former Its back into dialogue with the once-familiar world. Because the escapees' sense of self had been razed, it had to be reconstructed from the ground up. The Its had first eliminated all pleasure from their lives, which in turn led them away from human relations toward a communion with some otherworldly sense of impersonal life. To undo this, the deprogrammers simply ran that program in reverse: pleasure first, then human community. "Let me put it crudely: first you suck her breast, then you love your mother," said one tough-looking deprogrammer with a pock-marked face and slicked-back hair in a video interview that Mark found online.

Mark wondered how they got people to go with them in the first place. "Sympathetic touch," said the experts, while many observers on the Internet said, "Some kind of secret government hypnotics in the ash." The Its would roam the streets in small groups of five to ten, often though not always in particularly desperate or isolated locales, often though not always at night or in the early morning, and they would target people who appeared distraught or in need. They would surround the person and lay their hands upon him or her in a gentle massage that some said had a mesmerizing effect. Kneading and warming the tense muscles, they disconfirmed their target's former sense of isolation and entrapment within the bounds of the self and the problems this self had created. "Anybody can say you're not alone," said one escapee on video, her hair just beginning to grow back, her eyes still sunken from starvation and wide from fanaticism, "but the Its will simply *make* you not alone by touching you as you are, without any desire or preconception on their part. And if you've been in some kind of trouble, homeless or on drugs or in a bad relationship or just not right with yourself somehow, they give you the option of being held, of not having to do it alone, even if 'it' is just walking around in your own skin." Various experts and non-experts dilated on the potential experimental pharmaceuticals involved in this touch, narcotic tinctures that could pass from the surface of the skin to the interior of the body, presumably mixed in with the ashes the It people covered themselves with. Some even theorized that the drugs in the ash only worked in combination with the contact of two or more bodies, which was why they had to remain saturated with the stuff and in constant contact with each other. The likelihood that bizarre and unheard-of drugs were involved only leant credibility to the speculations that the It cult was tied in some way or another to secret state activity.

Because their activities were so often nocturnal or performed in scarcely occupied places, Mark found surprisingly few videos, only about ten or so, of the Its' recruiting. By far the most dramatic video, and the one with the most views on the video sites, showed a rare public demonstration, the act that probably brought them media coverage and wide attention in the first place. It happened back at the beginning of April, only a few weeks before Julia's disappearance. A man, middle-aged, thick-bodied and fat-necked but also frail-looking, stood in his rumpled undershirt with his back against the rail of a bridge, his arm draped over it, as if to lift himself up as soon as the mood struck him. The wind blew his head's sole flap of hair up and then let it fall and then blew it up again, like a trapdoor in a thunderstorm. He held his mouth rigidly open: he looked to be always on the verge of speaking. There were bored-looking beat cops talking to him while they probably waited for the social workers to arrive; they put out their hands in open-palmed gestures of sharing and trust, as they had no doubt been taught to do in some soporific seminar. More sirens whistled closer. Pedestrians and bicyclists, obviously including the unseen person who'd taken out his phone to record this moment, had stopped, forming a circle around the man and the police. The sun sparkled off the cyclists' gaudy lycra on their long, lean thigh muscles, and sparkled too off the silver cantilever that jutted from the top of the new public library, one of the first buildings on the city side of the bridge. The traffic over the bridge along with the wind caught up all the words and blew them away; Mark couldn't hear what anyone was saying. The middle-aged man raised the hand not grasping the bridge rail and thrust it up and down through the air, to smack away the concerns and consolations the police were enthusiastically lobbing at him. His mouth moved, but Mark couldn't hear what he said, if he managed to say anything at all: "I lost my job," or, "I've got cancer," or, "My children have disowned me," or, "I can't do what I used to do," or, "I'm sorry I banged my secretary," or, "My wife went off with her therapist," all the usual reasons.

Then the encircling pedestrians started to point away from the middle-aged man; at first it looked as if they were pointing at the person holding the camera, but it became clear that they gestured beyond or behind the camera. The person with the phone spun it, everything whipping and bobbing by in a blur of sun on cityscape and sun on water, and aimed the lens down the bridge, toward the bank of the river opposite the city proper.

Mark had read that the Its dress all in gray and cover themselves with gray ashes and consequently trail a fine gray dust with them wherever they go, but reading didn't prepare him to see it. The mass of them, about twenty slowly walking down the bridge in a circular formation, made the mind grope for analogies because they seemed so out of place. He had just been looking at the sun-walled mirrored fronts of the downtown buildings, and at the bright synthetic fabrics worn by the cyclists, at the phones held in the air by those who'd stopped to watch how the potential suicide scenario would end, at the streaks of red and silver that were the cars racing into and out of the city. Now here was a medieval procession from an old movie, all black-and-white filth and misery and renunciation, here was some leak of ink into water, graying the clear and the bright, some grim invasion of the timeless and colorless into the sun-struck pastels of noon. Mark told himself they were just disturbed people who had put on drab clothes and sprinkled dust on their faces, but that didn't account for the feeling he got when he saw them in the video, the feeling that the bottom of his stomach had dropped out and sucked the breath from his throat, as when you look up from the page of your bedside book to see a millipede scuttling up the comforter toward you, its legs rising and falling in rhythmic cascades that somehow interfere with the pulsations of your own heart.

They came on, the wind whipping ash out of their garments like so many beaten carpets, their bodies held rigidly, their feet barely lifting with each step so that they seemed to glide or hover in an ascetic parade. The shot kept widening as they approached, because the person with the recording phone kept stepping back as they neared, making wordless cries of surprise. Soon the recorder and all the other gawkers had gone so far back that the suicidal man and the police were included in the shot. As the Its fanned out and faced the man, the police too backed up, their hands nervously at the barrels of the guns in their holsters. The middle-aged man still kept one hand on the bridge rail and stared at them with his sorrowfully gaping mouth. Two of the Its took his free hand and ran their fingers up from his palm to the loose, mottled flesh of his upper arm. At first, he tried to contract his hand, and his muscle rippled beneath the skin, rolling a shadow-furrowed wave from elbow to shoulder; but then he relaxed and let them bear the weight of his hand. Slowly, like a snake leaving a branch, his other arm uncoiled from the bridge rail, and he slumped into the arms of the ones who were touching him. Just then, one of the Its who held him voided its bladder down its own legs, wetting the man, the front of his pants darkening, a black spot widening on the beige paving stones of the bridge. They handed the man along from one pair of hands to another until he stood in the center of their procession, touching him everywhere all the while, hands finding the sweaty small of his back and the inside of his thigh. When they enclosed him, they turned their backs in unison, and the procession went in reverse. A break in the traffic was filled up by shouts from the gawkers behind the camera.

"Hey! Where are you taking him? How can you let them take him away?"

The police turned and faced the camera.

"A guy can go where he wants. It's not our place to stop voluntary associations. Just be relieved he didn't jump."

"But they're a gang, a cult. Who knows what they are? They might be terrorists. They might have a disease. We don't want them on the streets!"

"Yeah, and if wishes were horses, then beggars would ride. If we stopped every group of like-minded people from getting together and trying to get people to think their way, we'd have to shut down the churches."

"But what about pissing on the sidewalk? I know that's illegal."

"Yeah, well, we'll send a fine to their address. Now don't you nice, professional people have somewhere to be? Beat it before we take you all in for disturbing the peace!"

This final flippant and authoritarian statement from the cop was often used as evidence, Mark found, for the conspiracy theories related to the Its that proliferated online: they were a creature of the American intelligence services designed to drain into mystical asceticism what would otherwise have been radical and dissident energies directed toward smashing the state; they were a creature of some rival states' intelligence services, Russia, China, Saudi Arabia, designed to deplete into fanatical impotence national strengths that would otherwise have gone into reforming America; they were created by or worked in the service of shadowy underground medical networks ostensibly built in secret to aid the poor but almost certainly involved instead in illicit black-ops-budgeted research into such authoritarian esoterica as mind control, which was always, speaking historically, performed on vulnerable and oppressed people pulled unwittingly from the streets; they were a mystery sex-and-magic cult like the pagan or else heresiarch sects of late antiquity, a further sign of Christendom's regression back to the darkness before the Incarnation in this late and faithless age; and, most oddly but also most obsessively pursued by one blogger in particular, who appeared to be some sort of renegade graduate student, the Its was a piece of conceptual artwork created to have revolutionary effects in the world by bringing forth the disturbed, lonely, and desperate as a reproach to our age of inequality and greed, a work of art directed from his fugitive hiding place in attempted atonement and expiation by none other than Frank Jobe, notorious perpetrator of *The Last Café*.

Mark lost all sense of time and read till noon, his eyes finally stinging, his back sore, his mouth foul, and his stomach empty. When he saw what time it was, he stood to clean himself up for the day and think about returning to the computer refreshed and dressed professionally, to put himself in the proper state of mind for his job search. As he stood, he saw a video in the sidebar of the conspiracy theory website he'd been reading; the frozen image advertising the video's contents somehow filled him with a sensation of sudden familiarity, even déjà vu, though it was just a pinkish blur, a torso caught in motion. The video's title was, *Another victim of It perverts taken from a church!!! Warning: Nudity!!* He sat down again, the stale sweat smell of his slept-in clothes rising around him, and played the video.

There was Julia. She stood naked on the steps of one or another of the abandoned churches throughout the city, her hair dyed bright red, a skull-and-crossbones tattoo on her upper arm, an infected-looking, badly stitched-up wound at her side, her face hardened and a little worn by the almost ten years that had passed since he'd last seen her. He recognized her instantly, without having to study the image; he had not forgotten the way she comported herself or the shape of her body or her long and gorgeous nose. Her face was strange, though, a picture of anguish struggling to lift itself into serenity. She had spread her arms and held out her hands, as if begging to be taken up and carried to safety.

The man with the camera seemed concerned chiefly with her breasts, however: the majority of the video showed them in close-up, indifferent to the rest of the scene, ignorant of the dusty gaggle of heretics or spies or double-agents or mind-control victims shuffling in grim procession toward her from behind the cameraman. Mark wanted to ignore them too. At the moment the shot widened, when bystanders could be heard to cry, "Stay away! Leave this sick girl alone!" and Julia murmured in a broken voice, "Let me go with them," and the phone spun to face the Its, he dragged the video counter back to where the close-up on her breasts began. He paused it. Leaning back in the chair, he peered at her nipples, rigid on her feverish flesh in the chill air of April. He couldn't see the half rings of fine brownish blonde hairs with which he knew her aureoles to be fringed, but he knew they would be there, knew they would still be there, wherever Julia was now, even if the fanatics had unsexed her. Like so much else he'd ever loved, Julia Bonham too was lost to him; everything he had treasured was falling away from him, spinning into a vortex of poverty and lovelessness, so that he no longer knew himself. While he had lost Julia a decade ago and had moreover not minded losing her in the least because he'd fixed his eighteen-year-old eyes on an apparently limitless future full of new loves, it now felt intolerable for even this girl who was nothing to him now to fall prey to a gang of gray fanatics. He loathed to lose this body he had embraced in his youth, long before he could have even imagined what it would mean to lose a job and a wife and an image of himself as a man in command of an intelligent and ordinary existence. He unzipped his pants, at first only to let his erection stand free. Then he gave in and masturbated at the frozen screen, at the icon he and the cameraman had made together of Julia Bonham's breasts. His strangled, whispered moans faded out into the empty room as they had done so many times before, when this house was still his home.

* * *

He would find that Mrs. Bonham still looked good. He certainly didn't. He had not checked the weather forecast before acting on his decision that afternoon to ask Mrs. Bonham if she would like him, for a fee, of course, to attempt to retrieve Julia from the Its cult. Now he called up the weather on the screen of his phone and confirmed what the choking atmosphere suggested to him, namely, that the heat wave not only continued but was worsening: it was a hundred and one degrees. Somehow the knowledge made him more unsteady and nauseated than the heat itself. Planning what he would say to her, he hesitantly walked up and down Mrs. Bonham's street in his blue silk dress shirt, which he'd packed for the sake of potential job interviews. His carefully combed hair disarranged itself into wet swirls on his beaded forehead as large dark patches spread over the back of his shirt. The houses on that suburban street, made of red or beige brick, white or yellow or pink siding, wavered in currents of heat-haze before his sweat-stung eyes, and the whirr of a hundred air conditioning units bombinated in his ears. He remembered why he had left this place: "You could die out here and no one would notice," he'd once objected to his father when he was a teenager, to which his father had replied that here, unlike in the city, there was no one to kill him, so he didn't have to worry about dying. All the empty yards and the streets without sidewalks and the pastel walls with people watching television and waiting to die of cancer or some other very suburban disease behind them filled his fluttering stomach with primal childhood fears: loneliness, emptiness, abandonment. He could assemble no coherent speech in his mind to make to Mrs. Bonham, nothing that didn't sound odd or crazy; nor, now that he was actually standing there on her street, could he convince himself as he had in the shower earlier that she didn't already have someone hunting Julia. The whole thing was folly, but Melissa still needed time to forget his mistakes and remember his merits. Where else did he have to go that afternoon?

He banished all thought from his mind and waded decisively through the brothy atmosphere straight to Mrs. Bonham's front door. The heat seemed to muffle the rap of his knuckles on the white wood; as he waited for her to come, he looked over the porch he stood on, the porch where she'd sat and smoked and watched the rain on the day he'd first had sex with Julia. The deep-cushioned pink wicker chairs still faced out over the lawn as they had a decade ago, just slightly turned toward each other with a hint of pastoral coziness; the small, glass-topped table still rested between them with its candle and its ashtray, though both were pristine now, untouched by any fire.

When she opened the door, the doorway releasing what felt to him like the frozen white smoke of a meat locker from the air-conditioned interior, he found that she still looked good. She obviously hadn't been eating enough, no doubt from the stress of losing her daughter; he couldn't find the shape of her body inside her ivory dressing gown. Her face, though, beneath the punitively bunned-up blonde curls, remained lively. Though it had appeared to be set into an sour and furrowed expression when he first glimpsed it as the door swung open, as soon as she saw him, or maybe just as the hot miasma of the hundred-and-one-degree air hit her skin, her cheeks reddened, her marbled green eyes opened wide, and her lips, already parted with a kind of distaste, now curled up in ironic surprise, almost as if she were on the point of laughing.

"Mark Weis," she said. "I'll be damned."

Her voice was unchanged, the high, youthful voice that used to confuse him in those days before cell phones, when he would call the house line and think he was talking to Julia, only to discover with embarrassment that it was a laughing Mrs. Bonham he'd addressed as "honey."

"Please come in," she said.

He entered an ice palace hung with pinkish crystals. She must have set the thermostat on twenty or thirty degrees, he thought and looked down his nose to see if his breath were visible. The sweat on his shirt seemed to freeze to his skin, which sent one violent shudder through him. Mrs. Bonham shut the heavy door behind him and sealed him inside the frozen atmosphere as the last wisp of boggy humidity rolled off his neck; inside it was like the kind of winter day that makes you feel you can see clear across the city and register every fluting and carving in every façade. In his experience, so many memories tended to abstract and purify a place to its emotional essence; a house he hadn't visited in ten years would fix itself in his mind as one color and one sensation, but whenever he visited it again, he was surprised to find that it was as many-shaded and variable as any place he was familiar with now. Mrs. Bonham's house wasn't like that, however. It had become more and more itself in his absence, the pink carpet and white walls brighter, the decorative flowers fresher and almost dewy, the furniture seemingly untouched, the crystal chandelier over the dining room table as unspotted as the day the craftsmen had washed the fine dust from the cut shards. It was a small house, but its front rooms were like museum pieces, reconstructed chambers of some royal villa.

"I haven't seen you in ten years," she marveled.

He moved his mouth a few times before anything came out, and then he said, "I heard about Julia."

"I didn't know you were in contact with her. Were you friends on the Internet?"

"No, not at all. I haven't heard from her since college, I only found out what happened yesterday. I just came to say I was sorry to hear it. To see if you needed anything."

"Thank you," she said. She searched his face, a mischievous and authoritative glint still irrepressible in her turned-up lips and narrowed eyes, that amused liveliness and transparent readiness to judge that he remembered so well, in contrast to Julia's impassive expressions and veiled actions. He knew that the loss of Julia hadn't destroyed Mrs. Bonham when he saw that she still commanded this fierce and unashamed mobility in her features, and he knew further that this meant she didn't need him at all. Finally, she said, "But don't you have a family of your own?"

Because you look out at the world, you rarely have a vision of your own face unless it goes into crisis. Now the scene, the frosted pink palace and the still-beautiful middle-aged woman with the ivory dressing gown and the mischief in her stare, was replaced in his view by his own visage: its multiple planes disarticulated, the mouth sliding off to the left while the nose drifted right, and the whole top half melted, running down in bulbous streams to the floor. He heard a lowing sound escape him as tears iced his cheeks. Though a tall woman, only an inch or two shorter than he was, Mrs. Bonham put her hands up, a gesture less consolatory than defensive, as if she meant to shield herself from collapsing rubble. He fell into her arms.

* * *

An hour later, they sat on her couch in the living room, sharing a heavy crocheted blanket draped across their legs. They had drunk half a bottle of zinfandel, and he'd told her his story. She had even gone down to some nook in the laundry room downstairs to fetch a pack of cigarettes she'd been hiding from herself.

"Divorce?" she was saying as smoke curled between them in spirals on the icy air. "I can tell you about divorce." She jabbed the tip of the cigarette at him: "Don't do it."

"'Don't do it'? But Julia used to say you hated her dad."

"She was a child: what did she know? I certainly didn't *let* her know, either. Julia's father was an infuriating man. He had more talent, more wit, he was even more good-looking, back when he was skinny anyway, than the rest of his loser family, a gang of barely-employed drunks who enjoyed thinking of themselves as outsiders and victims, you know, the resentful unassimilated immigrant type. But he was too much like them in the end. He mocked successful people, thought they were pretentious. He had enough intelligence to feel secure in dismissing what he couldn't understand or what he secretly thought he couldn't or didn't deserve to achieve, but not enough to learn the humility necessary to allow himself to take risks, to expose himself to failure. Of course, I told him these things, but he dismissed them as talk-show psychobabble. So I said, 'Fine, forget psychology, but don't you want to make more money?' Because he owned property, he was a super and a fixer in the city, and those were his jobs, which he'd inherited from his father, dead of alcoholism at sixty-one. Frank was amazing with his hands: he could fix anything. But I thought he could have gone to school. When we were nineteen, twenty, I said to him, 'Go, I'll help you pay for it, you could be an engineer, an architect, a designer.' But he took up his father's work. He said, 'You just want me to go to school so your family won't look down on me.' They did, by the way, they did look down on him. My father was an OBG-YN, my mother a traditional housewife; their fathers were a contractor and a steelworker, but they had worked their way out of those dirty lives, those lives where the men's hands are never clean, they worked their way almost to the top. And I was supposed to go all the way. They expected me to marry a doctor, a lawyer, a politician, maybe to become a secretary or a paralegal myself, certainly not to regress to some brute with a permanent case of dirt under his fingernails and a sneering sense of humor. They couldn't see the promise in him. But when I said, 'Come on, Frank, be serious, don't you want more money?' he got that maddening look on his face, that sarcastic smile that said he was so much smarter than you, that you were so naïve for believing in something he couldn't see, the look that said, 'Yeah, sure,' to whatever you'd told him. But for all that, he was a gentle man. When we had Julia after I graduated college and we married, I saw that being a father revealed a part of him that he denied in himself. The way he looked down at that baby girl, it was like no other look I'd ever seen on his face, not even the look he gave me. It held a purity: an implicit belief that the world could actually be a beautiful place, a home, a belief he and his people otherwise rejected. He needed that beauty for his daughter, even if he didn't think he deserved it for himself, even if he didn't really think I deserved it. Those first three years with Julia were the best we ever had. But having a child is not unlike falling in love for the first time, and here I speak for myself as well as for Frank. When the baby first arrives, it's like being with your first boyfriend: you could spend hours just staring into those eyes. Everything is precious, nothing disgusting, and you would do anything for this beloved creature. It makes you transcend yourself. You'll see, Mark, you will absolutely have the time of your life, no matter how many dirty diapers you change. But eventually your bad habits, your essential self, your basic selfishness returns, even as your child reveals her own fundamental independence in willfully disagreeable ways. Then it's remarkably like a marriage: you have to find a way to live with this person even in the absence of what felt like the divine inspiration that made you want to live with him or her in the first place. Let me tell you, Mark, you will make all sorts of compromises to hold onto this relationship, to do the best you can do for the other person, ones that look crazy from the outside. Honestly, men and women, *especially* women, who don't have children don't know the first thing about life. They shouldn't open their mouths about anything."

"Compromises. Like, well, you know," Mark spluttered, giggling with the wine. "No, I can't say it."

"Go ahead. Say what you want. We're having a vacation day, we're having a break from our painful lives, so say what you want."

"Like when you sent me up to the bathroom that day?"

"Oh, that," Mrs. Bonham said, lowering her face away from him, the blush coming back into her cheeks, her mouth at once embarrassed and mischievous. It was a girlish look, Mark thought. "All I'll say about that is she had to do it eventually. I'm not a prude just because I don't believe in being crass. But my God, she was eighteen years old: it was time. And I knew you were a nice boy, a responsible boy. So why not here, where I knew she was safe? And that's all I'll say about that."

"Fair enough," Mark said. "Sorry to interrupt. You were telling me not to get divorced. Something about compromises?"

"Yes, compromises, crazy compromises. That's where the librarian comes in."

"The librarian?"

"Julia didn't tell you anything about the librarian? Her stepmother?"

"No, never."

"Years ago, she was my colleague."

"You were a librarian?"

"Of course not, I don't have the attention span for book work. It's why my daughter thinks I'm a perfect bourgeois philistine, among other reasons. No, my college degree was in business: I worked as an accountant for the public library system, while she was head reference librarian for the natural history division. She had an appalling fascination with mutated fetuses and deformed lizards and tumor-stricken kittens and aborted rats and things like that. That was probably why she shared something of Frank's cynical and nihilistic attitude toward the world, even though she worked with her brains while he worked with his hands, she had a Ph.D. while he had been lucky to get out of high school. I knew right away they would get along. So I thought I would throw them together."

"You do that a lot," he said quietly.

"You're damn right I do, Mark. My daughter thinks I'm a very frigid or rigid woman. My ex-husband came to think so too. They think I inherited my parents' desire to excel and to prosper materially while also inheriting too much of their eventually accumulated privilege to have any verve or spirit left, to do anything unpredictable or just for the hell of it. Of course, my ex-husband and daughter were both prone to confuse having spirit with wading in a sewer, but that's their problem. What you should understand about me, Mark, is that all I care about is beauty. Look around: my parents couldn't have assembled this room. They would have put an ugly brown couch in the middle of it, because all they cared about was money, understandably enough, since they'd both spent their childhoods suffering from the lack of it. But money, properly considered, is a means to an end. Oh, I know you're thinking, 'You? An accountant? Beauty?' But there can be no beauty unless the ledger balances, unless you think and act very carefully and make very minute adjustments so that everything comes out right. Beauty is order, and only within order can you experiment or adventure. There was a part of Frank that knew that. He owned property, he spent most of his day fixing wires and pipes to make the electricity and water flow, which I don't understand at all. But there was a squalid side of him that thought everything was futile and purposeless, an aimless game in the dark, which was why he confused order with duty and freedom with anarchy. That was why he ran off with the librarian. He didn't understand minute adjustments, that was the problem. He also drank too much and ate too much, by the way. The man could dump a sugar packet onto his tongue. Have five cups of coffee before noon. He oversalted his pizza sauce; I used to tell him, 'The salt is not the flavor, it's to bring the flavor out.' You're married to a chef, Mark, so you can appreciate that. But he failed to see that I introduced the librarian into our marriage as a pinch of salt, a hint of contrast, to make him remember my virtues and merits. My flowers and rosewater next to her skulls and formaldehyde. But he was an immoderate man. He drank her down, he ate her up. He took to smoking fat cigars after he left me; he would light them with a butane torch. Eventually, I gather he understood what I had been trying to do, and he and the librarian made their own attempt. But they were careless as ever. They believed death was the only reality, those two. That gave them the idea that you could live for pleasure only, but believing that life is about more than pleasure is the only way to truly experience pleasure. And then there is my daughter. I suppose she must have come close to understanding what I just said; the last time I saw her, she had obviously reached the end of something. But with the immoderation of her father's blood she ran to the opposite extreme, and now she denies herself everything with those disgusting mental defectives in bad gray coats."

"Don't you want to find her?" Mark said.

"Of course I want to find her, but there's no point now, is there? She's not Julia anymore; she's wiped herself out as an individual. Even if I found her, it wouldn't be her. But if she makes her way out of this, I won't turn her away."

Mark, with the self-absorption of the drunken, said, "Do you think she'll take me back?"

"Your wife, you mean? She'd be a fool not to. And I don't just say that for sentimental reasons, though I have always liked you, Mark. A woman about to have a baby won't throw away a man willing to help her care for it. Oh, but I *am* sentimental, let's face it. Something Frank never understood was that I'd have taken him back too. He was far more absolute, far more proud, than I was. He knew what he did was wrong; he had crossed his own line and couldn't forgive himself, which was why he lashed out at me with such hate. He wanted to put the blame elsewhere, but he knew whose fault it was. He must have known, that pig-headed bastard, that I would forgive him. But he didn't think he deserved it. So he stayed with the librarian till the end, with the librarian and all her hideous carcasses and mummies and jars full of dead monsters."

"Why wasn't he around when Julia was a child? She hardly ever mentioned him."

"He saw her every weekend until she was twelve. Then when I understood what he and the librarian were up to, their irresponsible pursuit of sensation, I couldn't allow her to go there again. But that's all over. We shouldn't speak ill of the dead. Or the lost. If you want to know more about that, if you want to know about the person whose intrusion into Julia's life turned her from a sweet to a sullen child, talk to Alice Nicchio-Strand."

Mark's body jerked at the sound of the infamous name; he almost knocked his wine glass out of his lap and onto the pristine carpet. "Alice Nicchio-Strand? *The* Alice Nicchio-Strand?"

"Oh yes, the same one. There's no end to the damage that awful woman has done to the world. But I don't want to talk about it. It's all too atrocious. I'm sure I look very put-together, Mark, but to tell you the truth, I feel as if I'm flying apart..."

She gently took the wine glass from his lap and set it on the coffee table in front of them. She pulled him in by the collar of his silk shirt and kissed him on the mouth. Before he closed his eyes, as her face came closer, he saw Julia flicker for a moment in it: the long thin nose, the shape of the lips, and even, despite Mrs. Bonham's customary air of having discovered the absolute truth about life, the hint of hesitancy, fear, and self-disgust in the eyes. He kissed her fiercely, tasting first the cigarette smoke and the soured wine and then a hint of decay in the aging teeth and then just the raw flesh of the inside of her mouth, not unlike his own, but tinged by the perfume she wore, the soaps and lotions she used, a bit sweet but sharp too, honey spiked with clove. He threw off the blanket and put his hand inside her nightgown, fumbling for her breast. She firmly pushed his hand away and pulled out of the kiss, a filament of saliva joining them for half a second, glistening in the white of the room before it broke.

"This is just a little vacation. A little adventure, a pinch of salt, do you understand? Just a kiss. That's it, no more."

She pulled him forward again but this time kissed him gently on the forehead. The wet imprint of her lips whipped a convulsive chill down his spine in the nearly refrigerated room.

* * *

"There is something you can do for me," she'd said. "I was in a small accident, you know I've been very distracted lately, and my car is at the garage for the week. I have some shopping I could do, though, some exchanges to make at the mall and then some groceries to pick up. If you wouldn't mind."

He wandered quietly in his socks through the house while she showered and dressed for their excursion; luckily, she had made him take off his shoes before walking on the carpets, so now he could move undetected by her, creeping in his socks. The door to Julia's room was open, and he paused at the threshold, but felt it would be too great a violation to enter. Mrs. Bonham hadn't converted it into an office. In fact, she had made hardly any change at all. Because Julia must have taken most of her belongings with her when she left for college, the room was simply bare of almost all ornament. Even the reproductions of classic paintings that a teenaged Julia had cut from magazines and books, framed, and hung were gone. There had been a Caravaggio, a David, a Friedrich, he remembered, icons of the melodramatic and sublime tastes she concealed beneath her drab dress and inoffensive persona. The starkness and chiaroscuro of those paintings had been like holes punched in the plain white wall to disclose some elevated and superhuman vision. It surprised him back then that she didn't paint him in the same style, that she opted instead for the pitiless observation of his over-eager face and delicately crossed ankles: she had reduced and insulted him rather than putting him on the heights. The wall was empty now, as was the rest of the room, and whether Mrs. Bonham intended this to imply the triumph of her own aesthetic over her daughter's or an invitation for her daughter to return and hang her visions there again, whatever those were now, he couldn't tell.

On his way back down to the living room, he passed the open door of Mrs. Bonham's bedroom while she was still showering. All the windows were shaded so that the room was almost black, except that a blue TV glow played over the unmade bed's twisted sheets and battered pillows. A warm, stale, smoky, sour, prison-like fug seemed to exhale from the doorway, from the room that the air conditioning and the pink-and-white couldn't reach, as if she confined herself there day and night and left the rest of the house to its ice-glare peace.

He was standing in the kitchen, remembering the time he made Mrs. Bonham and Julia dinner under Mrs. Bonham's instructions, when she came down from her shower.

"What are you doing?" she said. The taut skin of her cheeks was flushed, probably from the hot water streaming down on it.

He had been running his fingertip across the roughness of a thin, scalloped dent in the wallpaper.

* * *

Arcadia Village Mall had declined significantly since his adolescence, when he and his friends would go there and wander around looking at salacious magazines in the bookstore, trying on colognes at the department stores' sample counters, sampling music in the record shops, daring each other to flirt with the cashier girls at various businesses, and eating pizza or lo mein in the food court. It was new and crowded back then, a novelty and a sign of progress, built atop a gray, silty slag pile on what had been a dumping ground for the mills' waste materials back when the city was a prosperous industrial center but before the suburbs had spread out so far. "When I was a girl," Mrs. Bonham said, "you could look toward this area from the city neighborhoods, and, if you went to a high enough elevation, you could see the whole sky glow red and smoky, as if it were the end of the world, when they dumped the slag." Since Mark's own youth, Mrs. Bonham reported, hard economic times caused a number of the mall's businesses to close and also led to rising criminal activity both in the building and in the parking lots. This drove out even more customers, which in turn ruined even more businesses, and now only a handful of stores were left. The decline itself, though, had solved the crime problem, and Mrs. Bonham no longer felt as if she were "taking her life in her hands," as she put it, when she went there.

As when his own mother used to take him shopping with her when he was a child, Mrs. Bonham ran her errands and left him to stroll at leisure through the mall after they'd agreed to meet in an hour by the fountain in front of the central department store. The fountain was no longer working; an empty, fenced-in construction zone covered it up. The basin of the fountain remained behind the plastic fencing, wrapped in a dirty plastic tarp, but the water that had spouted up in Art Deco arcs, underlit in shimmering aquamarine above the potted palms that ringed the basin, was long gone. He wished he could have back all the pennies he'd thrown in it.

The potted plants appeared dry and blemished, canker-blacked and unattended. Whole sections of the mall were dark with empty storefronts and switched-off tracklighting; in the absence of neon signs and busy windows, they looked beige and dusty, like abandoned closets. The carpet, periwinkle with off-center patterns of triangle and curlicue in warmer tones, vaguely reminiscent of a Constructivist painting, was scuffed and worn, long-faded from the glare that fell in through the dirty skylight. A zone of the mall where he'd spent so much time as a teenager, one with copper-colored floor cobbles and a photobooth and an ice cream shop, was wholly desolate now, its varnished tiles faintly shiny in the low light of the still-populated sectors like a menacing rain-wet street. He walked over the cobbles and into the dark anyway, because he needed to piss; there had been a restroom in a corridor off the ice cream shop, the storefront of which was now dark and gated. He groped through the dark to the men's room and shouldered open the door, but he found only darkness and humidity inside. It smelled strangely, not like a normal public toilet with its cheap liquid soap and urinal cakes and sedimented years of excrement, but rather like freshly turned soil and damp bark instead. A distant hole in the wall at the end of the bathroom opposite the door let in a jagged circle of sunlight. Mark took out his phone and used it to illuminate the room. A tree had grown through the wall, its leafy branches crowded in; they snaked over the stalls, their fronds pressed to the ceiling. His heart jumped, and he hurried back through the door, as if he had walked in on something obscene.

* * *

"Did you re-marry?" he asked Mrs. Bonham on the car ride back to her house.

"No," she said, "once was enough."

"But the article about Julia mentioned her father's name..."

"Yes, I went back to my maiden name, Bonham, after Frank and I divorced. And I had Julia's name legally changed to Bonham as well when I removed Frank from her life."

"But you went by 'Mrs. Bonham' even when we were younger."

"Yes," she said "I was a wife for many years: I earned my title."

* * *

Mark had met Fraternelli only once. He lay on his childhood bed in the sweltering darkness that night and tried to remember every detail as clearly as possible. Bits and pieces had been coming back to him all day, not only because of his discussion with Mrs. Bonham, but because the season had been summer, the day as hot as this one had been. Julia explained little to him about her relationship with her father, only that she saw him once a year, usually at the end of June, a kind of anti-Christmas. She'd asked Mark to drive her to the meeting place because it would be less awkward than if her mother brought her and had to risk an encounter with her ex-husband.

For most of the long ride out on the highway, Julia said nothing. She fidgeted compulsively, which was unusual for her; she normally comported herself with a reserve unusual among people their age. He was surprised at the length of the trip. At every exit, he expected her to tell him to turn off, but she kept silent. It was ten in the morning, so the highway was depopulated and the gray sky hung low like a dome over the road, sealing in the heat. His car's air conditioner didn't work; they had to sweat it out. He felt as if he would eventually drive to the wall of the sky and either crash through into the choking universe or simply be flattened against the blank gray. Julia kept rubbing the little notepad sheet the directions were written on, wearing off the pencil marks, eroding the paper down to smooth fabric.

"I think he likes to do this as far as possible from where either of us live," Julia said. "It's just for us."

After another interminable five minutes, she instructed him to take an exit down into a small, bleak township. The town center was crowded with decaying rowhouses at the foot of a sheer hill blackened with sooty-looking trees. Mark assumed there had been steelworks here earlier in the century and that these people had gathered around it like nomads around a campfire. Now that the fire had been snuffed, it wouldn't be long before the encampment scattered.

Julia told him to pull into a fast-food restaurant's parking lot and to wait for her in the car. They had already decided that her annual meeting with her father had the potential to be strange and strained enough without introducing a boyfriend into the mix.

"There he is," Julia said with a catch in her breath. She flung the door open and clambered out before Mark could say anything. He watched in the rear view mirror as Julia fell with surprising abandon into the arms of the huge man, her smooth pink camisole abraded on his oil-stained brown work overalls. Behind them, his big weather-beaten pickup truck squatted like a tank. His vast embrace pulled her feet clear of the ground.

Mark slid down in the driver's seat as they passed, her hand in her father's hand as she trailed behind him.

The heat must have put him to sleep, because the next thing Mark knew, he was brought anxiously upright, dashing his knees painfully against the steering wheel, by the sound of Fraternelli beating his big palm on the frame of the rolled-down car window. His dull wedding band clattered on the plastic. Julia, who was sitting next to Mark in the passenger seat, put a steadying hand on his arm.

Fraternelli said, "I'm Frank," and instead of putting his hand in the car to shake, he passed an ice cream cone through the open window instead. "Vanilla. She said it's your favorite. On me."

Mark's fingers grazed Fraternelli's hand, work-roughened like tree-bark, as he took the cone. "Thank you, sir," he stammered.

"Ha!" Fraternelli roared. A cloud of cigar-smoke wafted into the car. "Don't worry about no 'sir,' kid. I'm not her mother, you don't have to impress me. As long as you're good to her." He slapped Mark's shoulder with surprising gentleness. "As long as you're good, that's all that matters." Then he leaned down far enough to catch Julia's eye and winked. "Bye, baby."

In the side view mirror, Mark watched Fraternelli walk away, light on his feet despite the weight he carried. He sprang up into the cabin of his truck as if mounting a horse. Fraternelli's motions were entrancing in their odd grace. Only after the truck had trundled away did Mark notice that Julia was crying.

6. THE LAST CAFÉ

Sergey had a wrestler's body: a wedge-shaped slab tapering at the waist and propped on bow legs. When Mark told him why he had come to speak to him, his broken-nosed face tensed into a grimace so that he looked ready to charge under and toss Mark up into the air. It turned out he was just trying not to cry.

"I told her," he said, "I told her not to go anywhere near them. When we were in the tunnel, when I took her to hospital..."

"What hospital?" Mark said, remembering all the conspiracy theories about how the It people had something to do with underground doctors.

Sergey put out his hand to quiet Mark; then he took out his phone and made a call, his squat thumb fumbling with the numbers. He turned his back and spoke in a gruff whisper. Mark politely stepped away from the counter to look around the café. He tried to call up a vision of Julia moving among the tables in that cross-armed, cautious way of hers, bending to push in the chairs and wipe down the tables with her usual face of worried intensity, as if she harbored thoughts that absorbed and disturbed her. He couldn't put the picture together: the image of her in the Internet video and the image of her that he carried around from high school wouldn't coalesce. He couldn't make the nervous, assured girl into a woman so aghast at what she saw inside that she had to burn her very self down to the ash of those cultists.

What really stung him in the Asphodel Café, what pierced him so hard that it almost drew a beaded tear from the wounded eye, were the paintings that hung on the exposed brickwork. Julia had painted them. He would recognize her sensibility anywhere; he'd had to stab a fork through it once, after all. These were mostly portraits of animals: dogs, cats, rabbits, almost

100

all looking isolated, filthy, tortured, or damaged. A rabbit had only one ear, while a cat lay with its belly exposed, the pinkish white flesh bearing a fierce stitched-up gash, and a dog stared up from a chair out of an empty, blood-crusted eye socket. She'd volunteered in an animal shelter, he remembered reading in the article about her disappearance. Here was what he had seen: what people were capable of.

Sergey came to his side and said, "Her friend, Caroline, brought these here from the apartment she and Yuliya shared. She asked me to hang them. Now I am not stupid, Mr. Weis, I know pictures of sad animals, hurt animals, do not make people want to buy espresso. But Yuliya and Caroline had the fight before Yuliya went away, why I had to take her to hospital, she was hurt in that fight. Caroline forgave, though, and Yuliya is gone. Now I am a capitalist, yes, but I am a Christian too. So I had to say yes to the pictures. These are very sad pictures, bad for business, I am very sure. If she was here, you know what I say? 'Yuliya, why you not paint flowers?'"

The two men walked outside and stood in front of the café windows. Sergey lit an unfiltered cigarette. He offered one to Mark, who said, "Why not?" The acrid taste brought to mind Mrs. Bonham's brief kiss. It had been a week since he'd seen her. Melissa still refused to speak to him, even when he gave in and left her several voicemail messages and sent one impassioned email. The baby was due in a week; his parents would return before that. He'd received no callbacks from prospective employers. He had returned to the search for Julia, then, simply as a way of filling the hours, and he'd come here to ask her boss what her last days had been like. He sucked the smoke all the way to the back of his throat until it felt as if it were billowing up into his head to shroud his thoughts in gray clouds. He felt dizzy and leaned back against the warm pane of the window. The heat wave continued for the eighth day, and only Sergey's craving for a cigarette had been enough to drive them out of the air conditioning. While the burdened men stood and smoked, fit and carefree young people went in the café's door, their laughter insultingly loud and flippant; when they left, they were carrying clear plastic cups full of neon pink and yellow and red slush, the summer smoothies advertised on the Asphodel's clapboard sign, not espresso at all. Across the street from the café was the small park that ran along the river: the grass and the treetops looked dusty, parched, nearly shriveled. The sun, flaming in the overheated sky, had suffused the whole air and burned the raw green life out of everything. In ten days, it would be September.

"What are we waiting for?"

"My friend will come," Sergey said, "and he will explain the hospital. He met Yuliya only the once. 'Very sad girl,' he said, 'not surprised she made her choice not to live with herself.'"

"She wasn't sad when I knew her," Mark said.

"You were young. Young people should not be sad. When they are, it's because they have not enough to do, no jobs, no responsibilities. But then decade goes by, and, yeah, you're sad. Your mistakes, they pile on top each other like brick wall, all the things you lose. And then all the things you know you will never do."

"Isn't it the jobs and responsibilities that make people sad?"

"Why? Everyone dies, yeah? Better you're tired when it's time to die, so you lay down like you take a nap. But young people, no: they are not tired, they need something to do, otherwise they go crazy. I tried to give Yuliya lot to do. But I could see she was making lot of mistakes."

"What kind of mistakes?" Mark asked, trying to seem casual, concerned only for his lost friend, when he really wanted to know how her mistakes compared to his.

Sergey looked ahead pensively. His sorrow over Julia seemed to have tranquilly dissipated with the cigarette smoke. Now he mused disinterestedly over her story as if it were a parable, a cherry to roll around in the mouth until the fruit and juice were savored and the stone isolated.

"Fighting with her friend over some man, I don't know exactly the story. Then the fight is too much, I thought Yuliya would kill the girl. Now I'm respectable businessman, Mr. Weis, but I had my time when I would do anything. I knew criminals, very bad men. I did bad things, to tell you truth. And I have seen the look in Yuliya's eyes on the face of bad men. People who didn't try to control themselves except to get what they want. She tried to control herself, but she had something bad inside. She wanted to be an artist, to put those things out of her head in a good way, you know, in pictures. But she could put them out in a bad way, too. She was special girl, I mean it, deserved special life. But something bad too."

"You make it sound like a good thing she went off with the It people," Mark said. "Like she might have hurt someone otherwise."

Sergey agitatedly took another cigarette from the crumpled pack in his shirtfront pocket and lit it with the high-wavering flame of his heavy brass lighter.

"No, no, no," he finally said. "I come from Communist country, Mr. Weis, that is where I grew up. I know how it works, Marxist-Leninist plan to pretend evil will go away if we take away beauty and money and not let people be the best. You know how it works? It doesn't work. These stupid people in their ashes, they are like Marxists-Leninists without government to run, thank God for that. They think, Okay, let's take away choices, let's say nobody is different from nobody else. Then will all be okay, then we don't need cafés, churches, artists no more, everyone will be better. But you know what happens? Everyone becomes worse! Because I only can make myself better, you only can make yourself better. Maybe it's by work, maybe it's by making pictures, maybe it's by taking care of animals, whatever you like. Always it's by prayer: ask God to please give you strength to be good. But if you stop people from work hard for themselves, if you stop them from prayer, what is left? Just the evil. I saw it growing up, Mr. Weis, and I see it in these crazy people who don't want to be persons but just Its. Their ideas are, I'm sorry, they are absolute shit, because all they believe in is shit. It's why they shit where they stand, because what do they respect? Nothing. Makes me sick to think of Yuliya with them. But you had a pretty good country when I came, where everybody work hard and was free, and now you throw it all away. Where are your churches? You close them. Where are your artists? Your museums, they hire filthy murderers, your closed churches are full of pornographers, and your talented ones, like Yuliya is, have to be bossed around by old man like me all day because who is interested in a really beautiful picture? The Marxist-Leninists had no freedom, yes, but your country has no charity, Mr. Weis, no love. So where is for your sad girl to go? I hate these dirty cult people, they are like soul of everything I hate all my life. If I had my young days back, I would go fight them myself, I'd crack their heads with my bare hands." He flexed one hand, all brown-stained knobs and purple veins, in Mark's face; then he let it fall. "But where else was for her to go?"

From across the street, a plump man in a plaid button-down over stained medical scrubs and rubber-soled clogs came toward them. He moved his legs delicately, as if they were asleep, and his head spasmodically went up and down in an unpredictable rhythm. When he got closer, Mark noticed the luminous blue of his eyes, redeeming the wasted look of his pale face.

"Tom is homo," Sergey whispered to Mark, "but I get used to it." Then he laughed. "Is a free country, no?"

The two older men shook hands warmly. Tom took a handkerchief and wiped the sweat from his forehead as he looked Mark over. He said, "No offense to your business model, Sergey, but I'm going to need something stronger than a fruit smoothie if you want me to tell this kid what I've seen."

* * *

Sergey led Mark and Tom down to the dimly-lit basement of the Asphodel, where bags of coffee beans were stacked and wooden shelves sagged under giant bottles of sweeteners and flavorings. Its close air held a rich, dry, bitter aroma, as if coffee had soaked over many years into the wood of the overhead rafters. Mark wanted to close his eyes and pretend he was somewhere romantic and foreign, a fragrant flagon-walled caravanserai on the spice road in the twelfth century, rather than wasting the days before the birth of his first child on the trail of some psychotic old girlfriend whose ruined life was no business of his. Sergey sat them at the office desk he kept in the corner of the cellar and pulled from its bottom drawer a magnum of pear brandy; the light from the bare bulb over the desk swayed its gold reflection on the amber liquid as it sloshed between the round glass walls. He filled two coffee mugs with the sweet, burning liquor and left the men to talk.

* * *

Tom laughed when Mark asked him if the underground hospital had anything to do with the It people.

"Absolutely not," he said. "You can't believe bullshit on the Internet, let me tell you that. Dr. Grace believes in the responsibility of the individual. She doesn't just help people get better: she follows up on them after they're well. I've gone personally, under her instructions, to see former patients of hers and find out if they're squandering her gift or not. How do you think I know Sergey? She sent me to make sure he was still on the right path a few years ago, and he's been my friend since. When she first met him, a year or two before that, he had a bullet in his gut because of the life he was leading. But he went straight after she saved him. He bought this place, probably not with the cleanest money the world has ever seen, I'll give you that, kid, but what the hell, he turned things around for himself and now provides a service to the community and makes an honest living. When he brought your friend Julia to us, he was all kindness, he couldn't have treated her better if he was her own father. And he's one of our best allies; he's helped Dr. Grace turn other people around. No, Dr. Grace wants to help people not to make the kinds of mistakes she made in her life. She doesn't only heal the body. And when her former patients aren't doing what's right, well, then something has to be done. Let me give you some examples. Just yesterday she sent me up to check on a young girl, no more than twenty-five, brought in with an overdose last fall. Well, what do you think I find? This girl's living in absolute filth. I mean, her apartment smelled like a busted sewer pipe, and she's got a baby crawling around with a loaded diaper and a big black dog that would have been vicious except that it was starving. And the girl's lethargic on the couch, can barely hold her eyes open, and I saw that her mouth was missing a few teeth, you know what I mean? So I called Dr. Grace and told her what I saw, and two days later, she had some people, younger and stronger than me, bring the girl and the baby down to the hospital. She tied the girl's tubes right there and put the baby with a good family she knew until she could work on the girl some more, see if she could be saved and get her head right. Christ, she even had them take the dog to a no-kill shelter. And that's a sad story, but not a very extreme one. You can probably guess what Dr. Grace did with that knife of hers on some frat-boy rapist whose idiot friends dragged him in after a poor co-ed, as we used to call them, smashed his stupid face with a lamp. She didn't even wait for him to turn his life around; she just did what she had to do. Why do you think the cops are on her side even though she's running an illegal hospital underground? Because she stands for people being better. It's true she's a rare case: without having done such a horrible thing, she would have just been a normal person plodding through life in a middle sort of way, but now, because she ran down a kid, the woman's a goddamn saint. That's just my opinion, of course. But my point is, no way, she wouldn't help a bunch of confused people mutilate themselves because they can't tolerate the pain of this life or whatever other shit excuse they have for dropping out of the human race. I mean, come on: 'can't tolerate the pain of this life'? Well, welcome to reality, kids. You still have to do what's right. I've seen her turn them away, honestly. I've seen her turn them from the door when they're bleeding out from their botched castrations and mastectomies and whatever else, tongue amputations and all the rest of it. It looks cruel when she turns them away, but some things you just can't endorse. She's not religious, as you can't expect a scientific person to be, and I'm not either, I know we're alone in the universe, which is all the more reason to hold each other up, but when I asked her why the bleeding It types who showed up didn't have as much right to treatment as some troglodytic frat-boy rapist, she said the rapist hadn't yet totally thrown away his humanity the way those cultists had, that they didn't deserve to live. So no, forget what you read on the stupid Internet: Dr. Grace is the sworn enemy of the It people."

During Tom's monologue, Mark quickly drank down sufficient brandy to make him brave enough to ask the question that he feared would cause the older man to rage or cry or turn over the desk and fly back up the stairs.

"Are you aware that Julia once knew Alice Nicchio-Strand?"

Tom suddenly turned his trembling head down and to the left as if the woman's name had struck his face.

"Please tell me about *The Last Café*," Mark said.

* * *

Frank Jobe, then all of thirty-one years old, had crossed the planet on his mission to save art by destroying it as such, as an object that could be held as property or viewed from a distance and appreciated as merely beautiful. He wanted to make art instead a tangible force in the lives of those who encountered it. From behind his mirrored shades, his prematurely white hair waving across his tall forehead in the dry winds of the Hindu Kush, he'd told an interviewer, "They say it's all just signifiers, man, but what's the signification of this?" Then, infamously, he'd put his cigarette out in the interviewer's palm. Behind and above them flickered the anamorphic diagonal of holographic fire that Jobe and his team had projected on the steep slope of a mountain on the Afghan border, an opus commissioned by and assembled under the auspices of several non-governmental organizations for the sake of its "searing commentary on the horrors of international conflict." Jobe would later boast of his piece's effects. Warlords of various factions, in crossing the mountain pass, rounded with wide and suspicious eyes the illusionist's slanted flame until they saw the fifty-foot image of a human skull lambent within it; then they crashed their Jeeps or caravans and ordered their men to open fire on the high flame, momentarily suspending their own hostilities. It was this ambitious work of artistic anti-art, entitled *The New Ambassador*, that brought Jobe his global notoriety.

His inscrutable intentions helped his cause as well. He was a man of bombastic rhetoric without being very articulate. "Bourgeois art," he'd said, "is about something, it's supposed to remind you of something, and you're supposed to laugh or cry. Which is bullshit, man. I don't want to remind you of something, I want to be the thing. I want to be the thing you cry when you remember."

Was there any moral or political aspect to this or was it a creed of pure sensation? Surely, said Marxist critics, the purpose of protesting "bourgeois art" was to prepare for the utopic and egalitarian relations among a redeemed humanity that would flourish when the reign of the bourgeoisie was brought to an end by the revolution. Failing that, the purpose of his vital and tangible artwork must have been, as another of Jobe's critics put it, "to recall the subject to the materiality of existence and its attendant ethical responsibilities to the Other." Jobe wouldn't say; sometimes he said contradictory or incoherent things, leaving it to the critics and the curators and the professors and the graduate students to decide.

"What critical and cultural theories inform your praxis?" an interviewer had asked him in Germany during the opening of his piece, *The Marriage of Arbor and Rhizome*. For this installation he had planted parallel lines of oak trees at regular intervals in square dirt patches on the ground floor of a gleaming new white and glass gallery in Berlin. In fifty years, the oaks in stately colonnade would overtake the gallery. The branches' gentle force would lift and prise loose the glass roof until it would fall in a sparkling explosion among the acorns. The roots would ever so slowly swell under the white walls hung with their blank Suprematist canvases until they listed and fell in their turn. Eventually, no one would ever be able to tell that a gallery had been there at all.

"There are no theories," Jobe said. "Just praxis. People who write theory are undertaking the praxis of jacking off, which is cool if that's what you're into, but I'm into the real thing."

Mark, researching Jobe on the Internet after having spoken with Tom, read those words in a magazine profile published after *The Last Café*. The magazine writer levied his final judgment on the catastrophe with fine understatement: "In an art world whose habitués had perhaps grown too safe, too professional, brevetted by all the right credentialing programs and appealing to all the right money-men with all the right political views, Frank Jobe's willingness to back up his bad-boy persona with dazzlingly and grandly destructive works pointed to a horizon for American visual art beyond the cushy confines of over-theorized conceptualism and mind-numbingly P.C. cultural critique. It wouldn't be the first time that an unsuspecting citizenry, embarrassed by its self-perceived weakness, swooned for a martial rhetoric, unaware that it was in fact drifting toward its own destruction."

* * *

"Everybody who was anybody was there," Tom told Mark. "And I wasn't anybody, and I'm still not. But my boyfriend, Ricardo, now he was somebody. Professor of Comparative Literature, head of the department too, supervising five dissertations a year and publishing a book every two. He literally wrote *the* book on the evolution of love in western culture from the Middle Ages to the present. He claimed there was a suppressed tradition, bubbling just under Christianity and the Enlightenment, of trying to reach the divine through the human beloved. And this hidden current of thinking and behavior, he said, made a lot of nonsense of all our rules and norms, which we took on to promote the false understanding that this life was for work and the next was for happiness. But if you could reach the next life by touching the flesh of your lover, then heaven was here. And so was hell: all that awful toil and labor. The good news is if you're in hell, you can get out easily. Easy as a kiss. I didn't understand any of this when we met. Christ, I didn't understand anything. He found me on a park bench! That's how messed up I was. But he took me in and cleaned me up and explained it all to me. Jesus, you should have seen the ring of dirt I left in his beautiful clawfoot tub. He was a true believer, he read me Provençal poetry, me, who was lucky to get out of high school. I've known more handsome men, I'll say it, and men easier to live with. He wasn't that, because he was a goddamn genius, and you know how selfish they are, not in general, but with all the little things, all the little minutes they need to think in. Never do the dishes, never take out the trash, that kind of thing. But I'll never forget. His kindness to me, it was, it was..."

Tom swept his palm over his face clumsily, which only smeared the tears into a shiny film on his rough cheeks. He took a large gulp of the brandy, his chin too now wet and catching the overhead light. He rattlingly cleared his throat and inhaled sharply and deeply through his nose until he was calm. It took about a minute in all until he could continue. Mark, embarrassed, looked at the floor, wanting the whole time to throw himself forward across the table and take the suffering older man's hand in both of his own.

"We had five years, me and Ricardo. By the fifth year, I got complacent. He used to say to me, 'Don't get complacent,' when he would take me somewhere grand, some cathedral or museum or opera. It was part of his arrogance to tell me that, but he was right, so why the hell not say it? He knew the worth of the gifts he gave me, and he thought I would appreciate them more if I knew their worth too. But even he wasn't too excited to go to the opening of *The Last Café*, exclusive as it was, the new piece by 'the great Frank Jobe,' and in our little city, no less, thanks to the deal-making prowess of Alice Nicchio-Strand. Oh, Ricardo bitched about Frank Jobe for the whole week leading up to the opening. 'A thug's grotesque nihilism in our museum,' he said. 'Alice should know better. She is not a stupid woman, but a failed artist is a very dangerous person. They hate and resent all life, they hate beauty because they cannot create it, and that is Alice's problem, she is a failed artist, that is why she patronizes this grunting filthy pig, this Frank Jobe. It is all resentment. My God in Heaven, does no one read Nietzsche any longer?' That was Ricardo's opinion about the whole thing, and I remember it well because he said the same thing to me over the orange juice every morning for a week until the Friday of the opening finally arrived. He knew Alice Nicchio-Strand from way back, when she used to teach, and he couldn't believe she would fall for Frank Jobe's crap. He thought she was a sell-out, pure and simple, just trying to scare up some money any way she could for the museum in the midst of the economic crisis. Ricardo, despite his belief in screwing his way to heaven, was really an idealist at heart. He thought he loved the world, but he never saw the really rough parts of it. He had so many advantages over me, but that was my advantage over him. He was naïve, and it made him vulnerable, made me want to protect him as much as he protected me. I was the one who had to come into the bathroom and kill the centipedes while he kneeled all naked and pathetic-looking on the edge of the tub. And it was his idealism that Frank Jobe offended. 'They want money, they should show Caravaggio, they should show Titian, even, for Christ's sake, Beardsley. People are not stupid! They know beauty! They would line up for that! Like old women who put their last penny in the collection plate, the people would pay for that succor in dark times.'"

Tom pounded the table and, with a thick, moist accent, mouthed words he would never otherwise use, all in loving imitation of the dead professor, the Romance philologist from Buenos Aires, the man of great cultivation and learning disgusted by the upstart hipster artist and the cunning museum director who hoped to manipulate him for money's sake, this late scholar too good for a world that was, unbeknownst to him, about to vomit him violently out of itself.

An entire wing of the museum's ground floor had been made over into *The Last Café*, an expensive process that involved knocking out a partition wall, installing a wooden drop ceiling decorated with fake ducts and pipes, running real pipes and other plumbing to the end of the room where the equipment would be, hiring baristas and extra cleaning staff, and obtaining relevant licenses for serving food and beverages inside the museum. Frank Jobe designed the interior and the menu, and he was given final approval on personnel. He hand-picked coffee beans and suppliers for the opening and supervised the training of the baristas. He instructed them on the subtle performance of certain gestures, "no doubt derived from a superficial reading of Artaud," surmised a later critic, that would impart the quality of archaic and fatal ritual to their performance of their duties; they were only too eager to obey his instructions, since they were mostly actresses from local university theater programs. Alice Nicchio-Strand obviously took a financial risk in commissioning Jobe's project, but she calculated that the revenue produced by making a functional and relatively inexpensive coffee shop into a permanent museum exhibit created by the most renowned artist of his generation, with all the aesthetic credibility that implied, would pay for itself several times over. Unlike the fools in Berlin, she didn't even have to pay for the eventual arborescent abolition of the museum; it seemed that Jobe, as he got older, was settling into a less destructive mode, submitting himself to the merely routine cultural destructiveness of commercial nihilism under cover of irony.

"She looked like a true believer to me, though," Tom said. "Ricardo and I thought she must have been very cool and knowing about it all behind the scenes, but when we got there, all the investors and bigwigs invited to the private opening on that wretchedly hot night in July a little over a year ago, we saw that she seemed very, very serious. The doors to the café were closed, and they'd put a large bank of chairs in front of them along with a podium for Alice to stand behind. She stood there and watched us file in, the sweat from the heat outside still dripping off our heads, almost freezing in the frigid museum air conditioning. Oh, she looked resplendent, like a statue. Have you ever laid eyes on her? That woman must be six, seven, eight feet tall, with long, thick, black hair and big black eyes that are so opaque it's like she's looking at you from somewhere inside of them, but you can't see her in there. A fearsome, intense woman. She stood there and watched us file in, not glad-handing the crowd, no, she was way above that. And we sat down dutifully, on plastic chairs in the gray, cold, antiseptic museum corridor leading to the re-designed wing. We were mad about the delay because we'd been promised food, and goddamn it we were hungry.

But we sat down and looked around to see what other important people were there, because that would let us know how important we were. Of course, I wasn't important at all, but after five years of going to these things with Ricardo, I was starting to forget that."

Then, when they had all arrived, Alice Nicchio-Strand made a short prepared speech, a low-quality video of which Mark turned up later on the Internet. The video was filmed from behind, and the comments beneath it suggested that it had been shot by Jobe himself.

She spoke slowly, deliberately, and without emphasis: "There have been many attempts over the last two centuries to discover the end of art, where 'end' means both conclusion and telos, in a culture that has found itself no longer able to support the idea that art's justification lay in its reference to an ideal and spiritual perfection. Most versions of the 'end of art' that did not simply rest with art's impossibility in a disenchanted cosmos came to see art's proper role as that of a servant to the quotidian life of common people, from Constructivist advertising to Surrealist games to the various epic neo-classicisms that characterized the so-called workers' states, and on to the group-validating productions of identity politics in our own time. Frank Jobe's disquieting suggestion over the course of his extraordinary career to date has been that art's end might be nothing other than death: that art, rather than conferring beauty upon the everyday or legitimacy upon a political regime or identity upon an oppressed sub-population, might simply be death's embassy, if I may gloss the title of his first major work. But tonight we will find Frank Jobe in a different mood, the significance of which I must leave to you. 'What is *The Last Café*?' you will be forced to ask yourself. A corrosive satire of the status game the aesthetic becomes among the hip denizens of the coffee shop, blithely drinking the labor of distant bean-pickers as they hunch over their laptops and Moleskines? An attempt to contain and transcend that status game and, indeed, all commerce by replicating them to perfection within the artwork and the art institution? Or just a humble hymn to the everyday aesthetics of buying and selling common comfort? And, since there is always death with Frank Jobe, where is death in this picture? These are questions for you to contemplate as you enjoy a coffee and a sandwich in *The Last Café*. In the meantime, please give a generous hand to Frank Jobe."

Jobe came through the café doors to the side of Alice's podium and took an elaborate arm-spiraling bow in his silk paisley-printed shirt, his eyes inscrutable behind thick-framed sunglasses, his face four-days' bearded and his hair a thick wave of premature white threaded with strands of black.

"We all clapped," Tom said, "and then we stood to go in."

From the magazine profile of Jobe that Mark had found: "And what was it but a hip café? All exposed brickwork on the walls and weathered floorboards underfoot and aluminum ductwork overhead, with graffiti art on display and jazz fusion on the soundsystem and chessboard designs on the scored wooden tabletops, with real baristas, plainclothes rather than in uniform because this was not some trashy chain, with pink-tipped Chelsea cuts and black labrets, who tended to real espresso machines and accepted real gratuities. It was a real café, so real that, having gone there, you wouldn't need to go to another one ever again, simply because you will have had a visitation from the hip café's Platonic essence, of which all the extant hip cafés on street corners near university campuses or in gentrifying neighborhoods were only crude and primitive approximations. Its complete and total authenticity, at once raising and liquidating all of the last century's tiresome *ceci-n'est-pas-une-pipe* questions of truth and representation, guaranteed its status as a major work of international art. Could aesthetics ever hope to touch the real? Raise the yellowed ceramic mug to your lips and find out. By doing so, you would support the museum, which would of course collect all proceeds raised from the sale of drinks and food within the artwork."

"We were patrons of the arts," Tom said, "so we patiently lined up and ordered our coffees and sandwiches. Jobe had gone back into the little kitchen behind the counter, and Alice stood at the doors, her chin lifted in that regal way she had. But her eyes just a little too wide and worried, if you know what I mean, like a girl on the wall at the sixth-grade dance wondering if anybody will ask her. And the people were as insufferable as ever, Ricardo's annoying academic colleagues and various pretentious artsy-fartsy types. You should have heard the conversations; you could have cut the bullshit in the air with a butterknife. I leaned over and asked Ricardo if there'd be booze, but he just dug his elbow into my gut like he did every time I didn't act like his good little Eliza."

The artists, professors, critics, patrons, and investors bought their coffee from the violently gesturing baristas and sat at the round tables to argue among themselves as they lifted mugs and demitasses to their lips and broke off crumbles of plastic-wrapped cinnamon rolls. All their words drifted up to the beams and ducts and rafters, intermingled with the drum pulse and the dreaming horn that vibrated in the high-mounted speakers.

"I suppose I wonder if this is really what we need right now. Another piece of artwork-as-meta-sociology. Don't we get it by now? We're all inauthentic performers of our constructed and unearned privilege, okay. Wouldn't it be better to make something to alter this state of affairs rather than reifying it?

"You're relying on an outmoded surface-depth model of the text here, though, Timothy. What Jobe has given us is a practice. There is no representation of performance here; there simply *is* the performance. Real money for real coffee. Our privilege is material, not ideological, and it is actually being reproduced as we speak."

"Oh Christ, Jean, don't tell me you think this is a new and radical way to raise the moldy question of complicity."

"To the contrary, that would be as banal as appealing to the nostalgic concept of 'reification,' with its crypto-fidelity to some kind of medievalism that posits a once and future integration of the cosmos with man, and I *do* mean 'man.' There's no question of complicity in *The Last Café*, there simply is complicity. That is Jobe's genius. And why the hell do I have to explain the idea of praxis to a *soi-disant* Marxist?"

"Now don't get hostile here, Jean, just because you're a closet reactionary."

"I am not a reactionary, Abdul, I am the true radical, as radical as capital itself. You hate capital because its leveling force requires you to stand in a line on equal ground with a woman and listen to what she thinks. And Timothy's Marxism is a façade; you, Timothy, are a kind of John Ruskin or William Morris. You should design wallpaper."

"Well, despite Jean's creepingly capitalist and unwittingly raced attempt to speak for the entire chimerical sorority, as it were, I and my vagina must humbly dissent from proclamations of Jobe's genius. It seems to me that we have here the final nihilistic terminus of art's imbrication with, or better, construction *as* nothing less than white heterosexual patriarchy itself. But the inadequacy of Timothy's indeed nostalgic critique is writ large in the absence in his account of whiteness and, perhaps even more important because less visible, heteronormativity as the enabling structuration of this mode of commerce. Is the café experience a status dance or a mating dance? And for whom? Let me refer you to the music above, the expropriated surplus of the racialized subject's product, otherwise routinely abjected as criminal or dangerous, but here deployed as a small aphrodisiac to enhance the bourgeois heterosexual couple's inevitable reproduction as both *bios* and *nomos* over these oh-so-telling chessboard tables."

"Does this coffee taste exceptionally bitter to anyone else?"

"While the point about race is well-taken, Susan, I don't see how you can possibly neglect the queer dysteleology of exchange itself, as well as its inevitable disruption of racialized hierarchies; the true revolution will pass through exchange, not retreat from it. Its parody of biological reproduction ensures the discrediting of every naturalism. I can agree with Jean to that extent. Doesn't anyone recall that Dante put the usurers and the sodomites in the same circle of his *Inferno*? You and Timothy deserve each other with your ideologically doubled appeals to authenticity."

"Well, at least you admit this Jobe piece is located entirely within the register of parody. And my point, white and male as it may be, is that parody belongs to the last century."

"Excuse me, Timothy, but it's absolutely obscene of Gerry to conflate the tactical deployment of coherent cultural imaginaries on the part of the oppressed with the same ideological maneuver utilized cynically to bolster existing power structures by those structures' very beneficiaries. No offense to you, of course, Timothy."

"Of course. Let me put my objection another way: the museum's money would have been better spent bringing in an actual jazz musician. Speaking as a member."

"Speaking as a member of the empire in whose service Jobe's first stunt piece was produced. But I suppose Jean here will tell us that Jobe intended to subvert militarism in Central Asia with an invocation of the structuralist psychoanalysis of the anamorphic subject."

"Subversion, parody, these aren't the point, Abdul. The point is that Jobe has us not only talking but doing."

"But I can buy coffee anywhere, Jean. It will be less bitter too."

"But the redefining of the coffee purchase as art is the revelation of what art always-already was: both the token and the type, the form and the content, of sociality considered as the persistence through time of constantly renewed and stabilized identity structures formed by knowledge-production. I wouldn't be surprised if the bitterness were added by Jobe just so we don't forget the biological substrate of the subject's machinic reproduction. Tell me I'm not the only Spinozist here, please, for God's sake."

"But to what end? That is my question. To what ultimate end?"

"Well, we don't know, do we? It's only opening night."

"Where *is* Jobe, by the way?"

"Behind his creation so as to inhabit it fully, I would imagine."

"Sentimental religiosity, like the no doubt unconscious and therefore monumentally informative use of the word 'revelation' we heard earlier."

"Ricardo, you haven't said a word. Penny, so to speak, for your thoughts?"

"Well, my friends, this will not be to my credit among distinguished materialist reductionists such as yourselves, but I for one suspect that a revelation indeed is perhaps more in order than a revolution, not that either is a possibility in this rather grim café."

"Oh Ricardo, please. 'Only a god can save us'? Really? Tell it to Herr Goebbels, *mi amigo*."

"You know, I fear we're being quite rude to some of our patient company here, such as Ricardo's and Timothy's and Jean's partners, who do not share our obsessions."

"You're very kind, Abdul, but I am happy to leave the talking to Jeannie here. She's got the brains in the family. Luckily, I have the money. I'll say this for Mr. Jobe, though: he's really got us talking. Isn't that what art's all about?"

"I fear our talking has turned my poor Tom's stomach. You've hardly touched your espresso."

"It's true," Tom told Mark. "I'd been having trouble sleeping that week, so I took only a couple sips of the bitter stuff while the others were getting pretty wired, obviously enjoying their verbal spat over the politics of Jobe's art, a lot more than they would ever have enjoyed living in the just world they always talked about. And it was around the time Ricardo said that to me about the coffee that the convulsions began."

Ricardo's academic colleagues had received their drinks and were seated almost last of all the attendees. When a man across the room began to vomit and then to dry-heave forcefully, the choked noise that wrenched itself out of his esophagus echoing through the whole café, a few of the academics, after wrinkling their noses in disgust, failed to suppress a chuckle.

"The authentic touch of the real," said Timothy. "How could anyone say this isn't art?"

"I say it isn't art, and it makes me want to puke too," said Abdul.

"It would be a shame if they got sued, and all those profits they were dreaming of went down the toilet," said Susan.

"So to speak," added Ricardo, and then they all laughed uproariously, their fellow patrons of the arts and of the café staring at them nastily.

"But we didn't laugh long, as the saying goes," Tom told Mark.

The spasms started at the table where the man had vomited. The four people at that table, all very elderly and slow-moving, for which reason they had been encouraged to go to the head of the line when the café opened, now wore the tooth-baring grin of the demoniac. Their jaws clicked as their heads jerked in circles on their wattled necks; they looked as if they had caught a beat and were about to leap up, chairs clattering over behind them, to do a wild new dance. Their shoulders twitched, the arms flailing in limp curves, until they doubled over as if their stomachs had imploded like sledgehammer-struck vacuum tubes. Then they blew out of their forward hunch, heads thrown back, legs kicked out. The chairs noisily jumped across the floorboards with their occupants' convulsions before the old people lurched out of their seats and flopped in spine-cracking jerks, the limbs finally cruciform. Their cries for air sounded out like the lowing of kine. At the next table, a man's lips lengthened and contracted against smoke-yellowed teeth, and his wife's knee wrenched itself up so sharply that all the mugs on the table wobbled and tipped. One dropped off the edge and burst into shards that carried a glittering dust across the varnished wood.

"My legs feel strange," Ricardo had said to Tom.

Then the crowded café became a sea of flesh agitated by some deep invisible swell that surged through the room in peaks and troughs, all the muscles leaping and bunching and finally subsiding at one table after another in rollers spray-capped with vomitous spume.

"I turned back to Alice Nicchio-Strand, who still stood in the doorway, and I saw her, and I knew, despite what she did next, that she'd had nothing to do with this. Jobe had betrayed her. I knew because she'd simply lost control of herself: she looked like she was as poisoned as we were, her fingers buried in her hair, her mouth wide open, her eyes about to roll right out of her head. I knew she was innocent, even though the minute she caught my eye she seemed to come back to her senses. Then she calmly backed out of the café and threw the doors closed and pressed her whole body against them, as if she were afraid we'd get out and infect her with whatever we had. And only when she realized she wouldn't get it, because she hadn't had anything to eat or drink, did she start to scream. She screamed like a woman possessed; she was impaled on that scream of hers."

Then Tom had turned back to find Susan, Jean, Abdul, and Timothy trying to get to their feet, collapsing into each other, their faces frozen in the sardonic and contemptuous smiles that had been so much more mobile and alive when they'd entered this artwork. Their legs led them all around each other with raised arms in a chaotic quadrille until they spilled their torsos and heads to the floor. Tom's jaw was stiff and his calves twitched; he felt that his muscles were on strings being pulled this way and that by an unseen manipulator. He stood quickly and pulled Ricardo after him, though his lover was already quaking and trembling. He fell back against the wall, Ricardo's head leaping in his lap. A reflex climbed from his own nape to the pivot point from which it would send his head in its pendular swing for the rest of his life. Across from Tom another man who had taken very little food and drink stood with his own back against the wall in what was evidently an archaic instinctual search for stability. An abstemious old man in hound's-tooth, he kept his hands folded before him and his head turned slightly down, his thin lips fixed in a tender moue of compassionating disapproval; he watched the eruptions of toxic flesh through rheumy eyes behind thick lenses with an expression that suggested he had seen its like before, maybe more than once. Tom frankly willed himself, he told Mark, to lose consciousness, because he did not want to have to watch Ricardo die. Eventually he saw that the jumping and the lowing and the puking and the shaking had left off, and the café fell absolutely quiet except for the jazz. The barista with pink-tipped hair still stood at her station, frozen like the Gorgon-struck, tears leaking in a constant stream from her unblinking and stationary eyes. Later, Alice opened the café doors to a team in hazmat suits who zipped almost everyone but Tom and the old man into opaque white plastic bags and wheeled them out on stretchers to the faint rhythm of *Bitches Brew* still drumming out of the speakers high up in the ceiling.

Tom drank from the brandy bottle directly and sat, his shoulders hunched and head down, without any more tears or sighs, his face bobbing in and out of the light cast by the bulb overhead.

"And nobody ever found Frank Jobe," he finally said. "Some say he joined a terrorist cell he knew in Central Asia, some say his people had a private island, some say he just went to ground and founded these It people that have your Julia, some say he was working for somebody all along, maybe the terrorists, maybe the CIA, maybe the Chinese, who the hell knows, working for somebody who just wanted to make chaos. I used to say if I found him, I'd want an hour in a room alone with him, and at the end of the hour, you wouldn't even know that what had gone in there with me had been a person. But Dr. Grace showed me another way. I had to start going to see her because Ricardo and I hadn't made any preparations for his death, and I was left after he died with what I had before I met him: nothing. So somebody tipped me off to Dr. Grace, and once I got a bit better, I started working for her, both in the hospital and out in the world, following up with the people she helped to make sure they were living the right life. And that's my way now. I try to balance all the evil that son of a bitch did with some good of my own. But it'll never, ever balance. Nothing will make up for Ricardo. And I drink too much, and God knows I'll probably die soon, and, to tell you the truth, I hope to hell I do. But in the mean time, I try my best to keep people alive first, and on the right path after that. And these Its, well, I try not to judge, but they aren't right. The fact that people even think Jobe has anything to do with them tells me that. You should get your girl Julia away from them if you care about her."

"And how do you propose I get her away? Or even find her?"

"How the hell should I know, kid? Maybe you need to figure out what this sick cult is really all about. Maybe you should find Alice Nicchio-Strand."

Sergey came down the stairs with two coffees in to-go cups to sober them up.

"Did you find what you're looking for?" he said to Mark.

"I don't know what I'm looking for," Mark said.

Sergey, perceiving the red rims of Tom's eyes and the fallenness of his posture, stood behind him and kneaded his shoulders with knobby fighter's fingers.

"I thought you were looking for Yuliya," Sergey said.

"Yes, that must be it," Mark said and stood up.

He thanked Sergey and Tom with vigorous shakes of the hand; then he hurried up the stairs out of the dim cellar and back into the burning daylight.

* * *

Later Mark found the collectively-written blog of a renegade graduate student art-theory group that signed itself only as "the R.A.F.," or Radical Affect Faction. They'd posted several long essays on *The Last Café*, each with several hundred comments, due to their having been linked as outrage bait by several popular sites that compiled news and gossip. "Those Theory Bros You Remember From Your Liberal Arts Classes Just Defended Mass Murder," proclaimed one headline; the sub-heading asked, "Should they be outed before they kill?" Mark read through several paragraphs of the R.A.F.'s defense of Frank Jobe.

"It has long been a hallmark of the bourgeois order that it segregates all potentially disruptive affects into the anodyne zone called 'the aesthetic,' where they become the exclusive preserve of the feminine or the adolescent at the level of consumption and, at the level of production, of a small cadre of carefully recruited professionals, running dogs of capital, who exist to neutralize the threat contained in the concept and institution of 'art,' precisely by naturalizing it as concept and institution rather than radicalizing it as the immanent assemblage of the multitude. Art is energy, expropriated from the common by the proprietor and vended for profit as 'autonomous *objet d'art*' for the elite and as 'mere entertainment' for the mass, in either case a reified commodity drained of revolutionary potential. And all the so-called 'revolutions' that have been immanent to the field of art have exacerbated these reactionary tendencies, as Lukács, Bürger, Groys, and others have instructed us when they observed that 'modernism' so-called, a conservative capture of the very term 'modern' with all its intimations of emancipation, willfully remained within the bourgeois problematic of the artist-audience dyad and its impermeable boundary. Only the historical avant-garde, with its project to dissolve the illegitimate category of 'the aesthetic' and to disseminate it as lived utopia and general intelligence throughout the collective, had the nerve to look beyond this impasse. But their dire career should have served us all as a warning, for where is the historical avant-garde today but precisely on every commodity as ornament, its truest locus now where else but the fashion catwalk? No, designing new chairs is not enough to topple the imperial world-system.

"This is a lesson Frank Jobe alone seems to have learned. Honestly, we would have come to the defense of *The Last Café* for no other reason than the response it's garnered so far from bourgeois humanitarians with their endless 'human rights' blackmail, their evaluation of every act by the criteria of Amnesty International rather than that of correct praxis and emancipatory affect. But Jobe's praxis *is* correct and therefore worthy of defense on grounds other than striking back against the endemic Dickensian sentimentality of the good burghers who are always so aghast when the horrors the system that empowers them visits on Others across the unequal globe turn and strike at the heart of their own gentrified neighborhoods. Jobe's project is legible as *at one and the same time* a parody of the neoliberal system via its reduction of art to commodity, an enactment of neoliberalism's unstated policy mandate via its performance of exchange bound inextricably with slaughter, and a savage assault upon neoliberal aesthetic practices in that it literally liquidates their patrons. Jobe, in short, made a bourgeois art object so perfectly apropos of bourgeois murderousness that it killed its very audience. And he did so by poisoning that audience in such a way as to fatally excite the nervous system, releasing the revolutionary affective charge too long immobilized on the wall of the museum or in the pit of the orchestra or between the pages of the bound book. Jobe's audience was never so alive as during its death-gyrations. *Has any artist of the last hundred years demonstrated a keener command of dialectics?* But we partisans of immanence, we adepts of intensity, know that dialectics will never be enough; and Jobe appears to have come to this understanding as well. To crown his emancipatory achievement, Jobe has refused to allow himself to be capitalized as individual artist, modeled in the Enlightenment on the individual private proprietor, in the wake of the controversy over *The Last Café.* He has dissolved into the very multitude from whose heart he brought the energy with which he dispatched a fraction of its class enemy. That he in the process forever discredited the cynical curator, Alice Nicchio-Strand, former purveyor of naïvely subjectivist 'feminist' 'art' before she came clean and acted forthrightly as an agent of the art-world's money-men, is simply the icing on the current bourgeoisie's neo-domestic hipster cupcake. Whether or not Jobe has anything to do with the emergence of those gray brigades of anti-individualists who insist that they be called 'It,' their own praxis is in line with his in their revolutionary deployment of touch to assemble new collectives unhostaged to the capital machine. There is no question that as capital's current crisis deepens, more or more of those with nothing left to lose will join those itinerants in their promising insurgency."

Mark, his eyes feeling heated and dried in their sockets, leaned away from the screen. What did he have to lose? He wanted only to go to his wife, to be there for the birth of his child. Melissa still wouldn't return his calls. He did what he had not yet allowed himself to do during their separation: he navigated away from all his research about Julia and the It people and *The Last Café* and visited *All Tomorrow's Patés* instead. He didn't have a subscription, but he could watch a preview of a new video, one she had made since his departure. In the one-minute sample clip, she stood in their kitchen and awkwardly manipulated a potato ricer over a large bowl, a patch of her shirt that stretched over her distended belly already crusted with starchy paste. She laughed and swore, implicitly reassuring the audience that they could make good food gracelessly, that perfection could be a quality of the product despite the messy process, that, in effect, real women could succeed in the kitchen. Her fingers were streaked with potato mash, so she lifted the back of her wrist to push her glasses up on her nose and brush a coil of red hair from her forehead. Her smile was only for the cameras, he knew, but she was a good actress: she looked unaffectedly happy and seemed to be sharing that look with him. He couldn't find the tears massing behind her eyes, the shadow of a grimace in her smile. Like his parents' house, she was still there even though he had gone. He shut the web browser window before the video finished.

Then he opened another and typed "Alice Nicchio-Strand."

* * *

He'd expected more from her house. From the outside, it was simply a house, an old house at that, brown and drab, with a wrap-around porch and a picture window and one round turret on the right side with a weathercock spinning on its peak. It sat on a hill in a city neighborhood, and he had to climb a crooked, grass-grown set of concrete stairs set into the unkempt front yard to reach her door. The lawn had been neither mowed nor watered recently; some patches were brown like cigarette burns, while yellowish grass sprouted in tall arcs in other places. The heat wave was forecasted to break that morning. A desert-dry wind, abrasive and hot, blew clouds so purple they were almost black across the sky. His parents would return the following day; Melissa was due to give birth in three days. He had nothing to say to Alice Nicchio-Strand. He just wanted to hear her story. He wanted to hear the story of someone whose life seemed to be as ruined as his own.

He rang the doorbell. A dog, massive from the sound of it, growled and barked and clicked its nails on bare floorboards at him from behind the front door. Then he saw Alice Nicchio-Strand peer at him through the wind-blown curtains of the open front window. She fixed her eyes on him as he panted from his climb up the concrete steps and wiped the sweat out of his eyes. Her own large dark eyes were unblinking and fierce beneath sharp brows, eyes that would look at anything at all without fear; her face, while olive or tawny in its coloring, appeared pale against the dark fall of her hair in errant strands of black. "She was a striking woman," Tom had said, and Mark could tell that he was right, even though she was crouched over the back of her couch and spying him from the window.

"I don't talk to anyone," she called to him.

"No one at all?" he asked.

"Don't be cretinous. You know what I mean: reporters, researchers. Vultures."

"I'm not any of those things. I want to talk to you about the Its."

"But I've said a thousand times I don't know anything about that. And I don't know where Jobe is, if you're one of his disgusting groupies. I hope he's burning in hell."

"Listen, Ms. Nicchio-Strand..."

"*Dr.* Nicchio-Strand."

"Of course. Dr. Nicchio-Strand." He had to shout over the wind and the howls of the dog. "I want to ask you some questions about Julia Bonham."

She slammed the sliding window so hard into its sash that he was astonished it didn't shatter down on her. He put his face in his hands. He had nothing to do now but crawl back to his wife on his hands and knees and beg for forgiveness and then get a job bagging groceries. He couldn't pretend any longer to have some other purpose, to belong to a world of wildness and danger. He stepped down off the porch and wondered if tossing himself head over ass down the concrete steps would kill him.

The door opened behind him. He turned and saw her standing there, a head higher than him in her bare feet, a white robe draped around her in complicated and recomplicated folds. The dog, a huge black thing that would have been taller than anyone if it stood, stamped on the floorboards of the entryway, the beat of its claws mingling with the distant thunder.

She said, "You must mean Julia Fraternelli."

Part Three
FALL, ALICE

7. XERISCAPES OF THE HEART

The price they made you pay for the life of the mind was exile. Because you had the hubris to claim that thought could be adequate to your deepest needs, they punished you by forcing you to go wherever they sent you. They dared your self-admired consciousness to build a house anywhere, on alien or hostile ground.

Alice found herself in this lonely eastern city. To find oneself in a city at all was lucky enough: people she knew in graduate school who had come from cosmopolitan world capitals now spent their days staring at cows or mesas, and while it was possible that these new visions carved irreplaceable grottoes into their minds, she still felt fortunate it had happened to them and not to her. This city, though, had its four strong seasons: its winter so icebound the ice seemed like stone; the summers so burning she thought the sidewalks would melt; the fall with its apple-crisp air and ankle-deep leaves; and the spring, when everything, including the concrete, smelled green and wet like new shoots of wood. This city, small and old and to this day identified with the hard men who had built it and their steel virtues and vices, startled and jarred her senses. It made her feel the deep isolation that comes from losing a land, from learning that your place in the whole intricated reticulation of things was fragile enough to be lost forever with only the passage of a few years or miles. Someone else, someone stronger, might have imagined this mobility to be a form of power, the power to be at home everywhere, as some wise man or other had once said. To Alice, however, it had come with a great and diffuse sorrow, not enough to lay her out flat but sufficient to tint her every glance gray, because she thought of the move from her city to this city as her first death.

Alice came from a place in the desert hills above the ocean. A vast city in the basin between the mountains and the coastal hills spread out its lights beneath her town. There the sun always shone in the clear blue sky, temperately enough, though even the foliage appeared dusty and parched. Whatever steel or iron men had erected the city were long gone, it seemed, leaving only the contented or the desperate. The whole flawlessly desiccated scene was crowned by the drama of the landscape, the reddish mountains to the east, the western ocean that at evening washed the sun. This landscape with its moderate weather and severe topography moved Alice to poetry because it had the power to shrivel the merely human, to make all our arrangements seem meager and indifferent. Maybe the landscape's inhumanity explained why the scandalously inequitable city's affairs were so poorly and cruelly managed, she mused, but it nevertheless gave her, the privileged and ambitious girl, a broad expanse for her mind, or she might even say her soul, to grow in. Anyway, she lived not in the city proper, but in the hills that looked out over the beaches, far from the centers of commerce and entertainment and poverty to the east of her town. She very much needed the breadth the beach vista allowed her, because all her parents ever had or ever knew was money. Money meant love to the professional and progressive couple, Mr. Strand and Ms. Nicchio, so they spent their time earning it, both to love her and to show her that they loved her, and she didn't, then or now, lack gratitude for their efforts. Only a fool refuses money, after all, even if the person who pursues it to the exclusion of all else is every bit as foolish. Without the distance, observable from her bedroom window when she was a child, where the blue of the ocean vanished into the blue of the sky in a common indigo haze, she didn't think she could have developed an imagination.

Back in the cursed days when she used to have to teach, even though she knew that she knew nothing, she always observed the failure to form imaginations in her students from the suburbs. They'd also had tenderly money-minded parents when young but nothing compensatory to look at except treated lawns and beige bricks. Therefore, they never had the opportunity to extend their souls to the horizon. They shamelessly tried to cover up their lack for as long as they could with their mere intelligence, but Alice knew this was a poor substitute, however tempting.

With all the treachery of memory, Alice thought of a certain time in her early life, roughly from age twelve to about age sixteen, as a single, suspended, tremulous, liquid instant: the moment between her excited discovery of her own particular involuted consciousness and her having begun to grow sick of it, a sickness that remained with her forever. Contained in that instant, she recalled little but long afternoons spent sprawled on the sand, her hair saltwater-crusted, the pages of whatever luminous book she was then reading curled in the damp air. That instant held only one locale other than the beach: the little public branch library in the center of her seaside town. The library contained mostly books of instruction or fantasy for the money-mad men and women who could afford to live in the town above the unequal city. Just for the sake of the community's high-school students, who would be compelled to write reports on beautifully useless knowledge before they were allowed to make money down in the city in their turn, it also offered on its few short shelves several crucial and irreplaceable volumes in whose labyrinths she would spend her entire adolescence wandering, beach-towel-wrapped and barefoot, the way she no doubt falsely remembered traveling everywhere back then, her feet even now as broad and spatulate as a peasant woman's for never going shod. Why was it, and why was it so banal even to mention as she approached middle age, that, when she'd been fourteen, a half hour would somehow impossibly deepen into infinity like a magic corridor? For example, a half hour spent on the bench outside the library, with a photographic folio of Rodin's sculptures or a large anthology of English poetry massed in her lap, waiting for her mother to pick her up and not caring that she was late again because she had decided to stay behind in the mirror-walled city and earn yet more money. Those thirty minutes spread into a singular endlessness in which she could walk forever through the xeriscape that adorned the exterior of the little library, knee-deep in the wild and overgrown orange poppies and the wine-stained yarrow and the panicles of white desert lilacs, keeping her wary distance from the spiny cacti. At intervals in this dry garden stood or sat or reclined Rodin's heroic men and women, while all those birds who sang their way through English poetry rustled amid the hardy flowers, no matter that neither Rodin nor Keats had ever looked upon this garden or even this coast.

Surely other things had happened to her at this time in her life, painful things; she must have fought with her parents, been teased at school, done poorly on exams, loved unrequitedly. When, at the age of twenty-eight, she had moved to her new eastern city with its variable weather and endless green-treed and wet-looking hills, though she failed to remember anything of her early adolescence but days at the beach, days in dry gardens, years spent among sculptors and poets in an enchanted no-place between their land and her own, the place of her imagination.

In her late teens came the nights in the city, with its shag-headed palms slanted high overhead on fragile stalks, black against the ruddy sunset, the nights smoking clove cigarettes and laughing too loudly at street-corner bus stops until she and her friends could barely speak, until they found themselves touching hips or else dry-humping inside nightclubs in a strobing white glare that lit up the wobbled surface tension of every flung sweat droplet in mid-flight, the nights of eating foil-wrapped burritos so full they burst at one bite or tangles of soy-slick noodles at the bottoms of grease-stained paper boxes in strip-mall restaurants at midnight, the nights finally riding the bus home at three-thirty in the morning with a book of filthy poems open in her lap, alongside graveyard-shifters and night nurses and murmuring isolatoes all the way through the graying dark until the salt-sea air streamed in through the bus windows.

Some had called her a slut and a whore. Her half-dreaming nature demanded submersion in forces outside itself, whether xeriscape or sculpture garden or the lives of men, some alien element she could float or wander in. Different kinds of men gave her access to different modes of living: there was the athlete with his punishing regimen and long, sinewy slopes of thigh muscle moving beneath her; the musician with his caprice and his distance and his almost narrative kisses; the math expert, too awkward in his flesh to perceive the grace with which his trembling hands unclasped her bra. She didn't envy men. Some basilisk glare encoded either in their genes or in their societies froze them into these single postures for life: sweating all around a rubberized track or bent with calloused fingertips over a guitar or squinting hunchbacked at a computer screen. Men spent their lives striving to become the statues of themselves that the city fathers would unveil in the town square when they were gone. She, on the other hand, listened with equanimity to track statistics, chord progressions, and programming languages; she made each man's lovemaking a part of herself, even though his was all he'd ever know. They only became more and more themselves, but she became each of them in turn. She knew she was no slut: she was an artist, and she needed experience.

At first, she'd tried to write poetry, but she found soon enough that she lacked the strength to strip words of their merely descriptive function, to transform them into events in their own right rather than just labels for events. She wanted to make something happen, not chatter about something that had happened. When she reached high school, she turned to sculpture. Her art teachers recognized her talent and seriousness and allowed her to use what materials she wanted and to sculpt during study hall and lunch and the hour after school. A gallery of men and women, a veritable town full of people, emerged, moist as newborns, from her labor, before she fed them into the kiln's fortifying fire: naturalistically detailed and geometrically abstract, nude and clothed, suffering, luxuriating, reclining, leaping, dancing, singing. She liked to work in wet clay, to feel the body she intuited taking shape beneath her hands. It made her feel as if she had chanced upon a person in the dark and were palpating him or her for vital information with her sensitive fingers. She won awards; she received a scholarship to the most prestigious art college in the state; she came in second for Most Likely to Succeed in the senior yearbook but won Most Unique.

For all her success, her doubts were obscuring the future. She no longer discovered any souls in the dark when she sculpted. She did it because it had become the thing she did. She feared becoming not an explorer, not an adventurer, but a type: just another art-school trendoid, just another pretentious whore. The summer between high school and college tired her intensely. She would find her suspicions confirmed later, in her theoretical readings in graduate school, but she was able to surmise on her own that making statues of men and women differed little from writing mere words about experience. Both acts imitated, but did not create. From the bookshelves and dresser-tops and nightstands of her bedroom, her little men and women mocked her with their belatedness and falsity. She felt like the sorcerer's apprentice, who could manipulate matter but could not master magic. Her work was secondary to the world, and she did not want to come in second. She didn't want to make copies of the world; she wanted to remake the world itself.

She created very little art the summer after high school graduation. She contemplated rejecting her scholarship and not going to art school at all, because she knew she would be just another fashionable impostor. It was a strange, gray summer, dim and humid, not like the golden and azure summers of her childhood. Someone had shut the lid on the world; the sky seemed very close and the air felt scarce. For money, she worked in a florist's shop in her oceanside town in the desert hills. Without a thought in her head, she wandered around the tiny greenhouse at the back of the shop, misting the roses and lilies, the leaves of the plants kinking in the gray damp. She arranged bouquets and centerpieces and nosegays for rich old women. That was why she had been hired: she was an aesthetician. Sweat beaded and shone on her upper lip.

She had an abortion at the end of August. Her father drove her to the clinic in angry, compassionate silence, which she had been confident he would do. Her mother, on the other hand, would not have been capable of the compassion or the silence, because she believed, and she had often told Alice, that getting knocked up was a terrible way for a young woman to throw away her future. Alice and Mr. Strand agreed never to let Ms. Nicchio know.

The would-be father of her would-be child was an arrogant, scornful boy. He was dispatched by his grandparents during his summer stay at their beach house to pick up an order from the florist every Sunday morning to refresh the Sabbath tea table, while they went to church. He made bitterly sarcastic remarks about everything, because, she figured, he had been born rich but ugly, just as she had been born with talent but no genius.

"I don't honestly give a shit about flowers," he'd said the day she met him. "But I have to stay in their will, don't I? Hey, speaking of, do you have anything poisonous, something with a thorn that kills at one prick?"

His ugly mood mirrored hers, and she loved to look at his ugly, broad-nosed, freckled face as it sweated in the florist's shop. He was the incarnation of that weird, miserable summer. When the florist went to brunch one Sunday morning, Alice led him by the hand back into the greenhouse, because he was so ugly. He flung up her yellow floral-printed sundress in the peat-scented steam with a gesture of angry contempt. He looked like she felt, with his sweating, sneering lip: a slovenly monster among the roses and lilies. She sweated everything out. She was dry as the desert inside after that.

She felt as if someone had thrust a pushbroom through her soul. She lay emptily on her childhood beach the last week of that summer. She didn't regret the abortion in the least, but she was humiliated by it, embarrassed in her own eyes. Staring out over the cyclically brutal waters and the carnage they left, she observed the jellyfish, limp legs sprawling out of their melted gelatinous heads, strewn across the beach as if the ocean were trying to murder life itself by vomiting up its rudiments, its embryonic slime. She knew she had done what circumstances had forced her to do, and that is why she felt so ashamed: she'd always aspired to act according to her will, not the will of nature or God or circumstance. What else had she grown such an imagination for, if not to decide for herself in perfect freedom? She could not be the world's slave. It mortified her that she had made a decision whose consequences she was forced to evade in such undignified haste, on that embarrassed car ride with her father. She promised herself to act more deliberately in the future. She would live according to premises whose conclusions she could endure.

She still considered herself a pretender, her art exhausted, her genius barren. Without a thought in her head, she went to art school anyway, for no other reason than that she knew she had a lot to learn.

* * *

Well, she thought, she couldn't tell *all* of that to the boy who came in out of the rain and who wanted to know about little Julia Fraternelli. He was one of those young men she often noticed nowadays, those A-students with a bent posture and too much flesh at the middle and a simpering, compliant, but passive-aggressive manner, men who seemed to have absorbed all that errant estrogen in the water supply she'd read about. He was probably lousy in bed, too sensitive and polite and politically correct. Such qualities in a man never failed to suggest repressed murderous urges to her; those were the men you had to watch out for, the well-behaved little boys, the good citizens. Rapists all, she thought, if wish if not in act. She didn't intend to learn what kind of a lover he was, though: he was too young and not nearly fascinating enough. As she had told her graduate seminar back in the bad old days when she'd been forced to teach, "I don't sleep with students, because you are all too stupid."

Even so, she saw no reason he should have to put up with her in her current state, stale and filthy. This boy wasn't, as she was, indirectly but decisively to blame for the murder of twenty-one people by a sociopath whose frank sociopathy, whose active rather than passive aggression, had been precisely what had charmed her about him in the first place, and so he shouldn't have to suffer because she hardly went out of the house any longer. She left him in her living room, its every flat surface layered thickly with dust, the couch he sat on strewn with blankets that probably stank unbearably of her and of Matthias, her Doberman Pinscher. She commanded the dog to stay, and he reclined on his haunches by the cold, dark fireplace, his suspicious eyes on the visitor. The storm drummed on the roof.

She excused herself to the bathroom. There, she had to chip her fingernails untaping the square of corrugated cardboard that covered the place on the mirror where her face would appear if she stood straight before it. On the cardboard, she'd written out a quote from Pessoa: "Man shouldn't be able to see his own face: there's nothing more sinister. Nature gave him the gift of not being able to see it, and of not being able to stare into his own eyes." She threw the square behind the toilet, and there she was again: Alice Nicchio-Strand at forty-six years old. She was just one year short of the age at which her mother had died, she thought, as she studied with attempted dispassion all the signs of decay, the cracks extending across the hard clay mask: the lines around the mouth and eyes that told the world how she'd been habitually straining the skin of her face, certainly not in smiles or laughter; the whites of the eyes, taking on a horrid lactose appearance to replace the clarity of youth's vitreous bodies, like water clouding as it froze; the teeth that appeared to lengthen as they mildewed in the sour mouth; and the hair, brittle and wan and threaded with tombstone-gray. While she had known abstractly since childhood that this would happen to her, in no material detail had she predicted it, and still less had she predicted what the mirror didn't show, the low and droning constant headache, the sting in the lower back at every wrong move, the stomach ready to spasm at every affront. She had thought of her mother as someone taken too soon; now she imagined her as someone spared just in time.

If anyone had *taken* her mother, it had been Alice, after all. She took her mother and made a masterpiece of her: her final project at art school, the one that was to launch her career. The boy in the living room must have looked at it on the Internet or something if he had gone to the trouble to find out where she lived, to learn that she had once known little Julia Fraternelli.

My Mother's House; or, The Inside of Her; or, How God and Man Have Decreed That Woman Should Suffer. A structure, more or less the size of a domestic room, built of a hidden skeleton of wooden beams that were in turn enfleshed by globuled walls and a ceiling of molded Styrofoam, airbrushed in reds and purples to resemble the polypy interior of a human body, a woman's body. In this red room stood middle-class suburban furniture, much of it rescued from Alice's own childhood home: a love seat with white, leaf-printed upholstery; two glass-topped end tables with lilies in fluted purple glass vases, themselves fashioned to resemble petaled floral maws; a coffee table with coasters picturing snowy Christmas woods ranged around a candy dish full of gourmet chocolates; and a mantelpiece built into the organ-meat wall and bearing framed photos of Alice's mother at every stage of her truncated life, from baptismal font to poolside to prom to altar to office to baptismal font to office to deathbed. At the ovoid entrance, a blood-purple labial doorway, hung curled ribbons of red-stained white lace, strips of Alice's mother's own wedding dress. Alice's mother had died of ovarian cancer at forty-seven, just a year older than Alice was now. Alice was twenty at the time, one year into art school, and she'd had to take a semester off to return to the town in the hills above the beach and sit by the rail of the installed hospice bed in her parents' bedroom as the professional, money-making, middle-aged woman shriveled so much that she could be easily turned this way and that by strong-muscled nurses preparatory to being wiped clean like an infant. Alice's father, a kind and gentle man but still just a man, had quietly spurned his perishing wife with an unconscious glare of haunted fear in his averted eyes. He had worked overtime throughout her dying as if to make all the money she could not, and had once even complained, only to the hospice nurse, in the hallway, in the quietest and most concerned of voices, of the spoiled-raw-meat stench produced by his wife's rotting insides. He whispered it, but his wife and daughter heard it anyway. He still lived there, above the ocean, Alice knew, but she hadn't been to see him in two decades.

My Mother's House should have launched her career: everybody said so. She was never one to accept gifts graciously, however. She had no interest in the political ideology to which her teachers tried to arrogate the piece. In fact, she told them she felt rather insulted to hear critics place her work in the canon of what was evidently a religion of weakness invented by a lot of pious prudes who had learned to talk a vaguely Marxist jargon to disguise their allegiance to an ideal of pure and unsullied womanhood.

"But surely," one young male professor had said, "you intend irony and a pointed materialist critique of masculinist theology when you say that God has decreed that women should suffer?"

She replied only to correct his memory of her title: it was not *women* but *woman* who had to suffer.

A much older female professor, nearing retirement, had said in turn, "Well, sweetie, you'll go nowhere with that attitude. My advice is avoid the issue entirely and talk about something else instead. They don't cut a lot of checks in this world, or in this profession anyway, to people who speak their minds."

Speaking her mind wasn't her difficulty, though. She found herself unable to do anything at all after *My Mother's House*. The problem that had presented itself to her when she tried to write poetry and after she'd mastered sculpture came to her once again, none of its impassible difficulty alleviated by her greater maturity. After she made any work of art, she inevitably asked herself what would come next. She thought, I can't just do *this* again. What was she supposed to do, just become the feminist room-and-house artist? She could move on to her grandmother, her aunt, or any other relative with some portentously feminine paraphernalia in her living room and a conveniently gynecological disease: *My Third Cousin's Yeast Infection: A Philosophical Investigation*. The thought disgusted her.

She went on to get a Ph.D. in art history since they would pay her to teach for six years while she did so; if she couldn't make art anymore, perhaps, after careful study, she could explain to herself why she could not. In five years, she earned her Ph.D. with a dissertation on what she'd called "the iconoclastic avant-garde," a catch-all term for a century's worth of blank-canvas painters, concrete-block architects, photographers of light, and recorders of silence. On the basis of that study, she was hired to teach in this eastern city, far from her beloved desert hills and western ocean.

She took a brief shower and then put on a sundress that was inappropriate considering the heatwave's breaking in gust after gust of frigid rain that lashed the roof. She padded back out to the living room to tell the unimpressive young man what he'd come to find out. She let her long coil of wet hair dry on the bare skin between her shoulderblades as she spoke; that way, she could attribute any shuddering he perceived to the chill it sent through her.

* * *

Fraternelli owned a few buildings in the neighborhood where he grew up, an ethnic city borough that used to be full of immigrants' kids on street corners, half an underclass and half a new elite in the making, and now full of elderly women who'd outlived their husbands and all sorts of kids on street corners, mostly underclass now, alas, since the elite was more exclusive than it used to be. He ran these old buildings almost alone, with just a few unpredictable and brutal young men for assistance; he put himself at the nearly unlimited service of the old matrons in their eighties and the lone mothers in their twenties who rented from him. Alice imagined he spent most of every day on his back or on a ladder, behind a toilet or up in the ceiling, repairing all the hidden pipes and wires that strung the world together.

She went with him on his rounds once. She had asked permission first, and his wife, the librarian, had allowed it with that prim shrug of hers. All he said was, "As long as you don't try and start a union you can come, but I'm going put you to work."

They spent a morning together in a brown little apartment in high summer heat, the once-white blades of a dust-crusted box fan raking the hot air over them, air that would probably not cease to smell like cigarette ash until a wrecking ball knocked down the room's four walls. Mrs. Cassini, whose mouth had set into a squarish frown that made thirty-two-year-old Alice vow to smile more as she aged, brought them little saucers of coffee, black and bitter. She watched sternly with her hands on her artificial hips and a pack of smokes in her dressing-gown pocket as Fraternelli and Alice replaced the worn-out fluorescent lights in her kitchen and bathroom.

She asked Alice what she did for a living. Alice never knew what to say to those she thought of as normal people in response to this question, since "artist" didn't sound quite like a job and "teacher" conveyed the wrong impression.

"She's a college professor," Fraternelli said in Alice's silence.

"Well, la-de-da," Mrs. Cassini said.

The old woman didn't chain-smoke, but she lit up devotedly at regular intervals. Sometimes she coughed, her chest booming and sloshing like a barrel of wine rolled across rocks.

"Those goddamn things are gonna kill you," Fraternelli mumbled from the top of a ladder through the wire connector caps he held loosely between his lips while he stripped the ends of the new wires up in the junction box.

"For Christ's sake, I'm eighty-seven years old. How much longer you want me to live? I wish the shitting things would kill me quicker."

She watched them for the whole time they worked. Fraternelli did most of the job, while Alice handed him his tools or cleaned up the wire covers, plaster dust, and whatever else flew down out of the ceiling onto the drab brown carpet.

"It's nothing personal," said Mrs. Cassini when Alice noticed that she was surveying them. "It's just that in my day you had to take care of yourself."

The old woman would put in the occasional word of electrical advice, and Fraternelli would, with genial dismissiveness, tell her she was wrong; then he'd sweat and grunt for a while and come to admit that maybe she'd had a point. She would then turn to Alice and gesture up to Fraternelli with an accusatory upsweep of the arthritically clawed hand that said, "They're all the same, these idiots."

Once Fraternelli sent Alice up the ladder, awkwardly hauling the bright new fixture behind her, to strip its new wire ends, attach them to the old wires in the ceiling, and then bolt the whole structure into place. She got dust in her mouth and down her shirt, and her fingers bled where the wire-ends pricked her soft skin. She hadn't worked with her hands since art school, and they had grown tender and delicate since she'd devoted herself to mental life.

Mrs. Cassini, tired of all this electrician's work, turned up the radio, tuned to a channel that played the songs of her youth and early womanhood, and began to comment on each of the songs that came on.

"What a voice he had," she was saying as Alice blinked plaster dust out of her vitreum. "I wanted to marry him! I'll never forget the day I found out he was colored."

Alice had no doubt grunted in some way as she tried to maneuver the light fixture so that the holes at the top of it would align with the corresponding holes Fraternelli had drilled into the smoke-gray ceiling. With the sorrow of futility that eventually comes over all laborers, Alice foresaw that the pristine fixture would soon be as ashy as everything else in this place.

On hearing her grunt, Mrs. Cassini said, "Not that I have a prejudiced bone in my body, *professore*. It takes all kinds, don't it? There's a lid for every pot. And you don't look too colored to me anyhow. I took you for a Sicilian. You aren't colored, are you?"

As her fingers strained to hold the fixture flush with the ceiling, Alice spat through the nut and the screw gripped between her lips, "What the hell does it matter if the lights come on?"

Mrs. Cassini rasped out a noise half cough and half laugh that made Alice's chest hurt to hear it, and she said, "You got me there, honey!"

Eventually, the old flickering yellow fluorescent lights were gone, and bright new tubes threw a steady white glare all around at the grime-coated walls and window-blinds and linoleum. With dust particles jewelling all the dark coils of her hair and blood crusted around her fingernails, Alice felt less than satisfied with the job they had done; now she could see better, with some horror, all the work left to do, the mortal infinitude of labor.

Not that Mrs. Cassini was a dirty or slovenly person: she kept her apartment tidy and uncluttered, everything in its place, a vase of fake but convincing flowers on the kitchen table, a wooden crucifix high on the wall, a blue-robed Blessed Mother atop the radiator cover, family portraits of grandchildren and school photos of great-grandchildren magnetized to the door of the refrigerator, or, as the old woman still called it, the ice-box. She smoked two packs a day, though, and her arthritis, a word she pronounced with four syllables, bothered her too much to allow her to get up on a stepladder and dust or go down on her knees and scrub. She said it had gotten so bad that she hadn't even been to church in a year.

"Soon you won't be able to go if you want to," Fraternelli told her. "They're saying once all the old folks die off, they'll have to deconsecrate it."

"What's that mean?"

"It means it won't be blessed anymore. It'll be just another building. The diocese wants to sell it. They'll probably make movies in there. The artists will like the décor; it'll make them feel special." He limply twirled his hand through the air as he pronounced "décor."

Mrs. Cassini crossed herself: "Oh Madonn'," she said. "My useless pimp of a heathen brother-in-law would love that!"

As they were going out the door, refusing several offers of food, Mrs. Cassini said, "I'm not gonna ask what you're doing with this young Sicilian girl, Frank, and you with a little girl of your own."

Fraternelli said, "Good, because it's none of your damn business, lady," but he put both hands on her shoulders affectionately and winked down at her.

"Yeah, yeah," she said, "don't forget I knew your dad. I'm an old lady, but I know what people are up to."

Alice shook her dry hand, the fingers knobbed by rheumatism and nicotine-stained. When she withdrew her hand, she felt that Mrs. Cassini had pressed a warm, soft twenty-dollar bill into her palm.

"Don't let him push you around, honey," Mrs. Cassini told her. "These girls today are so stupid. They want to be college professors and senators but can't keep their men at home, can't cook a meal, can't grow a vegetable, can't sew nothing. I say let the men do the dirty work and then give them something to come home to. But what the hell do I know? I'm just an old lady."

* * *

Fraternelli, when she knew him: six foot six, with his big paws, the deep-ridged nails overtaking the squat fingertips like curved shells, their fluting ever caked with dirt, his pot-belly swinging slowly over his handyman's belt, and his flaky leather work boots. When he wasn't in the house, he kept a thick cigar fixed in the side of his mouth; it needed to be re-lit from time to time, so he kept a small butane torch on hand. Alice loved to watch the blue flame dart around the dry tobacco. He grunted as he dismounted the cab of his mud-spattered green truck on his bad knee, his body prematurely degraded at the age of forty-three from a life of labor and appetite. He had that permanently sarcastic glimmer in his left eye and that smirk at the corner of his mouth as he brought ice cream to her university office at the end of his working day and before her night class.

"This is fancy," he'd said to her with mild derision as he looked all around her large office, orange-shot with late-afternoon sun filtered through autumnal treelight. "I've never been to college. I was never that smart. On the other hand, we know you can barely change a goddamn lightbulb, so I guess we're even."

Fraternelli questioned and mocked and derided everything, his own actions included, which made her feel safe in this lonely steel and iron city, which had no beach and no desert flowers to tell her amid her doubts that beauty and chaos could both be permanent without destroying each other. Because he laughed at everything, he asked nothing of her; because he asked nothing of her, she could give him everything. She never did give him everything, though. The nature of their relationship made it impossible.

They met, if it can be called meeting, during her second year in the city. At this time in her life, she slept, taught her classes, researched in the university library, and revised her doctoral dissertation into what would become an influential, still-cited monograph on the iconoclastic avant-garde. On days when she could fill the hours no other way, she went to movies and galleries, and she'd found a regular café a few blocks from the small rowhouse she rented near campus. Even so, she kept trying to pretend she didn't live in this city, that she'd be leaving tomorrow or the next day, back to the coast. When her book was finished, though, she began to crave novelty, some jolt to recall her to physical life now that she had at last, after an almost fifteen-year epoch that began with her confusions during the summer after high school, explained some of her intellectual quandaries to herself. She needed some new stimulus to puzzle over, some affront to create new intellectual quandaries, if she were to go on thinking at all, some piercing mote to weave a pearl around. With no plan in mind, she began reading the personal ads in the newspaper; she had not had a lover in many years.

One bleakly bright summer morning, when Alice sat in the café, faced by a day with nothing to do, she found in the paper a detailed physical description of herself as she had looked the previous Saturday night, while standing in line to see a revival of *Belle du Jour*, from the plastic orange lily in her hair down to the sea-blue polish on her toenails. Her cheeks burned, as if everyone in the café could read over her shoulder. A couple had written the ad, MC seeking F; they said she'd caught their two pairs of eyes independently of each other, and that she had moreover returned their glance, which made them wonder if she would be willing to experiment with them. They told her to reply with a physical description of themselves if she happened to be interested. She hadn't catalogued their wardrobes, as they had hers, but how could she have failed to notice the huge, ursine man with the severe angular moustache that dropped in straight lines like columns on either side of his chin, his heavy hands on the thin shoulders of the tiny, flat-chested, librarianish woman in the plain brown pants, her eyes screened behind huge round glasses, her taut gray-brown bun at rest on his rough shirt-front? Alice wrote back, "You look as if Goldilocks's plainer sister had married one of the bears, and then they grew old together." At that time in her life, she was willing to try anything once.

Fraternelli had been married to the librarian for five years; she was his second wife. His first wife, a younger woman, some kind of suburban princess-cum-accountant type who came from privilege, always inspired scornful merriment in him, as if he had spent the decade and a half of their marriage being held prisoner in some bewildering country whose customs he had never mastered or grasped the inner necessity of: "She used to buy fresh flowers every week for Sunday dinner parties. Dumb bitch blew over a hundred bucks a week that way." Then he would blow a brown cloud of smoke and admit, "The place did smell pretty good, to give the bitch her due."

The librarian, on the other hand, spoke of her precursor with steely contempt: "She wants to live in a sentimental bubble; the thought of reality fills her with horror. She never picks up a book or thinks about the state of the world. And she thinks her lack of knowledge makes her a superior being, as if other people were willfully wallowing in filth when they try to understand reality. She's even filthier, though; she just doesn't know it. But Frank loved something about her. I think it was a maternal fixation: she was like the womb."

Alice didn't try to find out too much about their pasts. She learned only that Fraternelli had tired of his first wife's endless aesthetic demands for the perfect middle-class life and had left her for the librarian, a serious woman, a trained scholar of natural history, a sober teratologist, as committed in her own way as her handyman husband was in his to apprehending the fragile relations that made the world possible. Only once and by accident did Alice meet Fraternelli's only child, his daughter with the suburban princess; but this was a year into their experiment, and what she said to the adolescent girl one summer Saturday night brought their experiment to an end.

Why had Fraternelli and his second wife contacted Alice, she wondered? She concluded that it was simply because they had been married for five years. Each having been unsuccessfully married before, they knew the early symptoms of creeping paralysis, the way husbands and wives harden in each other's eyes like those moist clay figures Alice used to feed into the kiln, the way each sentence they do or could speak to each other comes to feel predetermined by their half-decade-old roles, the way leaving a marriage is never really about leaving another person but rather about abandoning a version of yourself that once was young and supple but has since petrified into a carapace around your living soul. Fraternelli and the librarian had both divorced already, though, so they both knew that ending a marriage did not automatically liberate the self into its suppressed possibilities; the self had to be altered willfully, divorce or no. They therefore decided to dispense with divorce entirely and change their selves in tandem, together, in response to a common risk; in short, they wanted to relieve the burden of marriage by making an adventure of it. Alice would be their adventure, they'd decided when they saw her in that movie line, this woman somehow redolent of saltwater in her white sundress purple-spotted with prints of vinous blossoms.

The librarian herself told Alice, in a clinician's tone, most of what she would come to know about the couple's histories and their marriage. Specializing in rare early medical manuscripts with gruesomely intricate engravings, she never said a warm word to Alice and seemed content to ignore or allow Alice's growing flirtation with Fraternelli. As for Fraternelli, all he said by way of explanation for their desire to bring Alice into their marriage was, "We were bored, but not exactly with each other."

The librarian did not maintain her scientific decorum in bed: she screamed and thrashed, her tiny fists mashing the bedsprings, her trim and firm body, which had never borne a child, undulating in shadow-troughed waves of muscle and skin. She was obviously the one who most desired Alice's touch, which, Alice thought, perhaps explained why she preferred not to speak to her. The first time, she recalled, Fraternelli faltered; he rolled off the bed silently, his limp dick flopping under his massed gut, and watched the women, his severe moustache a black frown in the dim bedroom. Alice had thrown him a questioning look from between his wife's thighs. "Don't stop on my account," he said. "I'm just enjoying the view." She thought she saw fear in his eyes, badly masked by the joke, but then the practical, pleasure-loving man was ready. It always happened the same way: the librarian would lay flat on her back, Alice would go down on her, and Fraternelli would take Alice from behind. Alice was the medium through which Fraternelli and his wife made love, a tool, a prosthetic phallus he used to satisfy the librarian. Alice told herself at first that she submitted to this because she too needed to crack the shell that had hardened around her. After all, publishing a book exceeded marriage when it came to fossilizing a formerly living version of one's own consciousness. At least you could, if you wanted to, dissolve your nuptials, but you couldn't recall your published thoughts. She slowly became aware, however, that she allowed Fraternelli and the librarian to use her as they did because she could feel all week long the huge, hot prints his hands made on her hips every Saturday night.

At the start, she was in love only with the librarian's house. Situated back on a hidden street that curved up behind a bank of woods, it was like a

Wunderkammer she had chanced upon while strolling through a forest. She found peace in its angel-topped backyard birdbath that whispered all through the summer nights; the folds in the mold-spotted melancholy angel's robe became the ribs of its basin, as if all things fit together rightly and the world knew no disharmony or conflict. Some Saturdays when they had finished making love, Alice would leave Fraternelli and the librarian in the new intimacy of their marriage bed to loll in their claw-footed bathtub, into which she would spirit one or two of the librarian's seeming thousands of mortifying cyclops-eyed and tumor-ridden books of historical teratology, trying to control her startled breathing as she turned the hideous pages that softened and wavered in the steam from the bath. She would remember forever the night that she'd crept on careful feet up to the attic as the couple lay sleeping, the night she discovered the cabinet of formaldehyde-pickled specimens, the long white worm spiraling in amber, the rat fetus never to be birthed from the pink travesty of an amnion it floated in; she'd flung both hands over her mouth, but streaks of screaming lit out from between her fingers anyway. If the couple had heard her, they never said so.

For six months, their *ménage à trois* went as planned. In those six months, she drafted and sold to a university press her second book: a creative piece, an artist's book, that described radical and probably impossible artworks that would not, if realized, represent existing landscapes but rather create new ones, unprecedented and dangerous. A lake shimmering at a forty-five degree angle on a mountain's slope, monstrously large orange fish dotting it here and there, hanging as if from their gaping mouths by the slanted, placid surface of the water. An open-air prison cage in the blazing heat of the desert full of parti-colored birds small enough to slip through the bars but too obscurely indolent to do so; the birds would die and be replaced from time to time. An art gallery that was also a meat locker, dim and frigid, the long rack-ribbed bodies and striated shanks dangling from hooks in dancers' postures suggestive of a cattle ballet; after their tour of the gallery, the patrons would reward the artists by purchasing the choicest cuts of meat. A beach where each liquid wave that crested and spumed fell as a pane of crystal, smashing and scattering itself in glittery crystals across the shingle. A xeriscape where amid the spiny cacti and orange poppies and wine-stained yarrow grew the bodies of women, long and sinewy fragile-looking stalks with thoughtful faces, who survived on little and would accordingly live long.

Her fanciful little book won her plaudits from the coterie of artists and thinkers she most respected and earned her comparisons to certain revered intellectual fabulists. Somehow it also certified her as a brilliant artist even though she had scarcely made a work of art since deciding to get her Ph.D., because she had not changed her mind about finding the imitation of reality pointless and the creation of more reality almost impossibly difficult, a task with a failure rate so high and a risk of repetition so great that it should only be attempted once or twice a lifetime. Her book struck a compromise: she revealed her extreme and even occasionally murderous visions without inflicting them upon reality. In this, she aimed both to honor and to censure all those hard men of the twentieth century who'd mistaken their dreams for something that had to be done to the world by force. Years later, when she was in the midst of another of her maddening dry spells, when she had abandoned teaching and abandoned writing and had taken up the directorship of the city's Modern Art Museum out of sheer imaginative exhaustion and desperation, this compromise could not protect her from the intellectual seductions of Frank Jobe, a creature who seemed to have stood up and walked out of the pages of her book.

While in the act of writing the book, she enjoyed herself, or even, they would have said under an older regime, *disported* herself, with Fraternelli and the librarian. She treasured those post-coital Saturday nights of sneaking around the long hallways of that hidden house while the couple kept to their marriage bed, the librarian's cat slinking warmly between her ankles, and she loved, with the wistful and yearning knowledge that it would all have to end someday, the times when she would sit in their kitchen and all three would eat a late dinner together with post-orgasmic appetite. They would drink too much red wine and eat Fraternelli's linguine puttanesca or chicken marsala, both learned by his mother's side in boyhood, and then his vanilla gelato trailing its milky swirls in espresso liqueur. He made these beautiful, perfect dishes in the same unsmiling attitude with which he repaired his tenants' broken toilets and blown wiring; but he oversalted his own servings, Alice observed, romantically thinking him a tragic craftsman who knew what proportion would be for others, even though his own palate was too coarse to abide it, a classic instance, like the deaf composer, the blind watchmaker, the wounded surgeon, and his weakness appealed to her as much as his strength. During those dinners, Alice would read to them from her manuscript, even though the librarian usually brought a book of her own to the table, a serious volume about the history of medicine, the philosophy of science, or the genealogies of the museum and the library as institutions. She hardly said two words to Alice, but she would look skeptically over the rims of her round reading glasses as she heard the descriptions of impossible artworks; she plainly disapproved of Alice's whimsy and lowered her eyes with relief to the illustrations of neoplasms or astrolabes in her own book. Fraternelli would say, "Well, it's not as if I'm an educated man, but it sounds pretty damn impressive to me." Then he would launch into disquisitions on the pragmatics of bringing what she described to life, a whole discourse of electricity and pneumatics and combustion that meant little to her. Her ignorance of practical mechanics ostensibly explained why Alice ended up asking the librarian, who only shrugged, if she could ride along with Fraternelli as he tended to his city properties.

Toward the end of their experiments' first half, after the day at Mrs. Cassini's, Alice regularly met Fraternelli without the librarian's being present: a drink in a bar, a lunch at a deli. They conversed very easily. A man who worked with his hands, who fixed things for a living, he took reality as it came. He listened to her without preconception as she explained her early life, which she never would have done in front of her academic colleagues, fearing the "discomfort" that their ideological prudishness committed them to feeling when faced with tales of sexual fearlessness and willing dissolution in the sensibility of a lover. Fraternelli, no intellectual, had an air of having heard it all and having forgotten it already. The stories he shared with her tended to be those of his tenants, their crimes and perversions and fetishistic photo collections and quotidian generosity, as if he had no story of his own, even though these stories revealed him more than anything could. He had come in to make repairs once for a tenant who was with a prostitute he couldn't afford to pay, and so Fraternelli settled the bill himself. He'd changed bandages on old women's suppurating wounds, he'd unblocked toilets as their turds swam on flooded tiles at his boots. He confessed to Alice that one of his tenants, with only weeks to live, had asked him to finger her on the day he came to remove her normal bed to make room for the hospice bed, and he had done it, he'd given her, bone-dry as she was, her final pleasure. He also confessed to Alice his selfish acts, his petty acts, his cruel acts in office: the smug child's toy deliberately smashed, the young woman spied on through a crack in the bedroom door while she dressed for the day as he was supposed to be changing a fuse. Once, he said he had been a bad father, as simple as saying the sun goes down in the evening, without judgment or self-pity.

When she told him in a bar about the summer of the florist and the ugly boy in the greenhouse, he said, "Well, sure. Sometimes you have to do something evil just to prove you're free." She wondered, as she sloshed her ice cubes around the bottom of her whiskey tumbler, whether or not he meant this as an invitation to kiss her. He lacked guile, she concluded; if he'd wanted a kiss, he would have asked for one. He penetrated her without looking her in the face and seemed not to desire what she regarded as the greater intimacy of an embrace. He always tried to pay for her food or drink, out of what seemed like an unquestioning sense of chivalric duty, relic of his immigrant upbringing's Old-World ethos, but she never allowed him to. Then came that night he brought dessert to her university office before her night class. Gradually, she let herself understand that she was falling in love with him. Her stomach floated up every time she saw him; every day, she reminded herself to tell him of some funny remark a student had made or some out-of-the-ordinary sight she had seen on her way back from the university. She checked books out of the library on wiring and plumbing, so that she did not disappoint him with her ignorance of the basic processes that made everything else possible: "Art's nice but what the hell good is it if you can't turn on the light and see it?" he'd asked her once. Every night that wasn't Saturday night, she missed him, his huge hands gently clasping her hips or her ribcage from behind. She would stand in her office door before her night class and wait for him, the emperor of ice cream, though in fact he only came the once.

On a Saturday night in September, she met Fraternelli's only daughter, his child with the suburban princess accountant: an adolescent girl, on the blonde side of brunette, about twelve years old, with all of Fraternelli's skepticism and none of his mirth. The look on her smooth face, with its *nez pointu* and narrowed eyes, mixed reserve with insolence, a combination that somehow came out as affectless fear. Alice imagined that little Judy or Julie or whatever her name was wouldn't amount to much; she seemed, in her white pinafore with a teen romance novel under her arm, to have taken after the mindless mother. When she'd been unexpectedly dropped off that Saturday night due to the princess's having to rush her own father to the hospital with a heart attack, Fraternelli introduced Alice to her as the librarian's old friend. Her face still flushed with orgasm, because the girl's arrival had interrupted one of their lovemaking sessions, Alice smiled cordially. Judy or Julie asked a lot of gossipy, chatty questions at the dinner table that required the elaboration of a flimsy mythology about Alice and the librarian's college friendship, but she only furrowed her brow with a bit of disdain at the answers. The girl seemed to fear silence and to be unimpressed with speech. Alice wanted to say, "You talk too much, you should only watch and hold your tongue." She wanted to say, "You want to seem worldly, but you seem prurient, like a spy." Alice felt grateful she had no daughter of her own. Yes, this girl would grow up to be a nag and a scold, always making inquiries and never being satisfied with answers that didn't conform to her sheltered and naïve fancies. A cruel thing to think of a little girl, Alice knew, but who cared? An artist had to be honest about what she saw. Alice, who had when she was just a little older than Fraternelli's daughter walked in a xeriscape around Rodin's sculptures and read the poems of D. H. Lawrence on a sea-bound city bus next to whores and sots and blood-spattered night-nurses, hated the girl's innocence and wanted very badly to stain it, smutch it, mash it like a flower in the dirt. When both Fraternelli and the librarian were out of the room for a moment, she leaned down to Judy or Julie and whispered, "When you came in, I was eating your stepmother's cunt while your father fucked me from behind." The girl flinched as if Alice had flicked her nose, and then she said nothing.

Four days later, while she was teaching herself the basics of electrical currents before she fell asleep, Alice's phone rang. Fraternelli's voice curtly informed her never to contact them again and hung up without waiting for a reply.

* * *

After Alice had told the young man with the immature face as much of her history with Fraternelli as she saw fit, remembering much more than she told, he stammered and stumbled his way toward asking her questions about *The Last Café*. The rain had subsided to a misty drizzle and the lightning and thunder had stopped, so she first thought simply to turn him out of doors as soon as he broached the subject. She began to wonder if he had cunningly intended to brandish the name of Fraternelli's daughter to get himself inside her house and, once inside, to spring his real journalistic trap and interrogate her about the fatal art opening she'd presided over. Even if she tossed him out now, she reflected, he could still write a piece about the dim and dank interior of her unkempt house, the hellish dog she set to watching him, and the salacious narrative she had recited of her ill-fated erotic adventures. Matthias was pacing around the furniture, his claws scraping and dragging over the floor as if he were too bored with all this somnolent human complication even to lift his legs to walk as he listened to it. She wanted to snap the dog to attention and thrust her finger at the girlish boy's neck so that the dog would leap up and chew his throat away in blood-slick, sinewy strips. She had only allowed him inside because the knowledge of whom he'd meant by "Julia Bonham" came to her simultaneously with the awareness that she had never really known the little girl's name.

She cut off his long, hesitant preamble about her notorious curatorial work and said, "So how did you know her? Julia Bonham, I mean?"

"We went out for a while in high school."

"That's it? That was, what, ten year ago or more? And you haven't see her since?"

"No," he said. "I know it sounds strange, but I've recently run into some trouble. Problems with my job, my marriage. And I've had some time on my hands."

"So you run from your present troubles to the lost utopia of your vanished youth and your old girlfriend? Do I have that right?"

"But you don't understand," he said. "She's gone. I'm just trying to find out why. Somebody should, and since I have nothing else to do right now…"

"Gone? What's happened to her?"

"She's with the It cult now," he said.

This news brought her out of her seat. She began to pace in a direction opposite to that of Matthias, but then he ran to her and circled her legs as she walked. She knew nothing about the It people, had no sense of whether the rumors that Frank Jobe was behind the group were true. Since she had scarcely left her house in six months, she had never seen them in the flesh. All she knew was that they put ashes on their faces, lived in sewage tunnels, touched each other all over, and voided their bowels and bladders where they stood, abjuring their humanity because the world was not yet just. It would be very like Jobe to bring such a hideous thing as this group into being, another of his defacements of the reality he so resented because he felt it excluded him. She hated them because they had given up; it wasn't as if she didn't know the despair that would make someone want to be nothing, but she had all her life sought a way through the tangle of meaninglessness, a way to live. She had taken a few wrong paths, of course, not least of them being the gratuitous insult to Fraternelli's little girl. She had not ever thought to sit down and die to the world, not since six months ago when she was sure the world wished her to die, and rightly enough. She felt a pain somewhere in the middle of her body as she walked around the living room much too quickly, quickly enough to make the boy on the couch think she was crazy. She searched her mind until she understood that the pain was a question, a question that, as soon as she voiced it within herself, sounded deranged and self-serving: had Julia's decline into the nihilistic fanaticism, the literal shit, in which she now immersed herself been initiated long ago by Alice's attempt to corrupt her, to stain her?

Just then, the young man's phone chimed from his pocket. She watched him pull it out slowly enough, as if it hardly mattered to him, but when he saw the name of the caller on the screen, he said with a cracking voice, "I'm sorry, I have to take this now." His fingers shook as he accepted the call; they trembled so much that he jarred the touchscreen and accidentally put the call on the phone's external speakers.

A young woman's voice, sweetly high-pitched but broken by tears and sighs, blared tinnily out of the small device: "Mark? It's me. I'm, I'm in the hospital. The baby's fine so far, but there's been a problem, I don't know, I can't focus right now. I've been in so much pain. I thought it would go away, but I couldn't even walk, so I had to call my mother. They're going to induce labor tomorrow. Mark, I didn't ever want to see your face again. Not after the way you hurt me, you lied to me, you made a fool of me. I've never been so embarrassed in my life, and I hated you so much for that, I swear to God I wanted to kill you, you son of a bitch. But when I was laying on the floor, waiting for the ambulance, all I could think was that I needed you there. Your face was all I could see. We'll figure it all out, we'll talk about it all later, but will you come see me, please? You should be there to meet your daughter. It's going to be a daughter, so will you just come over here, you bastard?"

Alice leaned over Mark's shoulder and ended the call. He rounded on her, his face so twisted with rage that she jumped back because she thought he might bring his fist around. She was glad to see him finally show some spirit.

"Get out of my house," she said. "Go to her. Go back to your family. Run as fast as your legs will carry you, stupid boy."

He half stood up, his face now tensed, mouth held open in a startled O. He looked like a sprinter poised on the blocks, all his muscles taut. Then his eyes furrowed with confusion, as if he were struggling to remember something important, and he said, "But what about Julia?"

"Forget about her. That's not your story. It never was; it was just a fancy you pursued when you thought for a moment you could have a different kind of life from the one with the job and the wife and the child. But you can't; you've made your choice, and now you have to live with it. Go back to your family. You're a family man now. These adventures will be someone else's responsibility."

She took his elbow in her tight grasp and led him to the door. The rain had stopped, but the sky was the dirty smeared white of old ice; the wind blew in cold gasps. Summer seemed to have ended forever. He began jogging down the slanted, cracked stone steps to the street when Alice suddenly called out: "Wait!"

She held Matthias's collar by two fingers and passed the dog to Mark. Matthias whined quietly, high and thin like air going out of balloon, just to register a protest, but he didn't resist. He seemed not to believe that he could change anything.

"He's very docile and well-trained," she said. "He's only two years old; he can be the companion of your daughter's childhood."

"But why are you giving him to me?"

"Because I'm going away," she said simply.

She shut the screen door on the young man and watched him walk down the stone stairs, more slowly now, dazed or drugged or under water; the dog trotted hesitantly behind him and tossed the occasional whining glance back at his former mistress.

* * *

While she was telling young Mark about her time with Fraternelli, she had mused aloud on what might have become of the man.

"You didn't hear?" the boy had said. "He died of a heart attack during a robbery. He and the librarian were robbed by the boyfriend of..."

He'd let his words trail off, aware they were carrying him toward some swamp of implication in which he would simply sink.

"The boyfriend of a woman who was to them what I had been," she finished.

He nodded in an abashed way. Her hair had dried completely; she couldn't blame on a chill the shudder that seized her whole body and rattled the chair she sat in. Fraternelli was gone, she thought; she hadn't seen him in fifteen years anyway, fifteen years alone, fifteen years in which she hadn't married or had children or had any serious relationship. Before she'd met him, and then again after, she thought herself incapable of love. Maybe it was so. Maybe her motives in life would never amount to anything more than a cruel curiosity, a hunger for experience for its own sake, a greedy desire for more, more, and still more. His commitment to repairing the world as it was had briefly shown her another way. When she'd stepped down off the ladder in Mrs. Cassini's apartment, she'd put her heel back onto a stray screw and twisted her ankle, almost collapsing to the ground; Fraternelli had placed both hands on the small of her back, gently, as if there were no urgency at all, and, for the briefest of instants, he was all that held her up, his huge warm hands. She felt she should honor it somehow, make her own form of repair, of reparation. Fraternelli was gone: so she would find his daughter.

8. THE BRIDE STRIPPED BARE

First there was some fasciculation, some nictitation, a twitch at the touch, a flinch of the neurons. Then a warmth flooded in from the sole of the foot and coursed all the way through until it saturated the brain pan and immersed the mind.

She worried she had waited too long, but here It was. A period of preparation, whose length she wouldn't want to attribute to fear, had delayed her a month, a month in which the news reported that the cult had grown so large, claimed so many, that what the local government and police had been willing to accept as a non-criminal outlet for the desperation of an increasingly impoverished populace now threatened the stability of the social order. You couldn't go out without seeing them anymore. Perfectly normal-seeming but actually despairing teenagers, who might otherwise have taken drugs or made feeble cry-for-help suicide attempts, now wandered off on ash-strewn feet instead. The city comptroller called a press conference to witness his own assumption by the Its; they dragged him offscreen by the legs. An entire graduate seminar in cultural studies, inspired by theories of "non-subjectivity" and "collective affect," walked out of the classroom and went away with them one night to submit those theories to the test of practice. Celebrities spoke in favor of them and signed petitions on their behalf.

"I think they're showing us the way, right?" a teenaged singer told reporters. "You don't need a lot of, like, stuff to make you happy. All this damaging discourse you see on websites about looking good and all that, being skinny and sexy like, it's all bullshit, isn't it? What is 'normal,' anyway? I wish I could go with them, but I'm under contract, you know what I mean?"

Public health officials warned that the insalubrious conditions the group favored, including their apparently ideological hostility toward the ordered disposal of human waste, could breed contagions not seen since before the rise of modern sanitation. Polls evidenced majority support for the forced dissolution of the It people.

"Well, I'm for freedom of religion, but not if it's breaking up families and spreading disease," said one half of an elderly couple interviewed on the street; her husband, hardly waiting for her to finish, said, "If they don't want to be people anymore, then I say put a bullet in them and let God be the judge."

There were even protests against the group held in the plaza before City Hall, mostly assembled and attended by well-off people whose children had become Its. When reports of cholera surfaced at a local hospital, the protest rallies became more violent; a gray dummy dressed in a tattered gray jean jacket was held up on a tomato stake, doused with gasoline, and torched in effigy.

The police faced a simple problem: while the group was clearly in violation of certain laws against public vagrancy and the like, there were simply too many of them to arrest or shoot. Where would they be held if arrested, for one thing, and for another, could the authorities run the risk of exposing the prison population to this cultic activity? Also, as a leaderless group, the Its could not be decapitated like an organized crime family, a terrorist cell, or a dictatorial government. They didn't speak, so there was no one to negotiate with. From time to time, their settlements, in underground tunnels or public parklands or abandoned buildings, were found out and razed, and then the group would just go somewhere else. The exasperated mayor put it as bluntly as he could to an increasingly aggressive press corps: "If a large enough percentage of the population decides to go crazy, there's not a lot the government can do. The city is only as good as the citizens." The city went on with its business and waited. The Its people would take over entirely, or they would incubate a plague that would desolate the city and leave the buildings standing for saner people and saner times, or they would run their course like any fad or mania, or they would make some kind of violent move that would unambiguously necessitate their destruction.

Alice waited too, though she couldn't say what for. She supposed she was waiting for someone else to take the decision out of her hands. In the end, no one did, so she went. She had no other plans, and she was running out of money. After the museum was forced to close due to *The Last Café*, she'd convinced her literary agent to get her an advance for writing a book about her part in the exhibition. She had no intention of writing such a book, of course, but she needed some cash until she figured out what to do. The book would not have been very edifying if she had written it, since it would only have reported that she'd been in a sufficiently fetid mood, artistically blocked and loveless and approaching middle age, to be tickled by the idea of inflicting Jobe's garden-variety, albeit especially thorough, nihilism upon the very patrons of the arts who had allowed men like Jobe to thrive while genuine visionaries went not only unrewarded but positively stigmatized. She hadn't suspected that Jobe's malice reached out beyond ideas and institutions to aim at life itself. Her own intention had been simply to unveil a *reductio ad absurdum*: an artwork so cynical and so militantly hostile to meaning and imagination that it would revolt its beholders, disgust them, sicken them, make them cry out through parched lips for a new work that, however crude or naïve or old-fashioned it would seem to the critical mind formed by theories of ever-more-rigorous negativity, sought to transform the world rather than sniping at it from a position of intellectual superiority. She was innocent, as the detectives who investigated her had been forced to conclude. She didn't know he would kill them all. It was as simple as that.

It was not. She'd been attracted to him, to his ugliness, his stupidity, his prematurely brown teeth and perpetually unwashed hair. The usual nihilists of the art world were poseurs, after all: well-coifed professionals with well-monitored bank accounts whose stated *épater-le-bourgeois* commitments simply represented the classicism or academicianism of their time; had they lived a hundred years before, they would have painted nymphs in exotic locales rather than constructing rooms full of politically allegorical baby dolls or shopping carts or tampons or river rocks or whatever. Jobe was not of this type. For one thing, he didn't cluck any jargon at her when he proposed that they actually charge for the café drinks. In fact, when a startled laugh escaped her after he'd said, "Let's make the assholes pay," he laughed even louder, which she took as a challenge to redouble her own merriment, and pretty soon they were holding on to each other's shoulders in her office, their heads bowed in breathless guffawing. He genuinely didn't seem to want anything. She was reasonably certain that his early work, at least *The New Ambassador*, was connected in shadowy ways with intelligence agencies, probably through open-secret front organizations bearing grant money, but he wasn't serving the agenda of any particular government out of ideological sincerity or fervor. He simply wanted to harness their destructive powers, to sow chaos, for his own pleasure. He really wanted the trees to overgrow the museum; he really thought the museum would be better off if its prime function were the provision of coffee. Most people who are smart enough to understand that all things are futile and meaningless leave some gaps in their nihilism, gaps big enough to allow children and paintings and social hope through. Not Jobe: he was smart enough to recognize the void at the heart of the universe without possessing the corrective emotional capacity for acting as if it weren't there.

Alice thought that if one couldn't find it within oneself to be what Fraternelli had been, a humble mocker who worked in the world and enjoyed its transient gratifications without expecting a reward or asking why, then one should be Frank Jobe: a man whose derisive laughter shattered glass and stones and made way for the vegetable kingdom. That's why Alice had commissioned *The Last Café* when she was halfway through her life, convinced that she would never make art or be in love again. She may not have expected him to kill anyone, but she had made Jobe the instrument of her own hatred; so how could anyone honestly claim that she was innocent?

Being guilty, then, she had to go. Her month of indecision, her blank September of sleepless nights without Matthias's dreamy fidgeting at her side, empty days in which her eyes would not focus on the pages of a book or the screen of the television, gave way to October. She illicitly ordered five hundred caplets of a general antibiotic from the Internet and inexpertly dosed herself with them for ten days. She spent hours on her front stoop, watching the leaves that filled the air flame up and then burn out and crumble. It was a proper fall, the kind she had never known as a beach girl, and she loved to inhale the clean smoke-tinged air of it.

Then one day, she threw on a kimono, slipped on her sandals, and carried a comforter over her arm; she walked into the city at dusk and bedded down in an empty alley. Research suggested that it would be fruitless to try to hide a phone on her person, still less a weapon; the Its way of life pragmatically forbade concealment. As with existence itself, so with the Its: she would have to enter naked and exit the same way. She had put twenty dollars in the pocket of her kimono in case it took so long for them to come for her that she would need to eat, but the media reports proved right: they were ubiquitous now, browsing on the desperate and miserable all through the night. They found her before dawn. The sky glowed with pale silver light when she awoke with a flinch and a twitch to a temperate, gritty touch on the sole of her foot, as if sun-warmed beach sand had adhered itself to her and sent a wave of comfort to flood all the chambers of her body. The touch was not unlike Fraternelli's: it had a quality of suspension because it asked for nothing, like wholly unreasonable and unconditional love. Fraternelli's love, though, had proved conditional on Alice's not smearing dirt on his daughter's pinafore or her mind. There was always a condition, she reminded herself, in love; so there must be some lie in this touch that promised everything. She had to discover this lie, so that she could stop little Julia Fraternelli from believing in it too. As the touch overtook her, however, as more hands were laid on and traveled from foot to calf to the erogenous hollow behind the knee, pressing in, kneading, wringing the heaviness out of her soul, she became weightless; she was the same density as the rest of the world, afloat in existence rather than stumbling heavily along its bottom. Her mind swirled up with the tide-borne sand and was carried away.

* * *

She'd wondered if there would be an initiation ceremony, but there was not. They put her in their midst and walked in a star-shaped formation through the pale pre-dawn, the walls of the city emerging into gray solidity as the darkness withdrew. The It behind her put a hand flat on her buttocks, and the one to her side brought her hand forward to touch the buttocks of the It in front. Both of them at her sides touched her on the hips. All of them were touching. In this way, they walked, hesitantly, slowly, so as not to break their formation, through the streets, until they came to a strip of park by the river. They filed through a person-sized cleft in a chain-link fence and passed into dense woods, the trees all autumn-topped, just as the orange of the new sun started to waver in glimmers on the agitated river. Jagged shards of the morning light spangled the dirt and leaf-mulch that chilled their bare feet, but they moved mostly in darkness. She felt like a desperately tired person on a bus, her wakefulness slowly pulsing in and out, her head dropping and then snapping back up. In a lucid moment, she decided to see what would happen if she refused to move on. She stopped. The It behind her bounced Its nose off her skull, and then It put Its palms on her back and pushed. She reached for the tree trunks to either side of her and hooked her fingernails into the bark. The It behind her wasn't strong and could neither force her on nor topple her over. The It in front of her turned around and punched her straight in the face. The blow forced her down on her back, blood streaming out of her nose, trickling, warm and then cool, down her cheeks and into her ears. The hands were on her again, like those of a mother who loses control and raises her fist and then rushes to console the child for the hurt, caressing the legs and arms, gently pushing on the palms and the soles, as if to draw the pain out at the extremities. Her wakefulness blinked out again, and when her head snapped back up, she was on her feet, though now nearly held up by the Its' firm grip on her arms. She returned to consciousness in time to disappear into some kind of drainage tunnel. They moved in dripping, stone-chill darkness, their feet plashing in a stream of shallow water that had collected in the central depression of the tunnel floor. A faint pressure in her bladder that had been with her since she'd awoken now swelled and jostled with each step. She wondered for a moment when they'd let her stop; then she remembered their way of life. Had she ever consciously relinquished control of her body anywhere but over a toilet since babyhood? Better here, she thought, than in whatever press of bodies they're taking me to. She let go: warmth spread down her legs, and the tunnel briefly filled with the sweetly acrid smell of her piss, which mixed up in her own swollen nose with the coppery blood crusted to the insides of her nostrils. Then the warmth turned cool; her legs felt mottled and clammy as they shuffled on through the stagnant water. Finally, the group turned down a tributary of the tunnel they had been trudging through, this one so narrow that they had to pass single-file, joined only at the hands. As they moved forward, the tunnel walls glowed brighter and brighter until they came out into some kind of a square clearing fiercely illuminated by a Klieg light at its center. The light burst on her eyes as they came out of the tunnel, and she dropped to her knees. She couldn't see much of anything when all the other Its reached down into a pile of ash and lifted it over her in cupped hands and let it spill down onto her face. They forced her down on her stomach and went at her with scissors, chopping and hacking and tearing at her hair so that it fell off in huge coiled clumps, sometimes less cut than torn from her scalp. After this, they ran a dry razor over what remained; the hair caught, pulled, and bunched until her scalp bled freely, no hair to obstruct the flow of blood. At last, they rubbed the ashes onto her burning, bleeding head. They pulled her to her feet and ran the scissors up the back of her kimono; it fell off her body without their touching it, its bright cherry blossoms trampled gray in the dust. They whirled around her then in a circle, pelting her with the ashes. From time to time, they would pause to close in and press them into her epidermis. One of the Its crooked a jag-nailed finger up her vagina and then her anus to detect if she'd smuggled in any contraband. Her vision had returned, though it was blocked by a square of blackness burned into her retina from the sudden flare of the Klieg light on eyes that had grown used to darkness. Around the square, she saw them pull a gray robe from a heap of rags and patches in one corner of the room; they put it over her shoulders and belted it around her, though it covered little and her breasts hung free of it. She felt little ability to act on her desire to resist these manipulations: something about their touch now had the ability to mesmerize her utterly. Her experience underground was like a continuous enactment of the last moments of a dream, when you slowly understand that you are in fact dreaming even as you continue to watch with bemused interest as the phantasmagoria reels on before you. This held a certain aesthetic fascination for her, this receptive paralysis, this powerlessness of the mind that has woken before the body and finds itself horrifyingly unable to animate the limbs.

Soon, they moved her body for her. In a mass, they passed on from the powerfully-lit clearing through another dank tunnel, this one more well-traveled, judging from the sharp air of old piss that pierced its damp. Whether beside or behind, the Its kept their hands on her, on her hips, on her ass, on her stomach, on her breasts, on the back of her neck, on her tender scalp. She had to palpate them as well. Bodies gave way to body parts. They were parts of one vast body, a millipede winding and skittering through the tunnel, its endless feet plodding in foul water. She felt she existed only at the points where she was touched. There was no her, there was only a spot at the small of her back warmed by three fingers, a span of the inner thigh where a back-thrust hand had wedged itself, and the ghost of contact that lingered as a sharp ache on the place inside her face that the fist had crushed. She was It now.

* * *

Crumbly cakes of flour and potato were handed down the line. How long since It had had food? It had no idea. Flavorless starch and powder in the mouth, a catch in the dry throat. A coughing fit that sent up a white cloud. A wooden bowl of water went from hand to hand. The water was becoming so filled with the flour and starch that soon it would be dough. It sipped, It lapped eagerly until the bowl was pulled away. The stomach rippled and contracted under the hand of the It to Its side.

* * *

They came to a kind of long trough and shat over the side. Something in It recoiled, something struggled to come to the light of consciousness, as It bunched up Its robes and squatted. Its bowels, roiled by such pale fare and such stained water, sprayed diarrhea in long sputters over the ledge. The tunnel echoed with gross air; the smell of spewed stomach juice rose in a high, invisible fog. It looked ahead and said nothing. What was inside, struggling? As It squatted and shat, one to Its side held Its hand and one on the other side rested Its foot atop Its. The whole million-footed beast writhed with flatulence over the trough. When they moved on, It moved with them, the hem of Its gray robe green with mineral-stained tunnel water and brown with excrements.

* * *

The beast wound up from the underground into a building, all long corridors, once white, now gray and green and brown, with handles along the walls for the feeble. Broken windows and empty beds. Rats scraped their claws over the floors to hurry away from the marching, winding millipede. Paintings hung askew with cracked glass faces on the walls; they showed blanched seascapes, rolling heather, still waters, anywhere but here. They spread out over the abandoned hospital. Two starved dogs, their bulging eyes crusted and milky, the flesh of their faces thinning and retreating into nothingness to leave only the long and black-pitted yellow teeth, their protracted racks of rib seeming to ripple beneath the meager, mangy fur, leapt out of an operating room. They flew into the side of the millipede, jaws indiscriminately scissoring down in mists of bright red blood that were like poppies blooming on the gray scene. The dogs' throats were almost choked by shitten cloth and bitten-through phalanges going down the wrong way. The Its fell on the dogs and eventually their necks were snapped until they lay stiffly with heads turned the wrong way around, blood like rust on the lolling tongues. Three of the Its writhed beside them with spouting wounds; two got up and struggled on, while one stayed behind. They continued on. Tonight they would sleep in the hospital beds.

No sleep before labor. They wound up in their file through the four stacked floors until they came out on the roof. It was an autumn afternoon, with light aslant, the sun too low in the sky, blinding on the diagonal. The roof of the hospital was piled thickly with soil, piled so high that when they came to the unhinged roof door the dirt was at the level of their chests and each It had to cup Its hands so that the It in front of It could put one foot in the cup and leap up with Its other leg onto the field. Then they stood on the level with the low sun, in the pinking clear sky, the wind that whipped the leaves in dusty vortices below catching at their filthy rags too and blowing the stench off them, the ashes reeling off their shorn heads as if from a bonfire.

Then something broke the surface: a *mattock*, the word, that is; she had found the word in some Irish poet long ago, had she not? It was the thing they put in her hand, the mattock, while for a moment they failed to touch her at all.

Hands pressed to the shoulderblades. It lost the word, all the words. It only held the mattock, its heavy iron head pulling it almost out of Its grasp, a splinter from the wood handle shivering clear into the meat at the base of the thumb. An It at the head of the beast began cleaving the soil to sow the potatoes, and then all followed in imitation, most of them clumsily. This was no work for the dazed, and splinters filled every hand. One of the Its clutched Its chest and tipped over into the soil. It was rolled to the edge and pitched from the roof. They worked body to body, sides touching, sweat mingling, their panting breaths synchronized. More than one blade fell badly and left a finger or toe in the dirt, another poppy on the black. They could not starve: it was necessary to reject the delusive pleasures of this world, but it would be a cheat to escape into death before death was necessary. They worked, their hands rising and falling with the mattocks gripped tightly, until the early descent of night chilled the sweat on their faces.

* * *

They wound back across the dirt, down the roof stairs, and through the hospital to their night-beds. They came in upon a rape. One of the Its had somehow stolen from the field with another and had thrown It onto a bed and was now ready to leap naked upon It, the penis bouncing in air like a rod on a spring. The Its fell on their errant member and held It fast in numerous arms until one came forth from the press and pulled a mattock from the folds of Its robe and held it high. The cock was still hard when it slapped to the linoleum; it detumesced and then shriveled before them as the blood pooled out behind. The rapist was in turn thrown onto the bed until a fire was started in the corner of the room to heat the mattock's metal head; the blood streaking up the blade sizzled and smoked. They shoved a balled pillowcase in Its jibbering mouth, and then they thrust the mattock smoking in the autumn breeze that came through the broken windows into Its groin to cauterize the wound. Its back arched up into the now meat-scented air, the muscles contracting almost violently enough to snap the spine, and then It fell into delirium, and whether it awakened or not was no longer in human hands. It seemed important to give the violator a chance to live. A violator deserved escape even less than the innocent others.

* * *

They slept four or five to a bed, curled in upon each other. Four squat fingers abutted the crease of Its labia, while Its own head nestled in the crook of a knee, the foot resting on Its chest. Awareness struggled like wings fluttering between bars. Above the foot and below the knee It felt old slash-scars on the leg. Some troubled young girl. The words came from where the word *mattock* had. Then they faded. While they lay in their beds, more ash was brought and thrown over them as if in a blessing. They were to sleep, but sleep seemed inseparable from their walking and working. What would sleep mean to an It? He slept, she slept; but It just was, and neither woke nor slept.

* * *

Sleep held its surprise: sleep here was like fever, burning with hallucination fueled by a few coals of fact. In sleep, she was almost herself, because some dream came from her and not from elsewhere, not from the fingers at her thigh and the leg above her head or the ash that they smeared everywhere to make the world look and feel as filthy as they intuited it was. When you sleep, you dream, whether It or not, but where could the dream come from if not from you and not from It? Perhaps, on the other hand, her dream did come from it, from the ash, from the one who had done all of this. She did not dream of herself, not of beaches and panicles and greenhouses and Fraternelli's setting a carton of ice cream on her desk. She dreamed of Frank Jobe, dreamed the life he had told her of in stray remarks made almost by accident, like a story he had heard in fragments from someone else entirely, though he'd said it was the story of his youth. Who knows? came a thought to her: maybe they all dreamed of the life of Frank Jobe.

* * *

Frank grew up in a rich little town on a vast river in the middle of the country. He was raised in one of the houses in the hills above the town center with its antique shops and rare bookstores and boutiques and spice marts. His mother bought his clothes at a specialty children's clothing store that looked out over the river, burgundy overalls and a tweed cap. Tourists from larger cities to the east and the west spent afternoons in his Christmas village of a hometown, and his first jobs were to serve them in eateries and shops. He waited tables in a restaurant in the tiny old mall built into the side of one of the hills that faced the water. After closing the restaurant, he would regularly exit through the mall and, when it was empty, draw a penis in red chalk on the abstracted, hammer-wielding laborer that appeared on a wall relief at the entrance. The relief dated from the time of the Depression; it had been moved to the mall from the exterior side wall of a long-gone grain exchange building razed when the town decided to capitalize on its powerlessness by re-baptizing itself as quaint.

By his late adolescence, he had come to loathe the place, had come to despise the preening blonde women who ate salads for lunch, as well as their milksop husbands, fat and bald and burger-ordering, and all of them always counting their money, wanting to argue about the bill, wanting to know how to receive the discount, making sure to get the parking voucher, and exclaiming about how sweet and cute it all was in this darling hamlet on the river. He eventually came to understand that he was living in a place designed to defeat experience by providing a very particular and controlled set of pleasures; these pleasures held no interest for him, since he didn't care about rare books or designer sweaters or imported herbs of interest only to the connoisseur of world cuisine. His parents did care about these things, though, especially his mother, with her spice rack full of curries and her bookshelf full of spiritual wisdom in moldering volumes. She was always off to meditative retreats on the weekends, even in Frank's early childhood. Then Frank would sit with his overworked father, who was content to watch whatever movies the TV saw fit to show on Saturday and Sunday nights, the more brutal the better, to let his own mind blank out and to keep his son quiet. Such movies gave Jobe a very early glimpse of a world where a person could take serious actions with permanent consequences, rather than a world where a person could buy a hand-fired vase not available even in the better urban markets. He gave no sign of these violent longings for most of his childhood; his parents had schooled him in the polite art of going unnoticed. He was not one of the troubled children who got into fist-fights after school or who tried to vivisect the neighbor's cat. Nor was he a sheltered, lonely boy, always in his room with a book, later to paint his face white and his fingernails black. In fact, he joined his friends in the mockery of such people, the fat girls with glasses and the skinny boys with calculator watches and the deviants with peculiar hair dye and make-up. He had plenty of friends, most of whom he'd met through baseball, a game he played avidly until high school. Nothing in life satisfied him so much as the hollow explosive sound made by the aluminum tube as it struck the leather-wrapped ball, like a length of pipe lashing a bone capped thinly with flesh: the patella, the skull. That was real, and all the pink sweaters and dusty folios were evasions of that reality. When he was ten or eleven, he could spend whole summer nights, from after dinner to before bed, in batting cages. His mother would drop him off after dinner and then go do God knew what and then pick him up before bed, his wrists still buzzing with the echo of those blow-ups at the end of his bat.

His dissatisfaction remained vague and inarticulate until he was about fifteen, expressed only as an obsession with hitting the ball faster and farther and as a relative indifference to everything else. He did enough schoolwork not to attract notice: a straight B student, for the most part. His parents destined him for a career in business, like his father's, a career that demanded not genius but a commitment to decent work bolstered by a motivating appreciation for the good life, the spiritually-rewarding life championed by his mother.

When he was fifteen, he took an elective art class because he thought it would be easy. No one could really judge art: it was an amorphous concept self-servingly invented by its lazy practitioners, he thought, the essence of the unreality he despised. He intended to take advantage of this fraud, get the good grade for doing nothing. Isabella Madison taught his class: a new art teacher, a woman in her late twenties with long black-dyed hair and a supply of morosely-colored headbands, maroon and indigo and gray, to hold it back; she wore black boots almost every day and often spoke of her long education with wistful bitterness. Her students enjoyed her sarcastic jokes at the expense of everything, from the latest pop stars to the duller students. When she lost their attention, she would get it back by mocking the other teachers' habits of unfashionable dress or poor hygiene. Isabella Madison discovered that Frank could draw. He couldn't draw the way some of the other kids could, the ones who pored over details, precisely penciling in every stitch in their shoes on the draw-your-legs assignment or calculating the angle at which the light fell on the onions during still-life days; those multi-talented students, who could probably also sing and master trigonometry, attained their effects through labor. Frank had no interest in labor: he drew fast, laying down thick, sweeping lines just to get his assignments done. Ms. Madison remarked that Frank's lines were the "right lines," the outline of an emotion, of a whole sensibility. The oh-so-correct kids bored her to tears with their fidelity to what they saw, but Frank instinctively transformed what he saw in the crucible of his soul into some other, realer vision, and then he slashed it into the paper with a contemptuous lack of self-consciousness, tearing at the surface as if he knew his vision would ultimately be found behind it and not on it. He usually ended up with drawings that looked unfinished, carelessly smeared with graphite dust, like figures half-seen in a too-strong light; the still-life onions were just a tangle of scribbled lines, some overlapping each other, the whole pictured bulb either occupying multiple proximate positions or vibrating very fast. His pictures *did* vibrate, Ms. Madison thought. The kids with the patience and the craftsmanship furrowed their smooth little brows at her when she held up Frank's work as a model. She quickly said some unintelligible stuff about theories she'd read in her M.F.A. program before lack of funds had forced her to go for her teaching certificate, theories about "artworks as processual events that made and remade the artist in the heat of his or her inscription." Her students only stared at her, and Frank didn't even do that; he only looked down at the desk, on which he doodled a broken-open baseball, its strings raveling out of the split leather like intestines.

Ms. Madison offered to give him private lessons after school every Thursday. He didn't want to take her up on it, but when his father found out about the proposal, he insisted that Frank accept. While he didn't particularly prize the arts or see any economic advantage in them, he also thought it would be foolish of Frank to decline any academic opportunities. Frank's mother agreed, for the rather different reason that she found art more spiritual than baseball.

At first the lessons took place in the art room and were an extension of the class: more exercises, more practice, draw your hand, draw my car keys, draw this glass of water, draw this photo of a city, draw what you see out the window, draw this, draw that. While he drew silently, even sullenly, she circled the room in an almost nervous state, putting away stray canvases, straightening up the closet full of magazines she gave to the students for reference, wiping down the tables with citrus-scented cleanser. For a while the only sounds in the room would be those of Frank's pencil scratching at the ridged high-tooth drawing paper and of Ms. Madison's heavy rubber tread in her thick-soled boots. Then, after a half hour or so, she would be unable to suppress herself any longer and would inevitably start talking. She gently mocked the student work she was constantly forced to clean up, making fun of the various high-school types and their predictable propensities when it came to drawing or painting or sculpting: the stoners with their bong designs, the nerds with their fantasy heroes and heroines, the jock guys with their pro athletes, the sweet girls with their horses and kittens, the pretty girls with their dresses, and the goths with their skeletons, razor blades, and headstones. She would talk to the artworks as if to the students who'd made them: "Nice try, honey, but in ten short years, you'll stop dressing in black, you'll have a husband and two kids, twins, and you'll walk them in their double stroller around the river wondering what ever happened to that black lace shirt you used to have, not that you'll be able to squeeze yourself into it by then anyway." Such comments often drew an appreciative snort from Frank, almost the only sound he would ever make as he bowed his head over the drawing paper.

"Not a lot of imagination around here," she'd say from Thursday to Thursday. "If I were you, I'd get the hell out."

"So why don't you?" he finally asked one day. "You're an adult. Do what you want."

"It's not like that. You'll see. You think it's bad now, because you have to live with your parents, but there are so many limits to what they can do to you. Now the world outside, *that* will do anything to you if you aren't careful. Things your parents can't do. Put you out naked on the street, lock you up in a mental ward. So you have to be careful, you have to keep your head down. Teach art, move to a little boutique city like something inside a regional museum, and dream your dreams quietly."

She had walked to the window and was looking out over the roofs of the town down the hill from the high school; she wasn't talking to him any longer, only talking.

"Bullshit," he said. "Come on. I think you just like hating stuff."

She turned to him. Her lips were slightly parted, her eyes opened wide behind her thick-framed glasses. He read a startled fear in her face, as if she'd suddenly remembered some responsibility she'd been neglecting, a friend's plant she hadn't watered or cat she hadn't fed for days. Much later he would come to understand that he was the plant and the cat, that she'd initially wanted to have some kind of fun with him until she realized she was his teacher after all and had to instruct him about the world so that he would not be unprotected in it.

Then he'd just said, "Hold that," and he flung her face down onto the rough-grained paper; a scatter of pencil dust clouded her almost maternally fearful expression.

The next Thursday, she drove him into town and parked at the end of a street lined with buildings. She sat with him in her car as he practiced one-point perspective. She smoked cigarette after cigarette as he drew, so that the car smelled of ash and graphite like a black-walled mill; the music she played was electronic and ethereal, women's wails afloat on cyclical harmonies, the sound, it seemed to him, of ascending into heaven. Eventually, he asked for a cigarette, and she held the pack out to him and then extended her old silver lighter with its high flame. Later she had to put her hand over his to guide his lines, which wavered and arched downward toward the vanishing point like missile trails. His habit of perception prevented him from seeing the world as linear, as a rational structure that could be arrayed upon a grid.

"Jesus, look at these people," she said as she stared out the car window at the bus-borne day-tourists, the old women and men, now sexually indistinct in their pastel-colored, elastic-waisted pants and wobbling neck-wattles, their rheumy eyes appreciatively shining at the small and humble pleasures of the pretty little town by the river. "Let's smoke these in a hurry so we don't ever turn into them. And turning into them is what will happen if you're lucky, Frank. That's if the car doesn't flip over or if you don't get on the unlucky plane or if the cancer doesn't come early: then you get to be that old, and limp around in retarded clothes with nothing intelligent to say any more, even in the unlikely event that you ever had something intelligent to say in the first place, smiling at whatever random shiny object gives you a split-second to forget that death stares at you out of the mirror every morning."

He balled up his failed perspective drawing and tossed it over his shoulder into her back seat, already cluttered with papers and shopping bags and empty water bottles and changes of clothes. He didn't say anything.

"I'm sorry," she said. "I guess I've been depressed lately. I thought by this time in my life, I'd be somewhere else."

"Let's go somewhere else then," he said.

She laughed a smoky, raspy laugh, shook her head with a youthful toss of the hair to tell him no, and drove him home.

The next afternoon, when he was back from school before either of his parents had returned from work, he heaved the never-used phone book down from the rear top of the refrigerator where they kept it. He brushed off the thick dust, affixed to the plastic cover with months of congealed cooking grease. Given the glossy and artificial black of her hair and the anti-social anger she'd confided to him, as well as her background as some kind of dissident student, he resigned himself to finding that she was unlisted. He assured himself, in any case, that it was simple curiosity rather than desire that made him take down the book. When he really did find her address printed in microscopic type, he felt a disappointed anger well up in him, because now this unexpected knowledge forced a choice on him. He would have to take responsibility for his curiosity or desire now.

She lived in an apartment on the eastern edge of the city, the one furthest from the river. He could walk there easily, just down the hill and into the city and out to its border before it ran into the highway. He left a casual note for his parents, explaining that he'd been invited to the mall with some friends. He set out in the drizzling November sunset and told himself that a young woman like her would not be home on a Friday evening. Calling to mind whatever he knew of artists and cities from books he'd read and movies he'd watched, he imagined that she would have set out driving immediately after school until she saw the lights rise over the plains, and when she got under the lights she would find concerts full of the kind of floating music she'd played in the car, galleries full of strange and disturbing images, and men with beards and drugs to accompany her through the night, to dance with her in strobe-lit basements and kiss her whiskey mouth in doorways and corners. When he got to her apartment building, though, his feet comically bright with the warmly-colored leaves that were pasted with rain to the tennis shoes at the base of his inconspicuous gray ensemble, he hoped she was there simply because he was cold and wet and didn't want to walk back up the hill anytime soon. He pressed the buzzer with a numb finger; within a minute, she was standing on the other side of the glass door. She stood silently, looking him over, her arms folded across her chest, that hint of worried care he recognized from their lessons vying now for control over her features against a smile of cynical resignation. Through the glass of the door's top half, he could see that she wore a black T-shirt with a picture of Holbein's anamorphic skull on it, the sideways column of shadow-pitted bone seeming to melt in a wave across her breasts. In the harsh overhead light of the entrance hall, in the cold wind that blew in through the open door, it was obvious that she wore no bra. He moved closer to the door, and she let him in.

"You can't do this," she whispered as they went together up the stairs. "You can't ever do this again."

He stood awkwardly near the door of her small studio apartment, his hands clasped in front of him. It smelled like cigarettes and like her perfume. A futon bed with tangled sheets and strewn clothes stood against the back wall, but otherwise the place was neatly kept, especially the three high bookshelves that stood opposite the bed, where a TV would have been in any other bedroom. The light was muted, diffusing in gentle waves of orange from a shaded floor-lamp near the bed; a small CD player on the nightstand played something where some kind of clarinet insinuated itself around drum-beats.

"What are we listening to?" he said, just to say something.

"*Bitches Brew*. Now make yourself comfortable. Take it all in, Frank, because you will never see this place again."

She prepared tea for him while he browsed her shelves of books and CDs. He occasionally took down a volume and paged through it, usually a compendium of modern or contemporary art, the kind of thing they didn't teach in high schools: video installations, site-specific work, performance pieces. Recordings of bloody animal predations, lions chewing the throats out of gazelles and the like, played in loops on indifferently-stacked TVs; four female performers on their periods crawled across tables laden with Thanksgiving dinner, menstrual blood smeared brightly in the mashed potatoes; a totem, twice the size of a man, erected from twigs and branches and placed in a gloomy forest clearing, was set alight to create a pulsing column of pink smoke in the green underwater atmosphere of the twilit woods. He had never seen such images before and didn't know that making them existed as a possible way of life. He stood rapt by them while Ms. Madison stood over the stovetop, hands braced on its warming edge, her shoulders tensed and contracted, until the kettle whined like an estrual cat and blew its steam in her already hot face.

She brought his tea to where he sat cross-legged in front of the bookshelf; she knelt to set it on the bare floorboards, and then she gently closed the book in his lap and set it back on the shelf.

"Did you bring drawing supplies?" she asked.

"No."

"Well, hold on then." She went to her closet and pulled from the top shelf a large sketch pad and a box of drawing pencils, which she tossed to him. The sketch pad spun across the smooth floor until the corner of its spiral binding pierced his knee, and then it came to a stop.

She crossed her arms over her head and pulled her T-shirt off. She lay down on her futon bed and slipped out of her sweatpants with a swish of the hips, and then finally pried her pink socks off with her toes. Frank had been examining the spot on his knee where the spiral-bound pad's wire had stabbed him; when he raised his head and saw that she was reclining nude on the futon, he involuntarily gasped, a gasp that ended as a small squeak. She smiled gently at him. The soft light fell across her breasts, which were larger than her everyday mode of professional dress made them appear; they rested plumply over either side of her rib cage, the aureoles so large and pale they seemed to dissolve into the surrounding skin at their edges, and the skin so fair that he could see the subtle blue glow of her veins from where he sat. Her pubic hair was brownish blonde and untrimmed; straight rather than curly, it stood in criss-crossed spikes making shadows on her thighs. He started to get to his feet, the wet soles of his sneakers squealing on the floorboards. Whether he intended to walk the length of the room and mount the bed or to run out the door and into the street was unclear to him.

"No," she said. "Don't come any closer than that. You're going to draw what you see. Take as long as you need to get it right. And then you're going to go home and never come back here again, never see me outside of class, in fact. This is your final lesson. It's the most important one, the one where you learn that a real artist, and I think you will be a real artist, Frank, a real artist has to give up wanting the world. Seeing it, and the special kind of seeing it that drawing is, has to be enough. The work has to be its own goal; don't confuse it with reality. Reality will destroy you. So look, Frank, look until you're not doing anything but looking. Look until you don't even want it anymore."

He sat back down and put the sketch pad like a shield in his lap, though it didn't stop the feeling that the head of his penis was magnetized to her, that it was about to pull his limp body over the floorboards to the bed. He had made out with a girl during freshman year, half on a dare, and he'd put his hand up her shirt too, but a woman had never lain naked in front of him.

"One more thing," she said. "Cut the drawing off at the neck. And please, for Christ's sake, don't tell anyone about this."

She closed her eyes and listened to the music, the music and the sound of the pencil as it moved with decreasing frenzy and increasing control across the page. The vacantly blissful look on her face said that she didn't really care any longer what happened to her. Eventually, the music ended. Then, as he drew, she hummed quietly, a tiny smooth-frequencied resonance down in her throat that resonated in turn within his ear: a little kiss blown across the room from larynx to tympanum. By the time he was finished, he sat cross-legged in a ring of orange and yellow leaves that had peeled away from his shoes and drifted to the floor.

"These are extraordinary, Frank," she said when she saw them. Now wearing a robe, she stood over his shoulder and examined the five sketches he had made of her body, headless and recumbent on the hillocks of mussed bedsheet. "Really. You are the real thing, kid." She touched the top of his head in benediction and then padded across the room to change the CD.

He excused himself to her bathroom. On the edge of the tub, one of her starkly black hairs lay in a long thin line with a crook at the end, the black fading to blonde along the line; he tongued his fingertip so that the hair would stick to it. He took down his pants, wrapped the hair tightly around the aching shaft of his penis, and almost instantly came into the toilet bowl; the orgasm flung his sighing torso back on tensed legs so that he almost fell over. He righted himself. As he bent to pull up his pants, he noticed the crusted splotch of dried blood on his knee where he'd been pricked by the spiral. He left her hair in where he had placed it, and, when he saw the milky clot floating slowly around the bowl, he decided not to flush the toilet.

"Not a word, Frank," she said as he prepared to go. "Think of how much trust I'm putting in your talent. Think of that if you're ever tempted to breathe a word of this. Also, get the hell out this of town, will you? I wish I could. Jesus fuck, if I were your age, I would do *everything*."

He nodded and left. He thought his knees would give way as he plodded down the steps of her building. When he got out into the gelid air, he began to run.

The next night, after his shift in the mall restaurant, Jobe took a crimson oil pastel from his pocket and slashed his first cock into the crotch of the worker on the wall relief.

He never spoke to Isabella Madison again outside of his art class. At the end of the school year, she informed the class that she had been dismissed, not for any infraction, but simply because budget cuts to the arts and music programs necessitated the termination of non-necessary faculty. Then, with a sardonic smirk, she said she had just quoted verbatim from the letter they sent her.

During the lunch hour of the last day of that school year, the empty art room burst with huge gouts of scarlet smoke. Bright clouds billowed out the door from a fire set in a trash can, its fuel apparently sprinkled with dyes. Jobe's last sight of Isabella was of her face in garish red light: the eyes were wide with sympathy and fear, while the lips just stopped short of smiling.

* * *

The only person he'd ever told about her was Alice Nicchio-Strand, because, he must have thought, what did it matter by then? Alice wondered if he'd ever been with a woman after that. Perhaps he had taken Isabella Madison's lesson to its logical conclusion, even later, even in the time of his fame, when he could have seduced many a starstruck young artist. He certainly didn't try to sleep with Alice; he only sat with her at bars, talking long into the night, not, if he could help it, about himself. While she had gone to bed with other men since Fraternelli, she'd limited herself to one-night stands. She sympathized with the spirit of Jobe's renunciation.

* * *

Yes, he'd told her most of his aborted love story, in his terse way, and she probably imagined the rest. All the images circled through her fever-like arid-mouthed half-dream as she lay uneasily with a hand on her inner thigh and a foot on her chest and a knee wedged beneath her buttocks: the

163

colored smoke, the unexpected breasts, the hair on the tub, the cock on the relief. If the Its were the work of Frank Jobe, where in this concatenation of mundane imagery was the source of it?

Then fireworks burst on the eyelids, the two racks of teeth cracked together with a click of bone, the taste of blood spread warmly in the mouth, and It, jarred from her dream, woke up to Its non-self: the It in front, the one with the scarred legs, jerked in a nightmare and twitched Its heel up into Its chin. It sucked Its bitten tongue and shoved both arms forward to knock the frail, scarred It who had delivered the kick out of the bed. It seemed to clatter to the floor, just skin and bone. On the bed, It blinked and strained until Its eyes adjusted to the darkness, to the moonlight falling in the high hospital windows, to the glow coming from the emergency-lit hallway beyond the room. It squinted down at the floor to see that Its robe had fallen down to reveal the protruding vertebrae, the ridges that notched the back all the way up the neck; It seemed to cry down there on the excremental floor, bereft of all touch, Its back to the It up there on the bed, Its shoulderblades clenching and unclenching like jaws. It rolled Itself off the bed, paddling Its legs as if in water to swim away from the fingers abutting Its vulva and the kneecap pointed at Its anus, to swim away from the omnipresent touch, to get down there with It, down on the piss-puddled and rat-shat linoleum, on the bestial floor.

* * *

Both awake, neither touching, they stared at each other with wide, startled eyes, the whites shining in the near dark. Alice saw that she was a frail girl with a wasted face and scars on her arms; her sternum stuck out between starved, shrunken breasts, and a pouch of skin hung from the violent concavity beneath the arch of her rib-cage. She hadn't been crying, for her eyes and cheeks were dry; she had only undergone a kind of emotional dry-heaving, the body wracked with a silent moaning. Then the frail girl insistently raised her index finger to her lips. If there was a principle valued more highly than collective and persistent touch among the Its, it was surely silence. What was language but evidence of the loneliness that only touch could cure, a sign that each man and woman was locked in the cage of the self and signaling for release? With the Its, release had come, assumption into the common of shared labor and shared skin. Speech and writing, having been obsolesced by this utopia, could not be tolerated within it.

Now assured of Alice's silence, the frail girl got onto her hands and knees and began to crawl across the floor. She waved her hand in the air, motioning Alice to follow. Delicately maneuvering their limbs over Its who slept on the floor, closing their nasal passages against the stench of urine and feces, they crawled out of the room and began to move along the corridor. Alice wondered why all this secrecy was required if the Its didn't prevent anyone from leaving. She wanted to ask why they couldn't simply walk out the door and into the moonlight and clear air, if that was what they wanted to do. She poked the girl's leg to get her attention and, when she turned around, Alice pointed first at her head and then toward the outside, as if to say, "Why don't you go?" Alice had to stay, of course, to find Julia Fraternelli, even if it meant suffering the type of degradation that she, who had always claimed to hunger for experience only, had always so delicately managed to avoid. The girl shook her head decisively on its fragile neck and pointed to the floor. Then, her gesture questioning and almost apologetic, the girl put her hand out and pulled it inward. She had to go down to the lower floors, and she wanted Alice to come with her, even though she knew she had no right to ask anyone such a thing.

Its slept in the stairwells, lit with dim back-up lights, and Alice and the girl had to step over their snoring, flatulent bodies and tiptoe past their piles and pools of waste. They made it down two flights; by Alice's count, they had descended beyond the hospital's main floor and were now underground. The girl led her down still another flight before they came through a door into a long hallway illuminated with a red emergency bulb. They were, Alice reasoned, in some kind of sub-basement now. No bodies littered the floor, and the corridor was relatively clean. They ran along its concrete bottom until the corridor branched, and then they moved down the tributary until it came out into a clearing with several rings of flickering candles in the center and about fifty sleeping bodies arrayed around the candles in a star-shaped formation, their heads pointed toward the flame and their feet toward the wall. The sleepers held hands as they slept, and moreover, the feet of those nearer the candles rested on the bald heads of the ones below them. Only the inner circle's heads were untouched, and likewise the feet of the those in the outer circle. The girl stepped very carefully around the arrangement of bodies, avoiding the clasped hands of the sleepers, until she found the one she looking for. It was another young woman of about the frail girl's age; she appeared to be in better health, and her gray robe was cleaner than that of the average Its, but her cheeks had a hollow and sunken appearance. The frail girl pointed down at the sleeper and then at herself and Alice, and finally she raised both arms diagonally, as if to say, "Up and out."

Alice would later learn from journalistic accounts in the aftermath that these underground rooms were reserved for those of the Its who had earned elite status, usually by electing to have some form of surgical operation to remove one or more of the organs that allowed for modes of individuation: sex, speech, sight, hearing. The Its prophesied a future of touch alone, pure touch, and such labor as sufficed to keep the touching body alive, lest anyone accuse them of having opted out of the struggle to devote their existence to pure mutual communion. This was the only legitimate resistance to the sufferings of humanity, which were occasioned simply by the illusions of individuality; our cruel delusions of selfhood prompted us to desperate and destructive attempts both to preserve the self and to provide it company, from reproduction to industry to all the vanities of culture. The ones who offered themselves to the knife, who were tormented even after all hands were laid on them and who consequently needed to rid themselves of some irrepressible inner source of goading and temptation to be other than an It, they deserved to be leaders of the Its as long as humanity remained so imperfect that even the Its still needed leaders. The frail girl had seemingly come in as a decoy just as Alice had: like Alice, she wanted to rescue one of the leaders, even though a leader, Alice thought, had made Its choice and needed no savior, except from Itself.

Alice stepped forward carefully and studied the features of the supine sleeper in the flickering candlelight, and something in the face, maybe the long thin nose or the mouth shut with wary and superior primness, as if to avoid speaking evil, even in sleep, reminded Alice of someone she once knew. Then the frail girl leaned down and shook the sleeper by the shoulders. The eyes and the mouth of the young woman threw themselves open as if they were the windows of a house on fire, and a scream spouted up out of her mouth as if it had forced itself up from the earth like a subterranean river. The last thing Alice saw before a blow to the back of the head knocked her out was the dark red hole of Julia Fraternelli's wide-open mouth: her tongue had been pared back to the root.

9. GADARENE SWINE

"Jesus fuck, look who it is," said Frank Jobe. He went from massaging Alice's temple to slapping it with the heel of his hand to wake her up. She lifted her heavy eyelids; he stood in front of the chair she was tied to. He wore gray army fatigues, and he had shaved his white shock down to the rough and fissured scalp. His face was jowly and impassive, hormone-starved, but his cynical smile on seeing her showed the same smoke-yellowed teeth she remembered. His first two fingers prised open her lips and tapped with their long yellow nails on her own front teeth, the click of horn on bone echoing amid the walls of her bruised head. "Solid," he said. "You haven't been with us long."

"Frank," she managed to say. Then her head dropped, and she lost consciousness for a moment.

He slapped her awake again. "Come on, señorita," he said. "Out with it."

"Whatever you've got planned, just let the three of us go. Me and those two girls." She looked to her left and right at the frail girl and her mute friend, who were tied to dingy split-cushioned old office chairs on either side of her. An orange light shone on their faces through high windows; dawn came like a fire on the hills in the distance. Alice jerked her head up to keep herself from falling unconscious again. When she swiveled her head all around, she saw that she and the young women and Frank Jobe were in the center of the hospital atrium. The walls were lined with Its, watching motionlessly and with no apparent interest.

"I'll let you go, Alice. Not only will I let you go, I'll come with you. I want you and your friends to watch. I want somebody with a mind to see."

"Watch what? What are you planning, Frank? For Christ's sake, don't kill anyone else."

"Christ got nothing to do with it, which you should know. And I don't have a plan. I just have a lot of people who are pissed off with the state of things. Too many people for shit to go on like this." He swept his hand around the room to indicate what could not go on. "It's time to broaden out. Sometime today or tomorrow, they're going to move on the city. I don't know what'll happen. Maybe the pigs'll drop a neutron bomb. Be interesting to see. And you always got me, Alice, fundamentally just *got* me, so I want you to watch with me. And if you want your friends to come, what the hell. Maybe we'll all be dead by tomorrow morning. But any asshole can say that, right?"

"Who are you working for?"

"Who are *you* working for, babe? Everybody's working for somebody."

"Frank," she said. "I need to know on whose behalf you implicated me in twenty-one murders. I am not a hysterical woman, not a flighty artist, not a moralizing critic. I'm not a cop, I'm not a shrink. I need to know for *myself*. You know me. And you know I need to know what all this has been for."

"Yeah, I know you, sister. Control-freaky, that was always your problem: you want everything your own way. I'm telling you, you control freak, that I don't know, and I don't care. The three or four links up the chain of command above me don't know either. Was there money? Sure, there was money. Crisp fucking bills, stacks of them, made a very satisfying slap-slap-slap when I flipped the edges. American money by the time it got to me, but who knows, maybe it started out Russian, Chinese, Saudi, or maybe it passed through them from the U.S. of A. in the first place. Maybe it ain't from a government at all, just some revolutionary groupiscule with a rich backer: Maoists of Peoria, Islamic State in Jackson Hole, white nationalists of Palos Verde. Maybe it's some bored ugly heiress who wants to see trouble on her news feed, wants to get emergency alert text messages to make her feel loved on those long wet-pussy nights all alone in the queen-sized between the damp silk sheets. Who the hell knows? Who cares? Don't play dumb, Alice, like some little girl saying, 'Daddy, why did God take Kitty? Why did God send the hurricane to blow away mommy?' Because I don't know. I *am* the hurricane. I'm just having fun whipping around, watching the landscape change under me. They don't tell me shit. What about you? What do you know? Do they tell you shit?"

She sighed with grim resignation: "No, I can't say that I know much of anything at all."

"That's the spirit, Socrates. Now I bet you know enough not to run if I untie you and your girls? Soon enough, there'll be nowhere to go anyways."

She nodded. As he leaned over her to undo the knots, she saw the void at his crotch and the bulge at his inner thigh. When she had one hand free, she ran it along the front of his pants. There was nothing, nothing but a thin tube that she followed with her fingers until they encountered a warm bag strapped to his upper leg.

"Go to town," he said. "It don't even hurt anymore. Who needs a cock and balls? If I could have found a way to take the pussies out of the girls, I would have, but you know, you can't remove a hole. The girls got a head start in that respect, especially the itty-bitty-titty-committee. But I think we're all equally nothing in the end. We were a mistake, a shit-stain on the earth. And this generation will show the way out, and then hopefully we won't have no more generations. It'll all be over. The trees will grow up through the buildings, and you won't be able to hear anything, and then the sun'll boil the sky, and that'll be the end of it. So touch it all you like, sweetheart. I don't feel a thing."

The frail girl, as he untied her, said, "Oh my God, will you shut the hell up? You just talk and talk and *talk*, while the only thing the rest of these assholes have going for them is that they have to be quiet."

"Somebody has to blow the last trumpet, sweetie. Might as well be me. That's why I kept this," he said, and he let his yellow-coated tongue drop onto his lower lip.

Julia kicked and moaned when Frank Jobe came to let her go; she had found her home among the Its and didn't want to be exiled. She was too weak to resist, though, and they carried her out of the atrium and back into the tunnels under the abandoned hospital, tunnels that ran out into the city.

* * *

A panel slid open in the door, and a bass voice cried, "Password?"

"Password is I got a gun," Jobe said. He stuck the barrel of the automatic through the panel and waved it around to create a metallic clatter that echoed through the tunnels. "Now don't be stupid, just open the fucking door."

The panel slammed shut so quickly that Jobe instinctively withdrew the gun as if it were an extension of his hand.

Julia, held between Jobe and Alice so that they could drag her unwillingly along, sullenly tugged at Alice's robe to get her attention. Then she stooped to the grime-strewn cement of the fluorescent-lit underground clearing and traced in the dirt the winged, serpent-twined rod.

Alice pounded on the door and screamed, "Caduceus!"

The door swung open so quickly that Alice almost fell inward. A huge man stomped out and, with a hand like a spade, swept the automatic from

Jobe's grip; it spun across the clearing. He calmly walked to retrieve it, and then he trained it on Jobe.

"Okay, folks, what is the nature of your emergency?" he finally asked.

Alice said, "These young women were with the Its cult. They're both dehydrated and half-starved, and this one has had a primitive amputation of the tongue."

A short, plump woman in a white coat and with a scar that jaggedly extended half her smile bustled out past Alice. "Julia Bonham," she said. "But I just saw you." She immediately took Julia's chin in her hand and opened her own mouth wide as a silent instruction. "Appalling," the doctor murmured as she peered into Julia's empty cavity, a nave without an altar. She took down Julia's robe to reveal a fierce scar on her abdomen, viciously pink like a slab of raw meat. The doctor turned to the frail girl next and looked her up and down, from her scarred legs to her jutting collarbones. "All right, we need to get inside right away," the doctor said. When she turned around, she found Jobe in her path. "And you are?" she said.

He only smiled, wickedly pleasant.

"Let me introduce Frank Jobe," said Alice.

The doctor squinted for a moment thoughtfully, as if the man's name were written on the opposite wall and she were trying to read it. Then her eyes widened. Though Jobe was a head taller than she was, the doctor brought the back of her hand up and around with swift force. One of Jobe's canines clicked with a bloody trail over the cement.

He laughed and rubbed his jaw and said, "Whatever happened to 'first do no harm'?"

She only walked around him as if he were shit on the sidewalk. She didn't address another word to him, though the company spent almost the whole day in her hospital. The huge man kept the gun trained on Jobe for the duration.

While she worked, her latex-sheathed fingers inside Julia's open mouth, the doctor spoke to her constantly in a low voice, the tone indicating that her words were both very insistent and very kindly. Alice couldn't hear what she said from the other side of the room. She was with the frail girl, who sat with a hunched back and an affectless expression, an I.V. in her arm.

"How do you know Julia?"

"We were roommates," Caroline said. She parted her lips as if to go on; then she closed them again and continued to sit in the underground hospital with only the doctor's murmured declarations and the hum, beep, clack, and whirr of the various medical apparatuses for accompaniment.

Eventually, Frank Jobe said, "We should probably get out of here soon. Who knows what's happening up there?"

"Why should I let you go?" said the man with the gun.

"We can't keep him," said the doctor. "It's not a prison. I just put people back together, and then they have to make their own mistakes all over again. Speaking of which," she said as she signaled to a man in scrubs who was attending an unconscious patient on the other side of the room, "please take a look at Mr. Jobe there; he's had a blow to the face."

Alice got up and walked around the vast yellow-tiled room that served as triage unit, operating theater, and recovery area. Along the rear walls, in shadows, was a line of cots. Two of them were occupied. In one lay an old man whose body was still and rigid except for its chest, which regularly swelled and collapsed under the pressure of a clicking respirator, the mask of which covered his face almost entirely. The other cot held a girl of twelve or so, the flesh of her face hollowed by some illness that burrowed and chewed beneath it, her body so motionless that she seemed to sleep; but, Alice found with a start, her eyes were unblinkingly, bulgingly open, the whites irradiating the gloom in which she was confined, so bright that Alice had to turn away.

* * *

The doctor had recommended that both Julia and Caroline be kept for observation, but Jobe insisted instead that they accompany him to the surface once both were rehydrated and disinfected and rested. Julia had given up struggling against her liberation from the Its, and Jobe in any case assured her that she may well join them again whether she liked it or not if they seized the city, that she might be able to escape once more the undefended exposed-nerve agony of the self and be warmed again by ash and touch. Alice herself felt a strange craving for the life of the Its now that she was gone from it: the hands always there, so omnipresent that if each It walked along a wire none would fall, or all would. The welcome burial of the monstrous I, with its tormenting temptation to engorge itself by consuming others, the torture of its memories that said its best days had passed and had passed moreover unrecognized as such. Only in sleep, had an I come back, but even here she'd evaded her own and had dreamed of Jobe's, standing at painful attention on the other side of a room from what its ferocious desire was barred from uniting with. She felt as she had during that long summer, her last at home with her mother alive, though she didn't know it then, a time of empty endurance, suspended between what she regarded, then and now, as a past of illegitimate happiness and a future of unforeseeable but unavoidable agonies.

They prepared to leave. They washed themselves in the tubs that abutted the hospital wall. Water streamed from their bodies and swirled above the drain, thickly sedimented with ashes pulled by the spiral into long black filaments. They all appeared to be crying black tears.

171

The doctor led them to a row of rusty lockers in which neatly-kept clothing was stacked and hung.

"Let me guess," Jobe said. "The people who came in these clothes left in body bags?"

No one said anything. They picked out their new dress in solemn, nervous silence, as if rifling through pockets on a battlefield. Jobe chose thick carpenter's pants with a huge tear up one leg, its edges faintly stained reddish-brown; over his naked torso he belted an oversized trenchcoat that hung down to the factory boots he had put on. He crowned it all with a broad-brimmed white hat and a pair of red-rimmed oversized sunglasses that covered the entire top half of his face, for he of all the company had to go unrecognized. Caroline wore a men's T-shirt and shorts that fell past her knees; they had to be held to be held up by a belt, which the doctor used a scalpel to make extra holes in. Alice dressed herself and Julia in long dresses of muted pastel blues and greens that she hoped would allow them, if necessary, to blend in with the gray-robed cult.

As they moved toward the door, the guard looked down at the gun in his hand and said to Jobe, "I think I'll keep this, sir."

"Go ahead," Jobe said. "Either we won't need it, or it won't help."

Dr. Grace put a hundred dollars in cash into Alice's palm.

"You take care of Julia," she said. "And take care of yourself too. We'll be watching you, both of you, to make sure."

"Make sure of what?" Alice asked, but Jobe, already through the door, shouted for them to come on.

They went back down the ramp and into the tunnels. Eventually, they surfaced at the mouth of a concrete pipe that opened onto a strip of woods near a bank of the river opposite downtown. A short walk under the thinning canopy of enflamed leaves brought them to a fence with a person-high breach cut into its links. Within minutes they were on a public street. It was a bright afternoon: the sun slanted down in golden shafts through which leaves spun on the light, crisp breeze. Alice had lost count of the days, but she figured it must be a Sunday afternoon from the way laughing families emerged buoyantly, the adults confidently sauntering, the children skipping in circles around them, paper cups of hot chocolates gripped confidently in their hands, from the door of the Asphodel Café across the street. She stared at the café door until it had centered itself in her vision utterly. If she focused on that zone of normalcy, of ordinary commerce, the exchange of money for pleasure, the orderly high spirits of domestic outings, then she could forget the gray swarm massing somewhere over the city that threatened to batten on it. Caroline followed Alice's gaze and then turned away, as if slapped, when her eyes rested on the Asphodel Café.

Then Jobe raised his hand and pointed up the street; the three women looked along the sightline his finger made. The intersection ahead led onto one of the bridges that entered the city proper. Like a slow stampede, the Its crossed the intersection. A car that had been in the middle of a turn jerked to a rubber-peeling stop, and the Its, each one with a force of thousands at Its back, continued over it, leaving ashy footprints on the windshield, while the driver inside gripped the wheel and screamed. A number of cars slowed to a stop in the mass, like so many goats and cows caught at a cattle crossing in a pyroclastic flow. On and on the Its came. The wind flung the ash from them in billows and clouds like smoke. Alice could feel beneath her borrowed sandals a slight trembling of the concrete sidewalk. Jobe turned his head in the opposite direction and squinted down the long river road toward the entrance to the next bridge.

"They gathered at the abandoned hospital," he said. "They all got together in one place."

"So they're only using one entrance to the city for their grand assault?" Alice said. "That's hardly good strategy."

"It's not a *military* strategy. They aren't trying to conquer; they're showing the new world to the old world. For a display, it's better they all be in one place. The convergence of the perspective on a single point, one last time, before all perspective is lost. A basic fucking aesthetic principle, right?" he said with a dry smile at Alice.

They walked down toward the other bridge until an empty taxi passed; then they squeezed themselves inside. Alice was wedged between Julia and Caroline while Jobe gave directions from the front seat. They had agreed to watch the approach of the Its from the top floor of the central public library, the tallest building that faced the bridge the Its were just then crossing. They had not even discussed running or driving in the opposite direction: somehow they all agreed without discussion that flight would be beneath them, would betray whatever necessity had driven each of them to the Its in the first place.

The cab driver turned onto the next bridge that led into the city. As they drove over the river, Julia opened her window and put her face into the autumn-barbed breeze. She seemed to stare at the library, the silver cantilever that adorned its roof like, Alice thought, a ship's prow. On the other side of Alice, Caroline, her scarcely-protected bones chilled by the in-blowing air, shivered and gathered herself against Alice for warmth. Jobe nudged the driver's elbow and pointed across the distance over the river to show him the amorphous, ragged flood of gray that was very slowly overwhelming the other bridge in a haze of soot and ash. The city at the end of the bridge stood in the gold and silver of civilization, the afternoon sun burning in the mirrored faces of the glass buildings, its pastoral trees with all their autumn heads on fire; it seemed, despite its solid stone and steel surface, unprotected against the colorlessness coming to claim it. Red and blue lights blinked at the entrance to the city, and helicopters chuffed in the sky: the authorities must have ordered the police to seal the bridge the Its had claimed. "Allahu akbar," mouthed the driver.

Alice looked away for now, to gather strength for the catastrophe; she calmed her eyes by resting them on the skin of yellow leaves that had formed on the surface of the river, weltering in soft undulations.

* * *

Though only a decade old, the library already looked tarnished and worn. Its high glass walls, brightly soaring atrium, and glittering silver cantilevered roof belonged to a potential future that had not and would not come to pass. The library was a failed prophecy shining in the sun. In the vanished future it implied, not only would public utilities have sparkled with clean reason and met the clear air of the sky as equals and partners, but their users would have also. Had the architects known what the building would in fact become, they would have made it like the cathedrals of old: a high-ceilinged flight to heaven, yes, but with enough smoky shadow and bleeding statuary to shelter and epitomize the wanderers, the beggars, the lepers, the madmen, the whores, the orphans, and all other lost souls whose raving curses and racking coughs and suppurating sores and moldering rags would be turned away from any other house. Now that the city's churches were being boarded up, the state's houses of worship were compelled to take any and all comers, but, on the evidence of their architecture, they hadn't prepared themselves to succor the weak. The library's transparent walls communicated the ease and assurance of strength, and the weak would just have to bend and curse and spit in the eerie haze made by the sky-high windows' shadow. Seeing themselves without illusion in the glimmer and shine of the crystal library, they might be moved to render final judgment on themselves. Four people had already committed suicide in the library that year, Alice had read: men and women who'd leapt to their deaths from the fourth-floor gallery down onto the atrium's marble, where brain and bone must have scattered in the smooth daylight like the luscious innards and glossy rind of a thrown melon. More security was put in place while better precautions were being investigated: so the newspapers, quoting the press releases, had phrased it. For now, though, the low silver rail of the gallery, just wide and flat enough to stand on, along with the bright empty air it overlooked, would remain a temptation for the wretched.

The library's thoughtless glass-walled clarity was an imposition, Alice thought, a piece of human arrogance. The nondescript little brown-brick library of her town in the hills outdid this gaudy display, because it left the imagination sheltered, thus free. The strained and showy grandeur of the city library forbade any true revelation by banishing the darkness that a revelation would necessarily have to emerge from, a darkness that could alone harbor the light.

Jobe, Alice, Julia, and Caroline, having arrived at the fourth floor, moved away from the gallery rail toward the building's other end, where a twelve-foot-high continuous wall of glass faced the river's opposite bank and therefore also looked out on the bridge. The general sense of panic that they'd seen in the streets during their taxi ride into the city had mostly emptied the library of all but the most bored teenagers and the people who had nowhere else to go. The four sat at one of the consequently unoccupied study tables next to the windows and stared down. The police presence, now including heavily militarized forces in black armor walking alongside what looked like small tanks, was now backed up almost to the library itself. Having herself been part of the automatic mass of the Its, she suspected they may well be capable of overwhelming the police force. Maybe the helicopters, she thought, carried enough weaponry to dispatch the cult ravening over the bridge. It had advanced halfway by now, and its approach made Alice feel a block of ice in her abdomen, a sensation of absolute powerlessness such as she had only felt once before, when the elite patrons of her museum had begun to jerk and lurch with spewing mouths like so many demoniacs. Not knowing what to do, she had rushed out the doors of *The Last Café* and had thrown them shut, pressing all her weight to them, like someone facing a tidal wave with touchingly useless resistance. She felt the same way now, and she prayed to no one in particular that the government possessed enough artillery to slaughter all these people so that her vicious, lonely I might be spared their drowning touch. Then she reflected on the grotesquery of the thought and, without rescinding it, began to laugh with bitter helplessness.

Julia started laughing too, a dry chuckle at first that sounded hollow in her empty mouth, and then a higher and more desperate laugh, almost a maniacal shriek. Caroline at her side caught the laughter too, and had to rest her head on Julia's shoulder to relieve her convulsive hilarity.

"That ain't right," said a woman near them, and then she pursed her disapproving lips.

Alice, looking from the one laughing girl to the other, turned to her side to see if Jobe too had seen the joke in the situation, but Jobe wasn't there anymore.

* * *

Just before the Its reached the end of the bridge, Alice decided she could no longer stand to watch helplessly as the Its advanced. Thinking she might, in her moments of individual consciousness, read a book, she walked away from the bright windows and wandered around the library's fourth floor.

She passed the computers arranged in a block near the welcome desk. Only one man sat before a screen, a down-at-heel professional-looking type, the kind of person who used to be called shabby-genteel. She stole a glance over his shoulder and saw that he was experimenting with fonts on his résumé. Then she moved among the long shelves of books, the aisles between them empty. She reflected that she had spent so much of her life in reading. So much of the I now perhaps to be swamped in the gray current of It-hood had been constructed from the words that entered her eyes like rays of light, the words that she rolled in her mouth like cherry stones, the words that were incised in her memory like the epitaphs of ideas. She idly wondered if her own books were in here somewhere. Wouldn't it be poetic to find one of them now? she asked herself, to clutch it to her chest, the only incarnation of whatever in her was not It, the thing that would be left when the It laid their hands again on her twitching limbs and took her under? She realized, there were no art books here, though, that she was facing instead a shelf of theological treatises.

Would it do her any good to peruse such literature now, at the likely end of her conscious life? No, it would do her no good at all to struggle with some priest's argument that the beauties and symmetries of creation not only entailed but constituted in and of themselves an argument for the necessity of an infinitely intelligent and infinitely loving creator. It would benefit her nowise now to be able to build up in her mind a logical refutation of this sheltered aesthete's theodicy. The words "nowise" and "theodicy" and "excrescence" could not sustain her while the end of her I was probably even now scudding toward her in a slow gray cloud unashamedly trailing its own excrescence, the inevitable daily residue of all the theologian's beloved beauty, shit's symmetry with the splendors of every feast being probably not what the theologian had had in mind. Whatever god took pleasure in the onrushing devastation, the near-certain bloodshed, would filigree and ornament his creation with cruel correspondences of human flesh, harmonies of wailing, more akin to the theodicy of the Its than anything that she and the theologian, those two benighted lovers of beauty, would be comfortable imagining. From this destroyer-creator, this cannibal deity, Alice wanted only relief. She couldn't lie to herself: that she held within herself all these words and all these arguments still made her feel herself superior to those coming toward her, even if they had eliminated loneliness. Like the god she at once didn't believe in and rebuked, she, by which she meant only her I, had the power to devise structures of blood and shit lovely to contemplate, and she knew she would probably never root out the faith, lodged very deep within herself, the very grain of sand she had pearled around in her long-dead mother's long-rotted womb, that this ability conferred something of the god-like upon her.

* * *

Alice walked back to the table and told Julia and Caroline what she had seen while wandering the stacks: "Frank Jobe is walking the gallery rail."

She pointed to where Jobe was almost dancing on the strip of silver, a sight hidden from the table where the women sat by the periodical shelves. She saw him as soon as she exited the theology aisle: he had pulled his boots off and was in the process of climbing onto the metal railing.

"I thought you didn't believe in suicide," she called to him.

He turned his boyish, nasty, yellow grin on her, his eyes concealed behind the sunglasses: "I don't believe in *anything*, sister. I believe in walking till you're stopped by something bigger than you. I'm just going walking on this nice little silver road here."

"He's walking it like a tightrope and making all sorts of aesthetic flourishes," Alice explained, "kicking a foot out behind him, intertwining his arms. People are gathering around, more entranced by him than by the bridge, asking him questions, shouting encouragement. But he won't say a word. He just walks back and forth. And when he starts dancing, they all get quiet."

She sat facing the periodicals and even turned her chair toward them and away from the window, as if to avoid a public charge that she had looked away from Jobe's agon with the void, even though she could not in fact see it beyond the magazine-laden shelves.

Silence gave way to a shriek followed by outraged laughter from the suicide corner. Jobe must have put a foot wrong and then recovered.

On the other side of the window, the sinking sun seemed to rest at the same height as Alice's face, and she couldn't look at it if she wanted to; its glow caused her vision to pulse and waver. Four stories below, sirens moaned dopplerwise toward the glass and silver structure, to reinforce the police.

"They're at the end of the bridge," Caroline said. "They can't go any further. And they keep coming onto the bridge too; it's getting more and more packed."

A certain tense vibration in the atmosphere told Alice that Jobe, unseen behind the periodical shelves, continued his silent crossing and re-crossing of the gallery rail.

Until then, the occasional screams that issued from the suicide corner had a squealing mirth as they rose into the cathedral-high spaces of the library. Probably Jobe's knees buckled, his foot slid, his arms rigidly wavered like old biplane wings, and the crowd, now comprising everyone on this floor of the library but the three women, whooped and tittered and let out high-pitched yells of perineum-tingling delight. This was a carnival, a

177

ritual: the man on the rail faced death in the crowd's stead, on its behalf, and as long as he held his balance over the empty air and the faraway marble floor, the crowd could contemplate his performance with a roiling equanimity and the nervous thrill of vicarious exaltation usually reserved for Oedipus, Hamlet, and the imperiled women in horror movies or on the local news.

Then a scream went up of sheer, unconscious, animal anguish, a throat-grating cry without any hint of play. The crowd's scream was pure worship: it sounded as if the earth had opened up and roared. The man on the rail had gone over. Frank Jobe was dead.

At the sound of the scream, Julia stood; she left her seat so fast that the backs of her legs, as they quickly locked into standing rigidity, shoved her chair over onto the floor. It was as if an idea had suddenly come to her, a solution descending out of the sky and lighting up the top of her head. Why hadn't she thought of it sooner? She began to turn. In a second, Alice saw the young woman's future course as clearly as if it were marked out in chalk on the carpet: she would run, this self-ravished Philomel, to the gallery rail and, having followed Jobe so far, she would follow him down to the crushing marble too.

Alice thrust her arm across the table and grabbed Julia by the hand before she could run. Julia didn't move. She remained facing the periodical shelves, one foot slightly turned, one knee slightly bent, in readiness to rush toward them, to the salvation behind them. Her back faced Alice.

"Is that all you want to be?" Alice asked. She lifted up her voice, as if to pronounce a judgment. "The next of the Gadarene swine off the cliff's edge? Will you accept all the world's devils into you and let them destroy you? Why? Because you behaved stupidly and cruelly from time to time? Because someone was stupid and cruel to you? You hurt the defenseless, you preyed on the weak, your mother didn't love you enough, death is the only sure thing and all you deserve: have I got it all right? And every word out of your mouth or, what's worse, every word in your head sounds like nothing but a petulant and whining self-defense. Your face is a monster's mask. Your desires are disordered. If people only knew what you really wanted, they'd hunt you down, lock you up. And what is it all worth? It will all be laid in a common grave, eventually, so why not today? Do I read you right, Julia?"

Julia kept her eyes fixed on the periodical shelves, her mind apparently tensed toward the suicide's leap beyond them. Caroline now stood up, though cautiously, so as not to alarm Julia. Alice gave her a steadying glance, her fingers still grasping Julia's hand tightly, bundling the girl's thin, cold fingers into a skewed fasces.

"Chance was the beginning, evil is the middle, and death will be the end. And given that, why tolerate the evil at all? Do I understand you, Julia, Julia Fraternelli?"

Now Alice leaned across the table and lowered her voice.

"When you were a child, I had an irrational hatred toward you. It seemed to be your innocence, your little white pinafore and that brownish blonde hair, that thin nose from your mother, which bound your father to a life I could never really share with him. And I loved your father's life; what was present in mine seemed absent from his and vice versa. What looked like our haphazardly broken edges would in fact interlock if they could touch. He was soft in all the places I was hard and hard in all the places I was soft. He never would have given Frank Jobe the time of day, for one thing. He revered reality to the point of crawling behind toilets to set it right; Jobe's nihilistic contempt would have disgusted him. But I never would have mistaken what you did to Mephistopheles for nihilistic contempt."

Julia jerked her hand away as if Alice's fingers were molten. Alice expected the young woman to round on her in rage, but when she turned, her mouth was twisted by sorrow and her face wet with tears.

"Oh yes, he told me. He never told the librarian or your mother, but he told me. And he told me that it made him afraid, afraid that he had ruined you when he left your mother, afraid that his actions had twisted you somehow. I accused him of being a self-centered philistine, and then I said that there is a way of loving things that inevitably runs of the risk of destroying them, them or oneself. He wanted to guard your innocence; it was that cynical, realistic man's single spot of naïveté, of sentimental blindness. You were the thing beyond the reach of his criticism, the thing he didn't want to have to fix, the one pure thing he had done in his life. But I knew you had no innocence to guard. You wanted experience at whatever cost, as I did. I saw you in your white pinafore, and I hated you not because you were different, but because I knew you were just like me, only you didn't know it yet, and I wanted to show you. Maybe I was wrong. Maybe I'm wrong now. God knows how wrong I've been before. But dying can't save you. Nothing can save you. You probably can't even save yourself. I know your secret, though, Julia Fraternelli: you were always such a curious girl. Desisting from your search is not worthy of you."

The crowd that had gathered on the other side of the fourth floor to watch Jobe's dance now antistrophed back toward the window; their reprieve from the potential gray apocalypse coming over the bridge and into the city had ended when Jobe's brains were dashed out over the marble of the atrium to the upwelling cries of those gathered below, and, with a begrudging sense of duty, the patrons now returned to the ashy submergence that approached them. They continued to make nervously amused remarks and to laugh with morbid hysteria, though a few among them dabbed their eyes. They paid no attention to the confrontation between Alice and Julia. Instead, they shaded their staring eyes from the late-afternoon sun and lifted their staring phones to the bridge, which was so crowded with the Its that some of their number were forced to creep along the exterior of the bridge rails and some had climbed the pillars between which the structure spanned. Police lights flickered on the bridge's far side; it seemed the authorities were determined to seal it at both ends. The Its, having paused at the first barricade they encountered on the entrance to the city, now seemed to have lost momentum. If they wanted to overpower the police, they were going to have to start crawling over them on all fours, loping like wild dogs into the city. For now, though, they didn't move, and the police held their fire; the helicopters circled and circled, no doubt recording it all for TV news and Internet livestreams.

Alice kept her eyes on Julia's, even when everyone around them drew in their breath at once in a common reaction of shock and then let it back out again in a variety of ways, from tearful groaning to a cheer accompanied by the clapping of hands. Then Julia, also not following the gaze of the crowd, turned to face Caroline, who stood next to her. The tears came pouring out of her eyes unstoppably, a steady stream pumped from the core of her, joining under her chin to run off in the steady plashing of a fountain. She dropped to her knees before Caroline. "Julia, you don't have to..." Caroline began, but Julia went even lower, almost on her belly, and clasped Caroline's bare legs and bathed their scars in penitential tears.

Alice, Julia, and Caroline did not see the bridge give way; none of them saw that the river seemed to boil with the agitations of sinking rubble and the struggles of the drowning before it closed serenely over them all, the drifts of autumnal leaves still rocking on the surface. By the time the women turned to the window, it was even too late to see the gray cloud that had hung for a few minutes before dissipating in the middle of the air where the bridge once was.

Part Four
WINTER

John Pistelli

10. BEGGARS WOULD RIDE

"You want a cigarette, Alice?" called the girl with the red hair and green eyes. Wrapped to her chin in a thick blanket, she sat on a low, flat tomb beneath the moss-pocked angel that guarded the remains of the tomb's occupant. She fumbled inside the blanket for the cigarettes she kept inside her furred boots, which were all she wore beneath the blanket other than a bra and panties. Her voice, chafed by too much orgasmic moaning, skimmed across the piled snow and through the clear winter air in high and low pitches, echoing from the surrounding trees and funerary monuments.

Since Alice, after selling her house and buying the abandoned property, had banished the pornographers from the church interior, the filmmakers became inventive about how to use the deconsecrated grounds for their own purposes. Filming inside crypts, they decided, leant a special piquancy, an imagined odor of moldering grave-clothes, to all sexual scenarios. While producing pornography in the nave had provided a reliably arousing sense of transgression, as proved by their Internet sales, recording the cries of orgasm as they sounded amid tombstones and burial chambers was to transgress against the brutally essential fact of death itself rather than merely against a contingent set of obsolesced social codes. The pornographers thanked Alice eventually, even though they'd judged her a pious prude when she ordered them out of the church.

"I have nothing against your work," she'd said. "No doubt it's more necessary than my own. But there is a place for everything."

This sounded absurdly small-minded to the pornographers, especially coming from this former avant-garde artist, and they raised all kinds of objections about the porous boundaries between art and pornography, about the irrelevance of the aesthetic hierarchies she'd tacitly invoked, and, above all, about their right to free expression. In the end she asserted the superior rights of property ownership, so they had to start scouting the grounds for alternative shooting locations if they wanted to keep delighting that portion of their audience who favored the eroticism of the profaned sacred. In the crypts they had to admit that they had discovered a worthy vision, and sales reflected their thanotopic breakthrough. When Alice asked what they planned next, they told her they had their eye on the convent.

When they asked her what she intended to put in the nave, in the empty space where the altar had been, she said, "Nothing."

When the actress had called to Alice, she had been standing outside the cemetery gate, with only her eyes and her fingers protruding from the layers of coat, scarf, glove, and hat that shielded her beach-reared flesh from the late-December wind. A very light snow had begun to fall in glittering shards amid the mid-afternoon's periwinkle light, but Alice went on painting. She had never learned to paint, neither in her naïve sculpting days, when she'd only cared to make solid objects, nor in her only slightly less naïve avant-garde days, when making experiences rather than representations had been her aim. A painting, a kind of imaginary window that hung flat on a wall, always somehow felt insubstantial to her; it failed to declare its own reality by standing in three dimensions as sculptures did. At least half of a painting's reality had to come from its viewer, and what artist, Alice used to think, would give up so much responsibility? As with all the endeavors we blithely dismiss while excusing ourselves from them, painting proved far more difficult to master than to criticize. Now she stood working over an image meant to suggest the snow-capped woods beyond the churchyard by an almost imperceptibly subtle transition from stark white at either end of the canvas to darkening shades of green toward the middle to a deep black strip at the center. She daubed the snow crystals themselves into the bottom of the canvas under the greenish white paint at the end of her brush. She did so on the theory that the picture she wanted to make would gain authenticity by being marked with snow, one of the very elements she sought to represent. Though she was trying to wean herself from it, trying to become more humble as she approached middle age, her passion for absolute reality had evidently not abated. The painting looked to her like a cheap rehash of the last century's increasingly meager leavings, and, worse than that, she'd so far failed to achieve the intended effect of incalculable subtlety. She thought it resembled strips of green and black on a white field, a soiled flag in need of a warm tone. These schoolgirl struggles to master the rudiments of art seemed bathetic and absurd at her age, but she knew it was good, even necessary, to begin again, to begin in ignorance. Her stupid painting made her want to laugh aloud, and she did, because she thought was alone. Then the actress called to her. She almost said, "I don't smoke," but found herself saying instead, "What the hell," and stowed her tubes of oils in the inner pocket of her coat to keep them warm. Let the snowdrifts bury the worthless canvas, she thought, and trudged in her boots into the graveyard.

The girl made space on the tomb for Alice; they sat together, so shapeless in their winter clothes that they looked like swellings of the earth only half-buried in the blue and glistering dunes of snow. It was the blue, Alice suddenly understood; her painting lacked the blue of the snow. She had painted what she thought snow looked like: she thought snow was white. Didn't everyone know it was? If you asked a child or a philosopher, they would say, "Yes, snow is white." If you look, though, especially in this wan winter light, it's really very blue. She almost bounded off the tomb and back over to her canvas, which she could see was shaking as the wind buffeted the easel. The girl had already lit her a cigarette, though, so she submitted to being sociable, even as she repeated her insight over and over to herself: it's blue, it's blue, it's blue.

"I haven't smoked since I was a teenager," she said. "We would smoke cigarette after cigarette on the beach. It was always like springtime, never like this, where I'm from. I certainly shouldn't smoke now. I'm only a year younger than my mother was when she died of cancer."

"Yeah, that shit creeps right up on you," the girl said.

Alice raised her eyebrows, because this girl was not a day over twenty-two, and whatever was creeping up on her, it probably wasn't a foreboding of her own mortality. She decided not to protest, though. She blew out the smoke in silence, marveling at how similar its color was to that of the massing snow.

"I fell asleep in there," said the girl, pointing with her cigarette end to the crypt behind them, with its angel-guarded door between Corinthian columns. "We brought in space heaters and got it nice and warm, and I laid down on the soft rug they put over one of the slabs while I was waiting for Peter to get ready. He was having trouble getting it up with all the death around, he said, and then Andy said, 'You're about to have trouble getting paid too,' and that's the last thing I heard before I fell asleep, because it was just so warm. They said I could only have been out for, like, five minutes, but I had this amazingly vivid dream, it was like a movie."

She stared into the wintry distance, as if trying to perceive the dream images out there on the bluish white screen of the world.

"Do you want to hear?" she asked.

"Why not?" said Alice.

"Okay, so you have to know something first. My sister, she went with the It people. At first I honestly thought it was a blessing. We hadn't been close at all since we were kids. She got into a lot of trouble, I'm talking serious drugs, teeth falling out, blowing whatever skeezy guys for a score. I mean, I know people criticize me for all this, but this is paying for college.

She wasn't going to college; she wasn't going anywhere. So when she went with the It people, I thought, Well, maybe that's what she needs. But she was on the bridge that day. And we lost her."

She said all this in tones as clear as the air; Alice's eyes felt more threatened by the pressure of tears than the girl's seemed to be.

"So," she went on, "I dreamt that I was there with her, and we all fell into the water. When we were down there, she wasn't dressed in a dirty gray sheet anymore. We were both wearing, like, Halloween stuff, we were fairy princesses, we had tiaras and high-heeled shoes that were too big for us and wings, we had wings. And we held onto each other's arms as we sank and sank, until the blue water started to turn black because we were so deep under. We just felt so happy to see each other, our faces were so happy. But then I saw her face get more and more scared as we got lower and lower, and I knew my face must have looked the same as hers, and I started to cry, except that you couldn't tell because we were underwater. Then I just thought, The hell with it, and I opened my mouth to take a big deep breath. And I could breathe just fine. When my sister saw that, she did it too, she opened her mouth really wide, and her face was happy again. We were breathing underwater, going deeper and deeper, and just holding onto each other."

"Then what happened?"

"Then I woke up because Peter climbed on top of me." The dreamy glaze of her eyes dissipated, and she laughed mordantly as she stubbed out the cigarette on the top of the tomb. "But you know what? That dream was a gift."

"I had a strange dream last night too," Alice said.

Andy the pornographer's voice caromed with good-natured exasperation among the tombstones: "Get your skinny ass in here before you freeze to death!"

"Shit, I've to go, Alice," the girl said. "Got to pay those bills, you know?" She climbed down off the tombstone and ran in her furred boots, the blanket billowing to either side of her, its wind-whirled hem flinging up bright powder. Without stopping, she turned and cried over her shoulder, "Merry Christmas!"

In the empty air, so silent she could hear distinctly the muffled pats of the soft falling flakes on the hard packed snow, she recited her dream to herself.

I am sitting in the back of the just about empty bus, going back home from the city, at three in the morning. The night has been infernally hot, but now it's cold, the way it gets in the desert, and I slide open the window next to my seat to let the wind rake over me as the bus speeds along in the dark. And I'm sixteen again, in my leather jacket, my throat sore from smoking cigarettes and drinking whiskey, my jaws aching from some desultory blow job in the bathroom of a club. But I'm trying to get my head in order in case my parents wake up when I come in, I'm trying to focus on my book, on the poetry I'm reading, when I notice this woman. She's in her late twenties, but I'm sixteen, so she might as well be forty or sixty to me. She wears some sort of dirty monk's robe and cowl and her feet are bare and her head is shaved and her bones are sticking through her face. Every time the driver stops the bus, she gets off, and then she comes back on a minute later with the bodies of street people, homeless people, beggars, some naked, some in rags, all rippling with flies because they are almost dead, near-skeletons barely identifiable by sex except for where slack pouches of wrinkled gray skin drop off them, at the torsos of the women, between the legs of the men. The woman lays each body across a seat, the legs hanging down into the aisle, until the bus is full. And when the bus is full, the driver floods the engine and the bus ceases to make any stops. It flies right past the small shelter at the bottom of the hill that my parents' house sits atop. The bus, going so fast I think the wheels will soon sail an inch above the asphalt, slows down as we near a deserted and pebbly spot on the beach, and then it turns to a shuddering stop along the seawall overlooking the sand. The driver gets out and crosses the deserted street to an all-night diner; the waitress in the window, soaping down a table, looks up at him and smiles, at first with more unconcealed glee than she's intended to display, which she then modulates into flirtatious coyness. I know I wouldn't be welcome to join them, these four-A. M. lovers, so I keep to my seat. Then, with infinite care and deliberation and patience, the bareheaded barefoot young woman takes each of her decrepit charges off the bus, carries them down the stone steps to the beach, and lays them out supine, hands folded over their hearts, on the rocky sand. When she finishes, I climb off the bus and survey her work from the seawall: the beggars all at rest, their heads toward the ocean and feet to the land. She steps out of her robe and sits naked, cross-legged at their feet; wavelets are just beginning to lap at their heads, to lift and to let fall wisps of their hair. I know somehow that she will sit there until the tide takes them, takes every one, and then she will do it all again tomorrow night.

Alice, her lips moving along with her story, felt that she was no longer alone. She looked up through the cemetery gate and saw Salvatore Cassini; he appraised her painting in that full-body way of his, reaching out to it, almost touching it, as if he wanted not to look at it but to palpate it. He hadn't noticed her sitting on the tomb, so she could watch him form a judgment undisguised by a concern not to offend her. His narrowed eyes bespoke fascination, his bunched lips frustration. The verdict would be a mixed one. Alice wondered if he looked frustrated because he could perceive that she was surpassing him. Then she wryly winced at her incorrigible, even if correct, arrogance, and, as if the courtly man were there in her head with her, she politely rescinded the suspicion.

When she bought the church, Salvatore feared she would put him out along with the pornographers, even though he had been coming there regularly to practice his superannuated art. He was bothering no one, he protested to her, and was certainly no pornographer, even if he did favor, in his pagan way, the nude. Instead of throwing him out, she asked the seventy-year-old man to teach her to paint. Five weeks of lessons passed before she understood that he was the younger brother-in-law of Fraternelli's old tenant, dead these fifteen years. She never said a word to the painter about it.

* * *

Melissa was surprised to see the squat, thick-muscled man at the door. She instinctively pressed little Lila closer to her chest. The man saw her take this precation and laughed and said, "I am friend of your husband's, Mrs. Weis."

"Ms. Nelson," she corrected him.

"Of course," he said with a deferential gesture.

She looked over her shoulder to see if Mark had come back from the bathroom yet. He had excused himself at the conclusion of a new TV special about the fall of the bridge and the end of the It cult; the show sought to explain, though some of course said that it sought only to cover up, what was known two months later about the mysterious tragedy. The reporters interviewed, among others, the man who had turned up one night and cried to Melissa about his wife's infidelity. He was in the process of making a feature-length documentary about the Its, he explained to the interviewer after being introduced as the acclaimed director of *Wasteland Wonderland, Sonatina*, and the forthcoming *The Night Has No Borders*.

"My wife, she was a troubled woman but a beautiful spirit," he'd said into the camera. "She joined the Its herself and she, she was on the bridge that day. And I never really knew why. So I have to understand what happened, what happened to make all those people give up like that. We have to learn what makes people hurt that way, so that we can end the pain. It's why we're here, to make this planet a better place. My work is about increasing understanding generally in the world. You can't hate what you understand. So maybe if we understand what happened to those people, we can stop it from happening again."

The interview unctuously asked if this would be a more personal work than his previous films.

"All my work is personal, I feel it all very deeply," the director said, the studio lights wobbling in the wetness of his eyes. "But to the extent that this is for her, that this is for her beautiful spirit, then yes, it will be an act of love."

At this, Mark had gone to the bathroom, ostensibly to pee or floss or whatever, but these days, after the birth of Lila, he cried at everything and nothing, and he knew that Melissa knew that he was sitting on the toilet lid with his face in his hands. Now he stood in the dark doorway of the bathroom, just out of Melissa's sight, watching her with Sergey. He was briefly immobilized by this irruption into his normal life, the second in one night, of a person he'd known during an adventure so distant from him now that he sometimes believed he'd dreamed it, though it had all happened just a few months before. He knew Melissa had nothing to fear from the café owner. Even if she had, that huge hound, Matthias, clicked over the loft's floorboards and now wove its long body back and forth between her and Sergey. Sergey stooped slightly to pet the dog's sleek neck.

Then Mark stepped out into the main room of the loft and said, "Sergey! It's nice to see you." He briskly crossed the room and shook Sergey's hand.

"So you do know him," Melissa said with a laugh. She apologized to Sergey and said, "You can't be too careful when you have a baby. It really changes everything."

Sergey smiled down at Lila's plump face, framed by a knit hat above and a blanket below, and said nothing.

"How do you two know each other?"

Mark said quietly, "He owns the Asphodel Café, down by the river. I used to go in there when, you know."

Her face furrowed at even this slight allusion to the troubled period in their marriage. When the documentarian came on screen, she had been content to treat the whole thing as a grotesque farce, because that would protect her from the reality of it: she and Mark could laugh at it together, if only he didn't insist on crying. To see a reminder walk through the door, however, creased her freckled brow. Mark knew he had to get rid of Sergey quickly.

Sergey said, "Can I talk to you alone, Mr. Weis?"

Melissa swiftly turned her face away from Sergey as if the man had lifted his hand to her. Then she said, in a superficially pert tone that only Mark could have identified as angry, "It's time for this little girl to feed anyway. I'll go in the bedroom and leave you two here."

She walked out of the living room, striking her heels to the floor with exaggerated violence to flourish the reserves of force she would be willing to use if her family were threatened.

When she was gone, Sergey sat heavily on the couch and took the dog's sharp face caressingly in his rough, scarred hands. Mark, trying to be subtly hospitable, remained on his feet.

"So what's up?" he said.

"You don't sound happy to see me, Mr. Weis."

"No, no. It's just been a rough year, and everything only recently got back on track." He lowered his voice. "I don't know if it was right of me to involve myself in that whole thing with Julia. And I was just hoping to put it behind me." Mark quickly sat next to Sergey, to show that he meant no offense.

Sergey laughed his unsettling laugh.

"Too much shit is forgotten," he said. "Whether you want to forget or no. Ever know somebody who was dying?"

Mark shook his head slightly, abashedly.

"They want it all back, Mr. Weis. The worst day even. Nothing behind them. Think about that."

He pushed Mark's shoulder with the heel of his hand, as if to impress the thought on the younger man's body. Not expecting this, Mark nearly tipped off the edge of the couch and had to grab its arm with both hands.

"Hey, you ever find job?" Sergey said.

"Well, no, not exactly. But my wife, she has this website, and it went viral, got all sorts of media exposure, her subscriptions are through the roof, and now there's talk of a book contract and a TV show. It all happened just a few days after my daughter was born; somebody high up found the site and it exploded. So we figure we can make do with her income for now: I can be the house husband."

"Nice surprise," Sergey said. "Nice coincidence about that website, somebody seeing it." He winked at Mark with an open-mouthed smile, the low light of the loft sparkling gently from a gold tooth in the back of his mouth.

"I don't understand..."

"Well, let me say this way: maybe someone was looking out for your family. Maybe someone put in a call, you know?"

"Why would they do that?"

"Didn't my friend Tom tell you about hospital? You get some help in your life from them, you better not waste it. He helped you with something, told you what you wanted to know. And some other people you know got even more help. And if they want to do you a favor, out of gratitude to the world, you know, just because they still have a life, maybe they did. But now you have gratitude too, no?"

Mark nodded without meeting Sergey's eyes; he kept his own fixed on the floor, his hands clasped in front of him. He imagined that he looked like someone undergoing an interrogation.

Sergey put his huge gnarl-knuckled hands on his knees and stood up. Then he pocketed his hands and made a circuit of the loft, remarking with quiet delight, almost to himself, on the beauty of the framed wedding photos of Mark and Melissa; Lila's newborn picture; Mark's framed master's degree and Melissa's framed diploma from the culinary academy; the small ceramic Christmas village, lit with blinking lights, that Mark's parents had given them last year; the miniature tinsel-strung tree with its baby's-first-Christmas ornament prominently placed. Mark surreptitiously lifted his eyes from time to time but dropped them immediately whenever Sergey turned back toward him. Eventually Sergey reached the front door.

"Well, I bother you enough, yes?" He laughed and went on: "You have a lot to be grateful for here, Mr. Weis. Beautiful baby. Beautiful little wife. Money from out of nowhere. And very nice apartment. Now all I'm saying is don't waste it. Be ready to give back. We'll be watching you."

Despite his wrestler's body and bearing, Sergey opened the door, went out, and shut it behind him with an almost soundless tenderness, like someone trying not to wake an infant. Only when he had gone did Mark realize that his heart was beating so rapidly he felt light-headed. He took several deep breaths and then went into the bedroom. Melissa sat on the bed with Lila beneath her breast; she had fallen asleep while being fed. Melissa handed Lila carefully to Mark, who placed him with patient slowness in the crib next to the bed.

"Is he gone?" Melissa whispered.

Mark nodded yes.

Then she said more loudly, "What the hell was that all about?" Mark understood then that she hadn't been whispering because of Lila, but because she'd feared Sergey.

He lay on his stomach next to her and said, "He met me when we were having that hard time. He just wanted to see if it all worked out. It's really nothing to worry about; I'm sure he wants the best for us."

She held her eyes skeptically wide as she looked at him, expecting him to say more. He didn't. He lifted his head and kissed her, because he saw then how irreplaceably beautiful she was: she hadn't filmed her show for a few days, so her hair was unwashed and unkempt, and it fell in orange tangles over her shoulders; her freckled face was free of make-up, with all the lines care had incised into her skin visible in the harsh light from the bedside lamp. Sergey had been right, of course: he had to be grateful for the company of this absolutely singular woman, with whom he had made another absolutely singular being.

Eventually, she fell asleep in the crook of his arm, as the baby slept in the crib on the other side of him. He couldn't sleep, though. He picked *The Scarlet Letter* up from the bedside table, where it lay propped open to the place he had left off, just a few pages from the end. He never managed to get through *The House of the Seven Gables* before he had to return it to the library, but he thought he owed it to the child he'd once been to complete that child's work. He determined to finish *The Scarlet Letter* at last and, in the interests of not wasting time, with his wife and child breathing softly in their respective dreams on either side of him, he prepared to the read it down to the last word that very night. He took it up and scanned the last page he'd reached for its first unfamiliar sentence.

* * *

Mrs. Bonham had not decorated for Christmas. She'd seen no reason; she had no immediate family living with her, no extended family to come for Christmas Eve dinner. She went from time to time to a bar with the girls from work, but at Christmastime they had their own families to attend to, and, though her two closest work acquaintances both invited her each year for their dinners at Christmas Eve and Christmas Day, she refused to trespass, to introduce her amputated self into intact families. She would treat Christmas Eve like any other night, and on Christmas Day she would go to church. As for the day after, she looked forward to returning to work.

She was an unmarried woman, after all, and was approaching what she regarded as an unmarriageable age. Her parents were dead, likewise her ex-husband, and her daughter was gone. Over six months ago, she had stood in the cemetery for Frank's funeral. It was her, the librarian, and two old ladies who had been his tenants: two middle-aged women, one with no child and one whose only child had as good as killed herself, and two old women who might as well have stayed in the graveyard when the ceremony was through. Maybe it was the rain keeping people away; on the day he was buried, it poured from dawn to midnight. It felt to her that everything was coming to an end. She'd said so to the librarian. They spoke briefly from under their umbrellas, their voices barely carrying through the rain.

"Why didn't you have another one?" the librarian asked.

"I had my job, Frank had his buildings. And you always think you'll have more time. Did Frank ever talk about having one with you?"

"Oh no, never. He knew my views."

"Which are?"

She lifted her hand and swept it out over the cemetery and up to the treetops, her palm escaping the umbrella's protection and filling with rain. "This," she said, "is no place for anybody. I think it's very cruel to strand a stranger in it."

"That's not our decision to make," Mrs. Bonham had said. "We have to live, not to judge life. It's not something in a book or a jar."

The librarian smiled obscurely at the ex-wife's undiminished bitterness. "Well," she said, "that's the difference between us."

She didn't say anything else; Mrs. Bonham stared at her face, its strange smile bleared only slightly by tears that twisted her lips and reddened her eyes. This woman, her interests and her appetites, would always remain opaque to Mrs. Bonham. In that moment, though, she reminded Mrs. Bonham very strangely of her daughter.

She had drunk half a bottle of wine by five o'clock in the afternoon of Christmas Eve, when it was already dark as midnight with snow falling quickly in unseasonable volume. During the evening news, she drifted in and out of sleep, and when she first heard the pounding on the front door, she thought only that something, the porch chairs or the screen door, had blown over in the blizzarding wind. When the noise didn't stop, she came fully awake and leapt up, looking around in confusion, her heart seized with sudden fear. "Who is it?" she yelled to the door. She was an older woman alone, after all, she told herself; it would be foolishly dangerous to open her front door to just anyone who came by knocking. The person on the other side said nothing and just rapped his or her knuckles more gently, as if tattooing a Morse code signal that Mrs. Bonham could not understand. She thought she could detect a softness, a selfless desperation in those knuckles, so she pulled the door open.

"My God," she said. "Jules."

It ended up taking a half hour just to undress Julia, because she had so tightly bound herself in pilfered jackets and scavenged bedsheets; she had no shoes but had thickly wrapped her bleeding feet in what looked like knotted pillowcases. Mrs. Bonham was too busy to weep upon seeing Julia's starved body when she finally got her out of her filthy rags, their outsides grimy with the dirt of the streets, the reverse sides yellow with rubbing against the young woman's skin. Her belly was like a stretched and narrow band of rubber between her rib cage and her pelvic girdle, which both looked like they were about to levitate through the skin at any moment. Mrs. Bonham had too much to do, however, to reflect on this; she had to focus on caring for her daughter.

Only when she got Julia into the bathtub and ran warm water in filth-bearing streams over stubbornly frigid limbs did it occur to Mrs. Bonham that her daughter had not spoken. She lifted her eyes to Julia's face, her father's dark eyes protruding out of receded skin, the cheeks contracted around the teeth, the prominent nose, always Julia's most distinguished feature, like a standing column in a field of ruins.

"Open your mouth, sweetie," she whispered.

She needed just a few minutes to herself, sitting on the toilet lid, facing away from Julia. She forced herself to make no sound; the eyes could squeeze out their tears if that's what they needed to do, but she would not convulse and cry, would not lose herself immoderately in uncontrolled sobbing. Julia bathed herself once the tub had filled. With her eyes averted from Julia and moreover blinded by tears, with all the mirrors steam-occluded, Mrs. Bonham just listened to the soft plashing that came from her silent child in the tub. She imagined it was twenty-eight years ago, that she had turned away for the briefest moment while her baby bobbed her fat little arms in the shallow, warm water.

When she was able to turn back to Julia, she told her how her friend Caroline had turned up one day about a month after the bridge collapse. Caroline's head was bald; she looked as if she hadn't eaten for days, and she had to lean on the arm of the man who accompanied her, a man with a hideous snake tattoo on his neck, whom she had introduced as her "partner."

"Can you imagine?" Mrs. Bonham asked Julia as she patiently unknotted and straightened her short blondish brown hair, which had grown matted and twisted from its never being washed as it crookedly regrew. "I just don't understand people."

Caroline, she went on, had told Mrs. Bonham that, despite what she may have imagined, Julia was not on the bridge that day. She had escaped the destruction of the Its safely, and then she had wandered off God knew where. Caroline said she couldn't afford to search for Julia herself, because she had to spend time re-ordering the mess she'd made of her own life with the help of the snake man, but that if Mrs. Bonham saw Julia, she should give her a kiss from Caroline and tell her that Caroline considered her a sister and would never forget her and would always love her. She also said to tell her that her brother, Daniel, was on the bridge that day: "Please tell her we lost him," Caroline had said. So Mrs. Bonham relayed these messages to Julia, who smiled in a distantly elegiac way on hearing it. "She was pregnant, by the way, your friend. I mean, she didn't say so exactly, but I knew."

When Mrs. Bonham was dressing Julia in her bedroom, dressing her in winter leggings and a black skirt, she mentioned the possibility of Julia's staying. Julia shook her head slowly to refuse, but she put her bath-pruned fingers on her mother's cheek. Her face was impassive. Mrs. Bonham knew that the girl was right, that she could not stay. Julia had crossed some verge, gone some way Mrs. Bonham not only could not follow but did not want to even if she could. In this ordered white house, what could Julia be? A monster in its cage, a specimen in a jar?

"But will you come see me again?" Mrs. Bonham asked.

Julia moved her head up and down, as slowly as if she were underwater.

Down in the entryway, Mrs. Bonham got down on her old and aching knees to tie boots on her daughter's feet. She tied them in a tight triple knot, to give the girl some reliable means of transport to wherever she was going, wherever Mrs. Bonham could not go and didn't want to. Mrs. Bonham had always tied Julia's shoes in tight triple knots, ever since Julia began wearing adult shoes with their knot-begging laces, so she didn't have to have her eyes open to do it. She kept them closed, to linger in the illusion that the girl was only three years old, that these were her first winter boots, that Mrs. Bonham had it all to do over again, that this time she would do something or anything or everything differently so it would all come out right. She opened her eyes, and Julia was still twenty-eight, dressed in her mother's old coat, in fine clean clothes her mother had kept for her, and she was standing in front of the door, ready to go out into the snow. Mrs. Bonham resolved to spend her Christmas Eve in just the way she'd intended, as if there had been no interruption.

* * *

Alice spent her Christmas Eve in the church. She stood in the choir loft in an old dress she didn't mind staining with oils, her feet bare, as when she was a girl at the beach, on the sheets she had lain down to catch the paint. No one was in the church now; all the other artists who came there must have had families to celebrate the holidays with. Salvatore had some girlfriend he didn't like to speak of, probably some young thing taken in by his old-world accent and courtly manners. Even the pornographers had someone to go home to.

Alice imagined walking down a long street across the blue snow, all the orange-lit Christmas windows hanging like portals amid the night's darkness, all the men in sweaters and women in shawls and children circling with excitement in their pajamas, the scents of roasted ham and crisp-skinned turkey and mulled cider drifting out with the pine-perfumed smoke that wisped from the chimneys. Yes, Alice would walk barefoot in the snow with the hem of her old dresses skirting the powder along the packed surface, her canvases under her arms, and she would whisper at the warm domestic windows, "*Ils sont dans le vrai*," but it wouldn't matter at all, because she had made her choice. She looked out of the choir loft over the dark aisle to the empty candle-lit nave; she was trying to paint the small flames in the darkness.

"Just worry for now about dark and light," Salvatore had told her. "That's the bottom of everything. Learn your dark and your light, and everything else will come."

The painting wasn't going well, though; every time she thought she had a success, as with her blue snow the previous day, she found herself embroiled in another failure. The canvas, with orange circles on a black ground, looked like a cheap Halloween decoration. One year when she was in high school, she came down to Christmas dinner in a black dress, and her mother had said, "It's not *Halloween*, for Christ's sake," and that's what this wretched canvas made her think of.

The painting looked even worse when one of the stray cats she allowed to share the church bounded, with startled eyes and an arched back, up the stairs that led from the narthex to the choir loft. The cat slinked in a gray swirl around Alice's legs; startled, she slashed an orange gash down the middle of the black canvas before losing her grip on the brush. She let out the breath she had sharply drawn in and bent to pick the brush up. While crouched down, she ran her thumb between the cat's eyes.

"Scared of your own shadow again, Medlar?" she said. "How am I supposed to become a great painter with you distracting me all the time?"

When she straightened up, she saw Julia walk from the stairhead onto the choir loft, dressed prettily under the snow that melted and ran in rivulets from her body. She had her natural hair color now; the hair was just starting to grow out over her ears and over her forehead.

Alice didn't say anything; she only stared at Julia with confused eyes. Then Julia pointed at two empty stretched canvases at Alice's feet. Alice shrugged and handed one to Julia, who propped the canvas on the loft's low wall. She walked over to Alice and started looking through the tubes of oils. When she was satisfied, she took them back to the canvas and sat down before it. She didn't do anything, though, because she was staring expectantly at Alice. She made a gesture with her hands to indicate that she wanted Alice to disrobe. Alice shrugged and took her dress off, but she didn't move from behind her easel.

"Well, come on," she said. "Paint me if you like, but I don't have any time to waste. I'm going to paint you too."

Julia stood and stripped herself down to her bones and her scar, and then she sat again and looked at Alice, who looked back at her. She indicated to Alice to move the leg that didn't bear her weight out into a more dynamic contrapposto. Alice did so, but she instructed Julia in turn to recline like someone at home in the world instead of sitting in a malcontented hunch. Julia obeyed, but, before she could begin, she motioned to Alice to lift her face out of the shadows and keep it in the light. Their movements looked like a patient dance animated by slow, obscure joy. Medlar wended his way around them both, rubbing his face on Alice's legs and Julia's arms as, in the choir loft of the deconsecrated church, the artists posed their naked bodies this way and that.

ABOUT THE AUTHOR

John Pistelli was born and raised in Pittsburgh, Pennsylvania and now lives in Minneapolis, Minnesota, where he teaches literature, writing, and other humanities courses. He holds a Ph.D. in English literature from the University of Minnesota. His fiction, essays, and poetry have appeared in *Rain Taxi, New Walk, The Millions, Revolver, The Squawk Back, Winter Tangerine Review, Atomic, The Stockholm Review, Muse, The Harpoon Review,* and elsewhere. His short story "How People Live" won Honorable Mention in the *Glimmer Train* May 2012 Short Story Award for New Writers. His novella *The Ecstasy of Michaela* was published by Valhalla Press.

Made in United States
North Haven, CT
27 April 2022

18636766R00111